Black Grapes

Eva Maclean

PART ONE

Chapter One

EFFIE WATSON AND I met on our first day at university. I guess that makes it easy to remember. October 2009. We were young, innocent and full of hope and the bad stuff was all in the future.

I had arrived a few hours earlier, hauling myself out of a taxi and shuffling across the campus with my capacious rucksack and my ancient wheely suitcase, standing nervously in line at the reception desk, overcome with gratitude to be given a key to a room which was mine alone. After a bit of leisurely unpacking and looking out the window at the block opposite, I was sitting in a mindless trance, overcome with affection for the single bed, the desk and chair, the curtains, the washbasin in the corner, drunk with the happiness of having escaped from home, when there was a knock on the door. And in she bounced. My next-door neighbour.

'Hi, I'm Effie.'

'Olivia.' My name sounded so much more cumbersome than hers. Too many syllables.

Blonde hair, blue eyes that roamed expertly and unashamedly over all my stuff. She sat uninvited on my bed in her faded jeans and oversized sweater, with long, droopy sleeves covering her hands, tucked her bare feet up under her and smiled up at me.

'You got anything to drink?'

I was struck dumb for a minute and then I was scrabbling mentally to catch up. It was obvious to me, even in that first moment, that she had everything I lacked. Perhaps if I stuck with her, if she let me stick with her, some of it might rub off.

As it happened, I did have a bottle of vodka in my rucksack. I had brought it in anticipation of the many lonely nights when I would be sitting alone in my room reading a book or watching a video or trying to write an essay. I wasn't counting on much of a social life. We finished most of it that evening.

Once we started to talk, there was no awkwardness between us, perhaps it was melted away by the vodka, but I think it was more due to Effie. I soon realised that she was one of those people who could keep a conversation going all on her own if nobody else chipped in. One of my aunties had been the same, people would lighten up and relax as soon as she got going. It was a talent I had always wished to have. Effie and I sat and exchanged confidences as easily as one might tell secrets to a stranger you won't see again. Except of course that we would see each other again, many times, over several years. Effie was the first person to whom I was able to explain the bizarre family circumstances that I had for so long sought to hide from all my friends. Her background was also unusual.

'My mum did a runner when I was eight' she said. 'She was working at an insurance company and she ran off with her boss. My dad threatened to kill the fellow but then he said it wasn't worth it. If he'd gone to prison, I'd have had nobody. After she'd gone, he had to do all the stuff like meetings with teachers and all the rest of it. He hated all that, but he did it. Actually, it was quite good for me in some ways. I think mothers are stricter about what you do and what you wear and all that. My dad just used to give me the money and let me buy my own clothes, so I had what I wanted. Not a lot of money of course, but I could spend it how I wanted. He's had a pretty rough life and he does drink a bit, but he's looked after me for all these years. I was glad to get away from Manchester in some ways, but I do worry about my dad and I miss him. I'm glad he's got Albert.' I must have looked confused. 'Our dog' she explained.

When we had finished our family histories and exhausted all other topics of conversation, we walked over to the social building to see what Freshers' Week had to offer. It was a large modernist building, looking like a couple of sugar cubes welded together, designed in that post-war period when architects could apparently get away with anything. The concrete areas were already showing signs of decay. I don't know why I noticed this. Maybe it steadied my nerves to fix my mind on something mundane and material. Once we got inside, there was no time to criticise the fabric of the building. There were bodies rushing everywhere. The crowds and the music and the atmosphere were almost overwhelming. The second-year students running things looked grown-up and experienced to me and I could feel myself shrinking, but Effie wasn't fazed by any of it.

'Mostly bullshit' she told me, tossing her head. 'Who wants to join a fucking chess club?'

I had been thinking that I would like to improve my very rudimentary chess, but I nodded and said nothing and we moved on. I was grateful to be part of this twosome, I wasn't about to assert myself at this point. After a while I realised that Effie wasn't interested in any of these clubs or societies.

She was looking for interesting people, specifically interesting men. The guy running the chess club, with his beard and acne, never had a chance. The rowing club, with its six-packs and biceps, was a different story.

And the rowing club was equally keen on Effie. For if Effie looked cool to me, the men were even more susceptible, and that was to become a constant in our relationship over the years. I never felt like the less attractive friend. I guess I was the less attractive friend, because pretty well every woman in our year was less attractive than Effie, but it didn't bother me, because we weren't in competition. I somehow felt that she belonged to me and the pride I felt in her was almost maternal. I loved walking down the street with her because I loved watching men crane their necks as she sauntered past - me sauntering vicariously in her wake.

Before I knew it, we were the nucleus of a large circle, because women were drawn to Effie as much as men. She had that knack of small-talk, of wittering on about nothing much, which broke the ice everywhere she went and drew everybody in, even if afterwards nobody could remember anything she had said. Women probably envied her looks but liked her anyway and wanted to be in the group that drew the men. Men were easy to attract, but some of them became more wary as they noted how quickly others were cast aside.

For Effie had a plan. A long-term plan. One that didn't involve getting shacked up with any of our redbrick university mates. They were all good for passing the time, and she was never without a man to tow around, but none of them had any place in her future, not as far as she was concerned. What most people didn't grasp about Effie was that she was really clever. Hidden underneath the ditsy exterior was a first-class brain. And while the rest of us were just enjoying our three years and wondering what to do when it came to an end, she was looking much further ahead.

'The thing is, Livy, you have to go where the money is.'

'Do you?' I was a bit nonplussed by this.

'Of course. If you want to have an interesting life. That's why I'm doing History of Art.'

'But art has nothing to do with money.'

She laughed and shook her head. 'Right now, art has everything to do with money. Do you know how much some of these Neo-Expressionist works are selling for? Art is one of the places people store their wealth.'

Wealth was an alien concept to me at that time, something a bit grubby, so I thought this was a bit of a strange conversation and I assumed that Effie would in time come to the same conclusion. I was studying French and vaguely hoping that it would lead me into something other than teaching, but that was as far as my vision of the future extended.

For the moment we were Effie and Livy and we were having the time of our lives. No matter how many other people were around, we were each other's primary person, like the sisters neither of us had. People invited us to things as a pair and if either of us needed somebody to steer us home or to hold our hair while we puked up after a really bad drinking bout, we knew who that would be.

Being constantly short of money we both spent most of the holidays working – shelf-stacking, call handling, waitressing – a lot of waitressing. Effie made a few trips home to see her dad, I made no trips home at all but did have a few meet-ups with my brother. It was an awkward experience for both of us because we were joined together by that part of our lives that we both wanted to forget. There were very few happy childhood memories to laugh about and we discovered that we didn't really know each other. I think we both hoped that we could put together some kind of relationship, but it was obviously going to take time.

During the Easter holidays in our second year Effie invited me back to Manchester with her for a weekend to visit her dad. They had a small terraced house in Denton and I got a warm welcome from Bernie and Albert. Bernie had a cleaner who came in once a week, but no resident female, so he kept the house exactly the way he wanted it. The coffee table had a dip in it right where he put his feet. On the walls were posters of concerts featuring old bands – very old bands. Grateful Dead, Rolling Stones, Led Zeppelin, Jefferson Airplane, Pink Floyd. Bernie had been an avid festivalgoer in his youth, Bob Dylan at the isle of Wight in '69 having been 'the high point of my life' (apart from Effie being born, he hastened to add). His most precious possessions were his turntables, his speakers and his vinyls. I was fascinated, picturing Effie growing up surrounded by rock music. It was not something she'd ever spoken about. I also couldn't help noticing that her speech, which up to that point had sounded pretty unaccented, became Mancunian as soon as we stepped off the train at Manchester Piccadilly. This wasn't something assumed, it seemed to be completely unconscious on her part.

In the evenings we went to the pub. Not a posh pub (Manchester has plenty of those) but Bernie's local, where he seemed to know everybody by name and where Albert immediately lay down under the table as if this was his second home.

Back on campus the months rolled on by and our busy social life continued. Right from the start there had been a steady stream of boyfriends and Effie was nothing if not generous. It was like a continuous audition process. Some of them got a few weeks, some of them got a few months, but the next one was always lined up. And she managed to move nearly all of them on with no hard feelings by the simple expedient of lining up their next relationship. Sometimes I was the recipient, sometimes it was one of the other women. And Effie's ex-men had the next best thing to references. If Effie had been out with them, they were officially not a dork.

Halfway through our third year Effie met Pete Grantham, who was doing an MA in mechanical engineering. When I say 'met', she walked up to him in the bar and made her pitch. Engineers were normally shunned as being non-intellectual, but Pete was sufficiently attractive to get through the gates. It was soon clear to me that this was more serious than her previous relationships – for one thing, she wasn't talking about it. This made me feel slightly excluded and I could certainly see what was attractive about Pete. Effie and I did seem to have the same taste in men. For that reason, I started to make a conscious effort to stay away from them. I had a few one-night stands over the next few months, but nothing that was going to change my life. For four months Effie and Pete were inseparable then, a few weeks before finals, she told me it was over.

'He really likes you, Livy.'

'Of course he bloody doesn't. He really likes you, and you've tossed him aside like all the rest.'

Quite why I was so angry on Pete's behalf I don't know. Maybe I sensed that he was a more grounded person than the self-regarding faux intellectuals we'd mostly been associating with and so more worthy of decent treatment. Whatever the reason, I decided that no way was I picking up this particular reject, and I went out of my way thereafter to avoid him.

Finals came and went and the post-exam celebration sessions got underway. I found myself outside the favourite student pub, full of ecstasy and alcohol, being backed up against a brick wall by somebody I didn't remember ever meeting. I tried the old joke about we haven't even been introduced, but he was too busy trying to get his hand down my jeans and my attempts to knee him in the crucial place had failed to find their target. Just as I was wondering whether to start screaming (surprisingly difficult when you're not used to making a fuss) he suddenly removed his grip and staggered backwards. If the wall hadn't been there, I might have fallen over at this point as there wasn't much else holding me up. When I had righted myself and blinked a few times, I saw to my shame that the person holding him in an armlock was Pete.

He sent my assailant on his way with a parting kick and came over to me. I was trying to pretend I was somewhere else, anywhere else. My legs felt weak, but the overriding feeling was embarrassment, as if what had happened was really my fault.

'Are you OK?'

I straightened up and put my shoulders back. 'Yes, I'm fine. Thank you for that. He was being a bit of a nuisance. OK now. No problem.' I gave him my best smile. Move along. Nothing to see here.

He took my arm. 'Come on. I'll walk you home. He might be hanging around.'

That was hard to argue with, so we walked slowly back to the flat I was sharing with Effie and a variable number of other people. There was no conversation. I'd already thanked him and I didn't know what else to say. I just wanted the walk to be over and he was also silent, probably regretting that he'd got himself into this. There was no way I was going to let Effie see me walking in with him, so I repeated my thanks on the doorstep and pointedly declined to ask him in. He turned, waved and walked off and that was the end of it.

Three days later I was pleased to see him going about with Melanie from the student house next door. Effie was obviously still co-ordinating the project. And she herself had taken up with one of the younger lecturers.

'We're all leaving anyway, so I think his duty of care towards me is pretty much at an end' she told me.

In fact, our whole lovely existence was now at an end. The outside world was not as impressed with us as we were with ourselves. Most of us drifted down to London, where Effie and I found a flat in Earls Court, shared with three other people and two cats. The building was stucco-fronted and had once been a beautiful family residence with the top floor, where we were, allocated to the servants. Being at the top of the building, we were safe for the time being from the damp that was making its way inexorably up the walls, but excessive insulation in the loft meant that we sweated and gasped in the summer and the winter was spent huddled over electric fires as the central heating installation had come to a halt on the floor below. Decades of neglect and sub-letting had left the steps up to the front door actually crumbling and flakes of stucco drifted down like confetti whenever the door was slammed.

Our landlord was a swaggering fellow with the sort of eyes you see on the slab at the fishmongers and a beer gut that always preceded him into the room. He was given to 'spot checks' early in the morning, presumably in hopes of finding us in states of undress. One morning while he was engaged in this pursuit Effie appeared and motioned him into her bedroom. He made it in there in ten seconds and shot out equally fast thirty seconds later. Effie never would give me any details, preferring just to wink, but there were no more spot checks.

Being in London was not cheap and the graduate premium seemed to no longer exist, so we had to consider our options. I managed to secure a junior admin role in a software company, which I decided would do for the time being, and Effie was accepted for the MA course in Renaissance Studies at London University, to start the following year. In the meantime, she got a job in a pub – not a smart pub, or even a wine bar, but one of the scruffier sort. When I queried this choice, she said it reminded her of her dad's local in Manchester and she didn't want to be serving drinks to posers. It was one of those large, tasteless London pubs, with the TV permanently on over the bar. Punters would come in, order their drinks, go next door to the betting shop to place their bets, then come back to watch it on the screen. There was a constant background hum of four-letter words and at the end of each evening the floor would be littered with discarded betting slips. It was a place in which Effie's looks and her talent for meaningless small talk were an immediate draw and would have been enough to offset any shortcomings in the area of giving the correct change or washing glasses. She was the target of much ribaldry and familiarity, which she ignored with aplomb. Then one day Jackson Welby walked into the pub and changed her life.

'He runs a gallery' she told me breathlessly the following week when I went into the pub to see her. 'In Mayfair. He just walked in one day last week and we got chatting. He's offered me a job.'

I looked quickly down the bar to make sure her employer was not within earshot. He was a soft-footed character who liked to sneak up on Effie – her response was usually to step back smartly and land innocently on his foot and she had taken to wearing heels for this purpose. He was watching the horse racing on the screen, swearing under his breath and oblivious to anything else.

'This guy Jackson, are you sure it's not you he's interested in, rather than whatever he thinks your accomplishments are?' I was sure any accomplishments would have been fabricated, probably very imaginatively.

She smiled and put a hand on my arm. 'Livy, you're always so negative. Jackson isn't interested in me. He's gay. Isn't that marvellous?'

I had to agree about that. It sounded very restful. I thought of Richie and Lawrence in my office - the easiest people in the organisation to talk to, no hidden agendas. A few days later we met Jackson for drinks and I discovered that he was anything but restful. He was in his thirties, dressed (amazingly) in a suit, clean shaven, with a lot of dark, messy hair – nothing punk or arty about him – but he was full of ideas and with a sober, cynical understanding of the art market. He seemed like the ideal employer for Effie and I told her so the next day. But I had one reservation.

'You're going to be a receptionist, Effie. That doesn't seem to be a good use of your degree.' In fairness, it was still a step up from the pub. 'And what about your MA course?'

'Darling, I won't need the course now. This is not like being a receptionist at the dentists. I'll be meeting clients and showing them artworks and in time I'll be curating exhibitions. People don't walk in off the street, they're admitted by appointment. According to Jackson, most of them are filthy rich and totally ignorant. They want something to hang on their wall which will impress other people, and that's what we provide.'

As usual, she was way ahead of me. Proximity to money. She had arrived there in record time.

Chapter Two

WHILE EFFIE WAS MAKING her way in the art world, I had managed to push my way into the publishing industry, courtesy of one of the contacts from my previous job. It's always about who you know. It wasn't fantastically well-paid, I think salaries are scaled down for the privilege of working with an acceptable product, but I wasn't about to complain.

Effie and I had both started renting separate flats by now. She stayed in Earls Court and I moved to Victoria, where I paid over the odds for a one-bedroom flat that was smaller than some studios, but gave me the massive advantage of being able to walk to work. It felt more grown up than the two- girls-living-together cliché and I wanted to be able to conduct my personal life without having it curated by Effie. She probably felt the same. So we started to see a bit less of each other and I was able to enjoy a level of cleanliness and tidiness that she would have derided as bourgeois. But we still met up regularly and it was in a wine bar in Earls Court that I first heard about Hugo Fincham.

We were sitting in a massive space done up like an American prohibition-era bar, with live jazz and waiters in shirt sleeves and a large array of unfamiliar cocktails. You really had to admire the amount of thought that must have gone into the place. We were drinking vodka martinis with bay leaf syrup and it didn't take too many of those to cast a rosy glow over everything we discussed. Nevertheless, I did have a few reservations about Effie's latest man. Looking back on it, I should have had a whole lot more.

Hugo had come into the gallery (by appointment, of course) looking for artwork to go in his house in Cheyne Walk ('Cheyne Walk!' Effie squeaked, 'Where Mick Jagger used to live!'). Jackson was out of town that day so Effie was Hugo's art consultant and at the end of several hours browsing the gallery together they arranged to meet later for drinks. Hugo met most of Effie's requirements – he was tall, nice-looking, wealthy (banking job and shares in a vineyard), passable sense of humour (she was unable to offer any evidence to support this assertion) and reasonably intelligent (we assumed, as he had an Oxford degree). I encouraged her to think of his shortcomings, which I was sure must be many and significant in order to balance all these virtues. She was unable to come up with any, which suggested to me that she was not doing proper due diligence (yes, I was learning all the business jargon now).

'The thing is Effie' I was suddenly aware that I was slurring my words rather badly 'he doesn't sound like our sort of person.'

'What's our sort of person then? Young and poor?'

I thought about this as best I could. 'Maybe. I don't know.'

'You can't just rule people out because they have money. It usually means that they're successful. Why do you want to go out with failures?'

I didn't have a response to this, but I thought about it. A few weeks later I met a lawyer called Jamie at a party.

Remembering what Effie had said, I agreed to go out with him.

Effie pronounced herself satisfied with his credentials. He was good-looking, reasonably intelligent and with good earning potential. For some reason this endorsement caused me to slightly lose interest in him, but it was good to have someone to go places with and the sex was good, so I hung onto him. After so many years of being assured by my mother that nobody would ever want me, I felt lucky to have someone. I was sure I would never be able to treat men as infinitely replaceable, in the way that Effie did. In retrospect, that was part of my problem.

When Effie suggested a meetup at a new restaurant opening in Notting Hill it was good opportunity to appraise each other's partner. It was one of those self-conscious openings with an over-designed interior and a tasting menu. This meant a procession of about ten small dishes, chosen by the chef according to whatever ingredients he needed to get rid of. All of the dishes were over-engineered, if not particularly tasty, and the people at adjoining tables seemed more interested in photographing the stuff than actually eating it. Each serving was preceded by a short homily in which the dish was presented and described with great reverence by the server while we all sat there looking suitably impressed and grateful. It was a very tedious dining experience. After the third presentation Effie had had enough. 'Just leave it there, love, we'll guess what it is.' The server retreated, offended, and Hugo, who I guessed had booked this restaurant, looked pained. He had a lot to learn about Effie, and I hoped he realised that. I was glad to see that she still had no patience with bullshit.

Hugo was exactly as Effie had described him. Tall, good-looking, well-dressed, obviously prosperous and very attentive to her – lots of hugs and adoring looks. So far, so boring. But what was more interesting, I thought, was that he was happy for her to run the conversation. A lot of men would have been interrupting her or trying to shut her up. Hugo did none of that. He sat in silent admiration while she rattled on and I realised that she was exactly what he needed. He was rubbish at small talk, but now it didn't matter because he had Effie to do it for him. She gave him cover and with her looks she diverted attention away from him. Any number of social occasions that he probably hated would now be easier because he had Effie.

When Effie paused for breath, the real business got going. The men sized each other up and then went out to bat. They started with cars. Both had expensive models which I can no longer remember. Hugo had two, so was probably the winner of this round. I had an old VW Golf and Effie had somehow managed to fail her test three times ('I just didn't like that examiner') so we didn't have much to contribute to this topic. Then they got onto sport (rugby and tough mudders). Effie announced that I had been in the university first rowing team and they gave that a nod and carried on. Careers were next of course and Jamie's prospect of taking silk sounded good until set against Hugo's family vineyard.

By the end of the evening, Effie's initial meanderings notwithstanding, the men had done most of the talking and we had done most of the drinking, so we both needed assistance to get home. I decided, as I tumbled into bed with a feeling like something had come adrift in my brain, that maybe Jamie was not the man for me.

When we met up the following week for a wander round the National Gallery, I discovered that Effie had come to no such conclusion in respect of Hugo.

'I think Hugo will be making me an offer soon' she said as we stood in front of Monet's various renderings of Waterloo Bridge. 'He stayed at the Savoy, you know.'

'What, Hugo?'

'No silly, Monet. He came over in the 1870s to escape the Franco-Prussian War and then again at the turn of the century.'

'But do you love him, Effie? Hugo, I mean.'

She turned to look at me and then wandered into the next room. I followed behind. We were done with Monet.

'I dunno' she said. 'Have you loved any of the people you've been out with?'

I gave this some thought. Most of my relationships could now be viewed from a distance, as it were, so they had been stripped of all angst and euphoria. 'I don't know either.'

'You see? It's a meaningless concept.'

'But if you're thinking of spending the rest of your life with someone...'

'That rest of life stuff is rubbish. Most marriages don't last more than ten years. Hugo has what I want for now.'

I couldn't argue with that and I thought about it a lot on the tube back to Victoria. My parents' marriage hadn't lasted much longer than ten years, although it had been dead long before the end, the frustration and resentment almost tangible whenever they were in the same room.

When I was fourteen my father evidently decided that his time had now come, and he decamped off to his mistress in Brighton, followed out the door by a flood of screaming recriminations and threats of suicide. If I had hoped that peace might be restored once one of the antagonists had been removed from the fight, I was soon disabused of that idea. My mother's dramatisations as the woman scorned were now directed at us. My brother managed, via football, cricket and motorbikes, to largely remove himself from the scene, leaving me as the main focus of her hatred and disappointment. It was always going to be thus. Even the worst mother will have a soft spot for her son. A daughter is too much of a reminder of her younger and more desirable self.

And so, for the next few years I kept my head down both metaphorically and literally, shielded by the pages of books. I kept on top of the household chores which my mother no longer considered to be her responsibility and counted down the years and months until I could do what my father had done and get out. When I was seventeen (I was a late starter, for all the reasons above) I met my first proper boyfriend. Felix was dark-haired and brown eyed and had a Honda 250, and sitting on the back of the bike as we roared down the road (no silencer), holding proprietorially onto his leather jacket, I felt like a new, exciting, escaped person. Unfortunately, I hadn't felt sufficiently confident to explain my domestic circumstances to Felix, although he probably wondered why he always had to pick me up and drop me off at the end of the road. One day he presumably decided to ignore this stricture and knocked innocently on the front door. This resulted in a disturbing confrontation with my mad mother, following which he promptly dropped me in favour of Beth, who was supposed to be my best friend. The pain of that betrayal far outweighed any feeling of loss in respect of Felix.

So I had seen plenty of evidence that Effie was right, the rest of life stuff was rubbish, and anyway she didn't need endorsement from me or anybody else. She had determined on her course of action. It might not have been the beginning of the end, but it was certainly the end of the beginning.

Chapter Three

INSTEAD OF A HEN do (thank God), Effie hosted a get-together in a pub in Maida Vale for all our university friends, or at least all the ones we were still in touch with. This would probably be her last seriously downmarket social occasion and I think she realised that. She stipulated no significant others, so we all more or less took up where we had left off.

There was a lot of stuff to talk about and lots to drink and some people had done impressive travelling or landed impressive jobs, but in the end none of this was much discussed. It says a lot, I think, for Effie's social influence that all other achievements were abandoned as conversation topics in favour of marriage, which most of us considered to be the least cool option ever. To Effie's credit, she wasn't having bridesmaids or a wedding list and there was no discussion of the actual event, but she sat in the corner with everybody around her and held a masterclass on the subject of her new husband-to-be. She answered questions concerning his net worth (she didn't know precisely, but it was substantial), his family (bonkers, most of them) and her plans after married life (shopping, travelling, whatever). It was a testament to how much we had assumed the priorities of the world of work that the pursuit of money didn't sound particularly outlandish to a bunch of people who a few years earlier would have regarded rich people with distaste.

Towards the end of the evening Pete came over to talk to me. He'd spent the summer in South America and was now working for a new start-up doing engineering animations (everything's being done by AI now). He looked tanned and healthy and quite a contrast to Jamie who had the complexion of somebody who spends a lot of time squinting at small print. Melanie was nowhere to be seen, so I guessed she was out of the picture. He was obviously taken aback by Effie's proposed nuptials and said he hoped she knew what she was doing. I wasn't able to offer any reassurance. As it happens, any reassurance would have been misplaced, but we didn't know that.

'And how about you?' he said, 'What are you doing now?'

I told him about my publishing job, which probably sounded more impressive than it actually was, but he seemed to think I'd done pretty well just to get into the industry. I was trying not to think about our last embarrassing encounter and he didn't refer to it. It was one of those times when I wished I was like Effie, able to just rattle on about anything, because I was remembering that I had always thought he was attractive, and now I wondered how on earth Effie could have given him up. It was important to keep up with the social chitchat in order to keep such thoughts at bay.

The next evening, I left my office and there he was, leaning against a pillar.

'I realise you're a very independent woman, but I thought I'd just make sure nobody was accosting you on the way home.'

I laughed and took his arm and all residual awkwardness between us was gone. And so it began. Three mornings later I woke up and looked at his face on the pillow and thought that maybe Effie was wrong. Love was not a meaningless concept.

Chapter Four

EFFIE AND HUGO'S WEDDING was held at St James' church in Bellingbury, near Windsor with a reception afterwards in a marquee in the grounds of Fawcett Hall, Hugo's family's main residence. If any of us had doubted that she'd go through with it, all bets were off at this point. And she deserved a lot of credit for not arranging something flash in the Caribbean to which we would all have had to travel at our own expense. Although I know now that Hugo's family would have considered that impossibly vulgar.

The church was a long way removed from vulgar. Anglo-Catholic and neo-Gothic with a tall spire and beautiful stained-glass windows, based on the original designs of some of the stained glass destroyed by Henry VIII's righteous looters. Consecrated in 1829. It was well positioned to fulfil that function of making those who only attend for weddings, christenings and funerals feel that they are lucky to be allowed in.

Effie's side of the church was university friends, ex-flat mates and people from the pub. Even her dodgy pub landlord was there, looking like he'd scrubbed up. A good cross-section of society in some ways. Hugo's side of the church also had a contingent of what looked like university mates, but the front few rows were definitely family. They wore morning suits, proper hats and fixed expressions. None of them looked round in surprised delight as the bride appeared – all the swivelling was on our side.

The bride looked lovely in a slim columnar white dress (not one of those blown-up marshmallow jobs with all the cleavage on show – not that she had a lot of cleavage). Bernie looked a bit shaky walking her down the aisle with a smile plastered to his face. I'd spotted him having a quick swig from a flask a few minutes earlier. Hugo, standing at the front, greeted her with a fleeting nervous smile and the only one who looked at ease was the best man, who a few moments later pretended to have lost the ring – well I was pretty sure he was pretending. When they finally walked down the aisle together Effie looked thoroughly pleased with herself and Hugo looked like a man who had made it through a fearsome ordeal and now needed a stiff drink.

The usual interminable photography would have been an opportunity to get a better look at Hugo's family, about whom I'd heard so much, but I ended up decamping to the pub for the duration with the rest of the younger crowd. I was told later that in fact it was much less interminable than usual because there were no bridesmaids, both sets of parents were only willing to do one shot and Hugo's brother and sister had unaccountably disappeared. So, after a bit of desultory posing around the graveyard by the bride and groom, the photographer gave up and took himself off. He was probably paid a fixed fee for the day, so that was a good half hour's work as far as he was concerned. We saw him driving off with a triumphant flourish of exhaust gases as we made our way towards the reception. It is, I think, one of life's peculiarities that people who are not particularly well-off hire expensive hotels, often in far-off places, for their wedding receptions and the rich hold theirs in tents.

The tent in this case was enormous, decorated throughout with swathes of greenery. It was difficult to spot a square inch of actual canvas. Beautiful young people in black whisked around with trays of champagne – coupes, not flutes – and morsels on crackers. They were being directed by a tall middle-aged woman with stylishly cropped hair and capable hands.

Most of the people there were Hugo's friends and relations, and I was keen to pick out the relations, to see who was in Effie's new family. Hugo himself was looking a bit tense, despite being centre of a circle of what looked like his rugby team. It confirmed what I had previously decided about him. Maybe he was good at one-on-one upmanship, but not so much at ease in bigger crowds. Or maybe he was worrying about his speech.

His younger brother Sebastian was very different. A slim figure, a ready smile and blonde hair that flopped becomingly over his forehead. Where Hugo was stiff, Sebastian was fluid, that's the best way I can describe it. A classicist, so Effie had told me, he had the air of a man who does what he likes and expects the world to adore him. In my, admittedly limited, experience, this attitude is self-fulfilling. People are generally very indulgent towards those with lots of self-confidence and scant regard for what anybody else thinks of them. Sebastian swanned around with his arm round his sister, Phoebe, saying he was keeping her out of trouble. 'Getting her into it more likely' said a voice I didn't recognise from somewhere behind me. I spun round and an elderly man smiled at me and raised a whiskey glass.

Phoebe had what people used to call 'class'. A well-proportioned face, good bone structure, what looked like natural blonde hair tied into a French knot, a simple, but probably very expensive, linen dress, practically no make-up and short fingernails. She made me feel blowsy and I wondered how much she and Effie would have in common. Not a lot, as it turned out.

I had worn a pair of unaccustomed high heels and the urge to remove them was powerful. I took my glass and wandered outside and let my bare feet sink into the grass. It was cool and soothing and had that lovely just-mown smell. It reminded me of being a young child and running barefoot on lawns. The air was warm and the sun glinted off a pair of tractors standing idle in the farmyard. In the field beyond were serried rows of sturdy plants. This was my first sight of the vineyard.

Back in the marquee, the formal part of the occasion was getting underway. Pete was looking less than enchanted by the whole thing. He said that he never liked weddings anyway and he would have been happy to sit it out in the pub. I laughed and gave him a hug. Hopefully he would change his mind about that.

Bernie, having excused himself from the speechmaking, had retreated to a corner by the bar. Hugo's father stood in for him and said all the right things with a stern, gravelly voice. The problem was that he said all these things about happy event and all the rest of it, without managing to look at all happy about it. I thought he was probably one of those people who don't smile much.

'Retired high court judge' the woman next to me whispered and that seemed to explain it. What he had given us was a summing up. The woman next to his retired honour looked like she'd rather be joining Effie's dad at the bar. At one point her head dropped and I thought she may have fallen asleep. Was that Hugo's mum?

Hugo was then called upon and said all the required things but it was clear that speechmaking was not one of his skills. Lots of pauses during which he looked around myopically, as if trying not to catch anybody's eye, followed by a quick shufti at his notes and the next bit rushed through to get it over with. Wouldn't have been much cop in the debating society. This was a speech which he couldn't leave to Effie, although she would have made a far better fist of it. Not so the best man. Sebastian launched with gusto into the standard recitation of Hugo's youthful indiscretions, no doubt substantially embellished, declared that the beautiful bride would have been better off with himself, then admitted that on balance maybe not, and finally (thankfully) proposed a toast to the happy couple, the whole peppered with bits of poems and declarations in Latin. I saw Phoebe cover her eyes at one point and Pete, next to me muttered 'Tosser'.

I turned to the woman next to me and introduced myself. She was Deidre, a retired district nurse with the sort of face that inspires confidences.

'I remember them all when they were little' she said. 'They've all grown up big and strong, which is what matters. Hugo was the one always in the wars – broken leg, sprained wrist and the whole raft of childhood illnesses – measles, mumps, chickenpox. His mum bought into all that business about the MMR – Andrew Wakefield and his bogus research. By the time the other two came along she'd come to her senses, so they had the jab, they never had to go through the illnesses. Anyway, look at him now. Makes my job all worthwhile.'

I tried to imagine Hugo as a small boy beset by illness, but somehow the picture wouldn't form. He looked as if he had been born grown-up and frequently annoyed.

I took Pete over to the bar to introduce him to Bernie and we spent some time talking. Bernie was unimpressed with the performance so far. 'There's obviously plenty of money about' he said 'but I've heard better speeches in a pub, made by people who were three sheets to the wind.'

When the formal part of the meal was over, Effie headed over in our direction, looking slightly rumpled but still beautiful. Her hair was coming down, there was a champagne stain on the front of her dress and she appeared to have lost her shoes (or she had discarded them, like I longed to do). We hugged and I whispered 'This is some family you've married into.' She said yes and gave me a rundown, although I'd heard most of it before. His honour is a bit scary, but she's sure she can deal with him. Verity, that's the mother, is constantly a whisker away from her next nervous breakdown ('full of drugs'), Phoebe is a clever scientist, probably the cleverest of all the family, Sebastian is naughty but gorgeous (I gave her a warning look at this point) and the whole show is kept on the road by Dorothy – the woman directing the staff. ('Nobody messes with Dorothy').

She had obviously got the measure of them all, but I didn't envy her the process of adaptation that undoubtedly lay ahead. Edward Fincham in his speech had not referred to her with any discernible warmth, neither Phoebe nor the mother-in-law had spoken to her at all as far as I could see and the only one showing signs of welcome was Sebastian. But he wasn't the one she had married. Hugo had the air of a man who was waiting for it all to be over. I hoped he realised that the being married part was not going to be over anytime soon.

'So will you be living here?' I asked her. I could see the attraction of living up here, the space, the trees and the fresh air, but maybe close proximity to the in-laws wouldn't be so great.

'No darling, Cheyne Walk, with the sheiks and celebs. It's the house that the family have had for about a hundred years, but they moved up here soon after Hugo was born. It's been let out most of the time, but the last tenants left about a year ago, so Hugo was able to move in. Although it's pretty nice here – and a vineyard, can you believe it? But it will be good to be a bit more central – for shopping and stuff.' Of course – shopping. I had forgotten that shopping would now be one of her occupations.

Effie was dragged away by Hugo to talk to what looked like a pair of aged relatives (earning her keep already) and I looked over towards where his retired honour (as I dubbed him to myself) was working the tent. Well, his part of the tent anyway, he wasn't going to head over in our direction. He must have been pretty attractive when he was young and he'd aged quite well. Grey hair is death to most women, but it tends to not look bad on men and he had plenty of it. People were falling over themselves to get his attention but he was looking over their shoulders all the time, scanning the room to see if there was anybody more worthwhile. Dorothy went past and he gave her a brief smile – his Woman Friday. All in all, I decided I wouldn't like to be standing in the dock facing him. He wouldn't be too understanding of the grubby sins most of us get up to.

The older generation melted away before the dancing started, including Bernie, who was one of the first to leave.

I could understand that he'd seen enough of what was on offer and was happy to escape. I couldn't see him forming any kind of bond with Hugo's dad. Effie ordered him a taxi and waited outside with him for it to arrive. I thought that was a nice touch – still in her wedding dress.

By the time she came back inside most of the 'grown-ups' had gone. Left to ourselves, the younger generation spread out and relaxed. Effie and Hugo staggered unceremoniously onto the dance floor and ordered everybody else to join them. Obviously, no rehearsal or dancing lessons had taken place and too much strong drink had been taken for any stylish performance to be possible. I put my arms around Pete and decided that I was probably the lucky one, more so than Effie. By the end, of course, luck would have deserted us both, but I mustn't get ahead of myself.

Chapter Five

THREE WEEKS LATER, FOLLOWING her return from Antigua, I went to visit Effie at Cheyne Walk. You don't have to be famous to live here, but you do have to be rich. That river frontage doesn't come cheap. Number 183. Not one of the houses previously occupied by the famous, but any house here has that cachet – harking back to when Chelsea was raffish and cool, rather than just disgustingly expensive.

Ellie and Hugo's house of weathered red brick had a small but immaculate front garden surrounded by a brick wall, a dove grey front door and highly-polished brass. I wondered who polished it – surely not Effie?

I was almost surprised when Effie opened the door herself and I said so.

'God, you thought I'd have staff? I'm not that far gone. I do have a cleaner, because quite frankly I don't feel competent to maintain a place like this, but nobody living in. Actually' she stopped and thought for a moment, 'the idea of somebody living in doesn't seem so bad. I wouldn't mind a lodger, somebody to chat to.'

She had that faint sunny glow that fair-skinned people get after a holiday in the sun and she was wearing a loose dress from an expensive label, but I could see from the way it was hanging on her that she had lost weight. And really, she didn't have any to lose.

Looking around the place I thought I probably wouldn't like to be responsible for keeping it perfect. The windows were smudge-free and nothing showed up when I swept a fingertip along the mantelpiece. Effie said Dorothy came in and got it ready while they were away. The wonderful Dorothy. The floors were polished to a silky sheen, the curtains pooled over them like water, the sofas were brocade-covered and sinkable. The rug was amazing paintbox shades of indigo, burnt umber and magenta, but had that slightly worn patina, which made it clear that it hadn't come from some showroom. Probably been laboured over for years by underage weavers in Uzbekistan.

And there was quite a collection of silverware – snuff boxes, perfume bottles with silver stoppers, wedding photos in silver frames. There was a really good black and white wedding photo of Effie and Hugo in a heavy silver frame. So that photographer had come up with the goods after all. I opened one of the snuff boxes and sniffed. Nothing.

Effie had flopped into one of the overstuffed armchairs, which looked like it was trying to consume her whole. I replaced the lid on the snuff box.

'I guess this stuff is all valuable.'

She shrugged. 'I'm sure it is. Not my style of course, but Hugo likes it.'

For the first time in our history neither of us knew what to say to each other. The house had silenced us. I had this weird feeling that we didn't belong here. It felt like we were two housebreakers who had broken into some rich person's house and were just making free with their possessions. That was reinforced when Effie suggested coffee and I followed her into the kitchen. She didn't have much of a grip on where everything was, and we had to rummage around to find the coffee and the percolator. We had broken into somebody's house and now we were going to try making coffee in their kitchen. It was a long way removed from the stylish hostess Hugo probably thought he had married.

The kitchen was a surprise. Maybe because, when this house was last renovated, nobody had the idea of entertaining guests in the kitchen, it had escaped whatever refurbishment had taken place elsewhere. The cupboards were a nasty shade of mustard, the sink was cheap stainless steel and the cooker looked pretty much like the model we had in the kitchen in our hall of residence, the one that stood next to the fridge from which we nicked each other's milk. The window, which gave a view of an admittedly beautiful garden, had those elasticated frilly curtains on the bottom half. Everything was clean – Effie's cleaner did a good job – but Homes and Gardens it wasn't. It reminded me of footage I had seen somewhere of Margaret Thatcher in the kitchen in the Downing Street flat. I guess we all expected it to be well posh, as we were all paying for it, and it was a shock to see how crappy it was.

Then I thought, maybe I've got it wrong, maybe the best people, like Hugo and Prime Ministers, have crappy kitchens, maybe that's a sign of U (as opposed to non-U). Maybe having one of those taps that do chilled, fizzy and boiling water out of the same spout marks you out as a prole. Actually I think it's more that rich people never enter their kitchens, they leave that to the staff, so they're not interested in boiling water taps.

While I was standing around thinking all this ('wool-gathering' one of my teachers would have said) Effie had managed to rustle up two mugs of coffee and we carried them carefully back to the sitting room and placed them on the coffee table where expensive magazines were carefully displayed. I put mine on Vogue, right on the face of some pouting celeb, and hoped it would leave a ring. You have to get your kicks where you can.

I told Effie she'd arrived. She was one of the rich now. Although in truth she looked like an orphan washed up on a desert island. If it's possible to be oppressed by *stuff*, that's how I would have described it.

She tucked her legs up under her, picked up her mug and asked for my news. I didn't honestly have much to report. The job was still going well and there was an outside chance of promotion. I really loved being able to work with books. They were paying me reasonably (nothing like the allowance she was probably getting for not working, but these things are all relative) and I was still in the flat in Victoria. Oh, and I was still with Pete, of course.

Effie smiled. 'See. I told you he was the one for you.' I was happy for her to claim foresight on that.

'So tell me everything. How was the honeymoon?' We had exchanged a number of texts while she was away, but now I expected to get the full version. I expected her to be bubbling over with it, Effie who had always had something to say. She was strangely non-committal.

'Everything is pretty good. The honeymoon was fantastic, did I send you the pictures? The house in Antigua was amazing of course – and a butler, can you believe it?' She got up and fetched her phone and I duly admired the beautiful house, the private beach and the gardens – the butler alone was pretty gorgeous.

'So are you pleased to be back?' Somehow she didn't look pleased, but it had to be asked.

She hesitated a moment. 'Well it's a lovely house, there's plenty of money and I can pretty much do what I like.' She spread her arms as if inviting me to admire it all.

'So why aren't you happy?'

'Oh Livy is it that obvious?'

'It's screaming from the rooftops. Is it Hugo?'

She looked up sharply, picked a non-existent bit of fluff off her dress and shrugged her shoulders.

'Hugo's fine. I don't see that much of him because he spends his days at the bank and weekends at the vineyard. And I'm fine. I guess maybe it's just that anti-climax thing. You know, you have this goal that you work towards, and then you get there. And what are you supposed to do after that?'

'I think you have to have a new goal.' I wasn't sure about this, but it sounded right to me. 'As you have lots of money now, maybe you could look at ways to do something good with it.'

I knew that was a mistake as soon as the words left my lips. She rolled her eyes and crossed her arms.

'It's not my money Livy, I can't go throwing it around. I can't set up the Effie Fincham Foundation to end world hunger.'

I was beginning to lose a little patience by this point.

'Effie, first world problems. You need something to do. It doesn't have to be huge or worthy, it just has to be something to do. Nobody can do nothing. It drives people insane. You can't sit around on your arse like some kind of mentally-challenged trophy wife. You need to be out doing stuff.'

You have to laugh. Here was me, with an entrance-level job and a tiny flat in Victoria giving lifestyle advice to a woman with a house in Cheyne Walk and an allowance. Really, she should be sorting out my life. She looked slightly chastened and I wondered if I'd been a bit harsh.

'Perhaps you should contact Jackson. I didn't see him at the wedding.'

'No, he was on holiday. Actually, I do miss Jackson.'

'OK, well he probably misses you too. Let's meet him for lunch, see how he's doing.'

The following week we met Jackson for lunch in the Coach and Horses in South Audley Street, an original Georgian pub with many original features but overlaid with expensive additions to ensure the comfort of its well-heeled patrons. A large table of expense account drinkers was making enough noise to drown out everybody else, but maybe it would have been worse to sit in a silent pub, feeling that everything you said was being overheard.

It was a relief to see Jackson. Here was somebody who knew Effie almost as well as I did and would have her best interests at heart. That was the picture I was painting at any rate. Perhaps he could get her enthusiastic again, where I had obviously failed. Perhaps he could let her have her job back.

Jackson seemed to have had a much better holiday than Ellie. He looked tanned and relaxed and his hair even had a bit of sun bleach. He described at length the Greek island where he had spent a fortnight with his boyfriend – the sun-warmed stone floors of the villa, the morning swims in the sea so clear you could see all the rocks beneath, the leisurely breakfasts of yogurt and honey, the sailing, the grilled squid at the taverna – no butler, mind you. He hadn't taken many photographs, for which I was grateful, but listening to him I really wanted to be there.

Now that he was back, he had lots of news about new acquisitions and upcoming exhibitions. He was sponsoring several young and exciting artists that he was sure were going to make it big. If Effie wanted to come back, he was sure he could find a space for her, but she probably had other plans.

I think I realised at this point that Jackson had a business that he cared about. It wasn't his job to make Effie happy and he would make sure that the gallery did well with her or without her.

Effie remained unusually quiet throughout Jackson's recitation. A few minutes later she went off to the loo, attracting a lot of attention from the expense account table as she went past, and Jackson leaned towards me and assumed a more serious tone.

'This is a disaster isn't it? I blame myself for her meeting him. I was really hoping it wouldn't come to anything.'

'Why not? What's wrong with him?' I whispered, half-afraid that Effie would come back and catch us.

He sighed. 'It's the Finchams as a whole, all of them. They're good customers of mine – lots of money, very keen on artwork - but I wouldn't want to be personally involved with them. It's a strange family, lot of stuff going on. The dominant father and the neurotic mother, how were the kids supposed to turn out?'

Effie reappeared at that point and Jackson sat back, smiled and began telling me a joke about a gorilla and a stick of celery that made no sense whatsoever. Effie seemed to have reapplied her make-up and was looking more cheerful. We ordered more drinks. No worries

Chapter Six

EFFIE NEVER DID GO back to work in the end. After a while I had stopped nagging her about it. After all, work had never been part of the plan. She had chosen Hugo as the alternative to work. Instead of going back to the gallery, she threw herself into redecorating the house in Cheyne Walk (well that kitchen really did need an upgrade, I couldn't argue with that) and any idea of working was then terminated altogether.

About six months after the honeymoon, I met Effie for drinks in her old pub and she told me she was pregnant – three months gone at that point. She was drinking tonic water as she said she couldn't stand the smell of wine and she claimed to be desperately tired most of the time, but she was still looking more animated than I had seen her in a long time and she had that healthy early-pregnancy glow.

'Hugo must be pretty pleased about it.'

'Hugo? Oh, yes of course. He's thrilled. He wants a son, but we'll see what he gets.'

With the topic of Hugo out of the way, we got down to discussing the details – the morning sickness (not so far), the bloating (waiting for that to start), the tiredness (I could sleep lying down on the hard shoulder) and the examinations (apparently by the end everybody's had their hand up you, and you no longer care). I winced a bit at that last one. The birth was to be in a private suite at St Mary's in Paddington, which was already booked. Effie was busily researching the subject of water births. She wanted a natural birth (don't we all, to start with?) and had bought into the idea that the warm water would make pain relief unnecessary (I think she had that a bit wrong).

There was not a lot of support forthcoming from the Finchams for this water birth idea. Hugo didn't want a birthing pool overflowing onto the expensive rugs at Cheyne Walk, although he had conceded that Effie could give birth in the bath if she really wanted to, as long as she had midwives there to deal with it all. Really, he wanted her to give birth efficiently and discreetly at St Mary's and after the unpleasant stuff had all been cleared away, he would be available to wet the baby's head, or whatever. St Mary's probably rolled their collective eyes when Effie suggested a water birth at the hospital but came back and said it was possible as long as her husband arrived with the birthing pool and erected it himself. The idea of Hugo trying to put together a birthing pool, like someone wrestling with the innards of an IKEA wardrobe, while his wife laboured and yelled in the next room was so entrancing that I told her she must pursue it.

In the end, as so often happens in the baby business, the birth plan and the birthing pool went out the window. Effie's pains began a week early, nobody was prepared for it, and after six hours the pain was so excruciating that she was screaming for pain relief. All thoughts of a natural birth were abandoned at that point. To give him his due, Hugo did do the first shift in there, mopping her brow, but after being repeatedly sworn at in words some of which he had never heard before, he retired from the field and I took over.

After twenty hours the medical staff had a bit of a think and decided that if nothing interesting had happened by the time they returned from their tea break, they'd consider an emergency caesarean. And so it transpired. As Effie had refused an epidural, the caesarean had to be done under general anaesthetic, so my last view of her was of her tiny contorted face, lost in the plastic shower cap, as they wheeled her into the theatre.

Forty-five minutes later she was out, all screaming over, clutching a tightly-wrapped bundle which she presented to me as Mabel. Mabel and I looked at each other (although in her case the focussing was probably a bit off) and I had that sensation, which I think is quite common with babies, that I knew her already. Something in the shape of the eyes. Effie let me hold her and I breathed in that lovely newborn smell. 'She's gorgeous' I told Effie. 'Good job.'

She smiled proudly and I handed the baby back. Both of them looked ready to fall asleep.

'Why Mabel?' I liked the name, but I was curious just the same.

'After my grandma – my dad's mum.'

Maybe I was imagining the satisfaction with which she said this, but I wondered if it was one in the eye for the Finchams. Hugo had been hoping for a son and heir, and instead he got Mabel.

Chapter Seven

MABEL'S CHRISTENING WAS A grand affair, held at St James church with a reception at Fawcett Hall. The weather was still warm(ish) so we mostly sat at tables and chairs in the garden and in a large orangery at the back of the house (I think that's what rich people call their conservatories. I didn't see any orange trees growing in there, but there were a couple of Mexican orange blossom bushes, so maybe that's all it takes). Effie had taken some time to recover from the birth and her scar was obviously still hurting, so she was looking tired and moving slowly. But she had made the effort, in a pale lilac wool suit and a cloche hat with a tiny veil. I couldn't imagine how much her outfit had cost, but it looked like money well spent.

Hugo was looking more at ease than he had at the wedding and even made time to talk to me and Pete. He told us that two of their wines had won awards at the London Wine Competition – one silver medal and one bronze. He invited us to the next tasting. I wondered if he was feeling better about himself now that his manhood had been validated, or whatever.

Phoebe was there with a new husband, Andrew, a City trader of some sort. Theirs had been a quiet wedding to which I had, of course, not been invited. Effie had been there briefly, as it was a few days after the birth of Mabel. It seemed a bit curious that they had arranged their wedding to take place at the time when Effie would be giving birth, but there did not seem to be much of a bond between the two couples. Effie was dismissive about the match. Money attracted to money. But maybe also brains attracted to brains. Phoebe was clever and commodity trading would presumably require a certain amount of intellect. Well, that was what I thought, anyway. I didn't know much about commodities or how they were traded. Effie had described Andrew as boring but rich. And in her book rich could make up for quite a lot of boring. Andrew didn't seem all that boring to me, he told a couple of very funny stories.

His worship didn't appear to have altered much since Effie's wedding. He didn't look like a man celebrating his first grandchild and he wasn't paying much attention to the woman who had produced it for him. His wife looked just as wired as she had at the wedding, although she did at least seem to be taking some interest in the baby, and actually sat and held her for a while. I couldn't take my eyes off her until she had handed the baby back, I just felt she could drop her at any time. Probably unfair of me. Sebastian, who was acting as wine waiter, brought her a glass of fizzy water and she smiled vaguely at him.

'Still the nightmare mother' said Effie in my ear. 'Nervous breakdown, or 'nerves' or whatever, rattling with prescription drugs. Apparently she used to regularly threaten suicide, even in front of the kids, when they were small. Of course, she never actually *does* anything, so she won't be much of a granny. Hugo says it's been Dorothy holding things together all these years. His lordship's right-hand woman.'

I realised then that neither Effie nor I referred to Edward Fincham by his name. I thought of him, kind of cynically I guess, as his worship, or sometimes his honour, and Effie was now referring to him as his lordship. Probably none of these salutations were correct as he was now retired anyway. I think it was just that we didn't think of him as a person like anybody else.

I was interested in Verity Fincham, she looked to me like she might have something in common with my mother – all the 'nerves' stuff for a start. She was a slight woman with short, expensively-tinted hair and a determined chin. 'Brittle' was the word that came to mind. Her jewellery was understated, so presumably valuable. She was well past middle-age but there was no sign of a double chin or baggy arms, so she wasn't a complete slouch, whatever Effie said. Maybe she was a secret gym-bunny. It was obvious that she was on drugs of some sort – anti-depressants maybe – because sometimes she gave the appearance of being about to fall asleep and a few moments later her eyes would flick open and dart from side to side as if warding off danger. I wondered if her husband had attempted to stray, like my dad did, but hadn't been able to carry it off. So now he was attached for life to her frustration and resentment and the nervous episodes were the punishments he had to endure. Bit fanciful on my part, no doubt, but she certainly didn't look like a restful person to be with. There was something operating furiously behind the façade, but I felt it was something I wouldn't want to know about.

I hadn't had a chance to look around the main house at the wedding, as the reception had been in the marquee, but now I took my chance to rectify that and slipped away when nobody was looking in my direction.

It was what is usually called a 'mature' house, built in 1869, so Victorian – not so old - according to the stonework above the main door. My heels echoed satisfyingly on the flagstone floors and I tripped lightly up the wide stone staircase. The stairwell carried a procession of paintings, several of them were portraits of grim-faced elderly men. Ancient Finchams perhaps? Seemed unlikely, as the house had not been in the family that long. Or perhaps they had been brought here from Cheyne Walk. Just as well really. Effie would probably have wanted to get rid of them. A trip to the bathroom gave me a chance to snoop into the rooms on the first floor, which had high ceilings and big windows. I admired the view out of one of the bedrooms and spotted Sebastian and Phoebe walking around the back of the house, apparently deep in conversation. He put an arm round her and they moved closer to the house, out of my view. Seeing this slightly altered my opinion of Sebastian. He obviously had some empathy and cared about his sister. I wondered if things were not going as well as they seemed with Andrew.

There was a step behind me. I swung round to see Dorothy looking at me quizzically. She wasn't going to do anything to put me at my ease. No point trying to pretend. I gave her my best smile and forced myself to speak slowly, no nervous gabbling.

'Hello Dorothy. Such a lovely room I was looking for the bathroom, but I couldn't resist sticking my nose in. The view from here is amazing.' I could tell from her expression that she didn't believe a word of it. I was just a cheap snooper.

She was silent for a moment and then came over to join me at the window. She had been about to say something else, but evidently thought better of it. She was going to let me off. It was important to keep things civil.

'Yes, we're quite high up here, so on a clear day you can see the Castle.' She pointed and I squinted hard. 'On a wet day the mist settles and you can't see a thing.'

She turned away 'Let me show you where the bathroom is.' I followed her out, feeling like I had been escorted off the premises.

When I got back downstairs Pete was talking to Effie in the orangery. She had discarded her hat and her shoes. She saw me first and waved me over.

'I think we all need some space. Let's take Mabel and go for a wander outside.'

That sounded good to me. Ellie led the way to the back of the house where the outdoor stuff was kept. There were about twenty-five ancient Barbours and other varieties of waxed jackets and raincoats hanging from rusty hooks. Most of them looked like they hadn't been disturbed in twenty years, and they probably hadn't. We kicked off our shoes and sorted our way through piles of wellingtons, some encrusted with mud, some with holes in the bottom, some in pairs where each boot was a different size. Eventually we emerged, looking like three farmhands. I was glad that Effie had covered her beautiful lilac suit with a grungy old mac - I didn't think any grade of dry cleaning would remove a mud stain from that. It was a lovely sunny, blowy day, we didn't need to wrap the baby up, and I found I loved pushing the pram around. Maybe, I thought, I'll get one of my own to push one day.

As we got outside, we were joined by Sebastian who was presumably also playing truant from the occasion. He offered to show us round the vineyard. It struck me he was really playing the host that day, more so than Hugo or his father.

I was surprised by how much I loved the vineyard. Walking in the sun between the rows of vines gave me a kind of holiday feeling. Effie slipped her arm through Sebastian's and I wondered briefly where Hugo was. We came to a huge barn and Sebastian led the way inside. Apparently, this had been where the lambing had taken place in the sheep-rearing days. Now it was a high-tech, sterile environment. When we got to the pressing machine, which was gleaming and enormous, not one of those rustic wooden ones that you see in pictures, Pete was suddenly much more interested and Sebastian answered all his questions as if he knew what he was talking about. And maybe he did. It was easy to underestimate Sebastian, indeed he invited that, with his laconic attitude and refusal to take himself seriously. I realised for the first time that there was a lot more to him than that.

Coming out of the shed we saw Dorothy, who had also found a reason to excuse herself from the reception. Presumably the waiting staff had all been given their orders and could now be relied upon to carry them out. She was also wearing wellingtons, walking around with an old paint can, feeding half a dozen geese, who followed her every step, honking as they went. It reminded me of those scenes in the West Wing, where the President is walking through the White House with a whole babble of advisors whispering in his ear and vying for his attention. I watched the grain arcing out between her strong, flexible fingers.

'Just for domestic consumption' said Sebastian.

'The geese you mean? Isn't that a bit ...difficult?' I know I'd find it difficult.

Sebastian shook his head. 'Nah, country people are used to that. Country people and Dorothy.'

Chapter Eight

AND SO BEGAN WHAT I think of as the golden period of my life. Pete and I were living together in Victoria (despite its miniscule size, my flat had turned out to be better than his) and with two salaries the rent was not a problem. Pete and I enjoyed each other's company, we laughed at the same jokes, we bought bikes and spent weekends cycling round London, discovering parks and bits of canal towpath and going up and down the Embankment. I was even thinking about getting a dog. Sometimes we called in to see Effie at Cheyne Walk and then we would chain up the bikes and all go for a walk with Mabel in the pram. She had become much more animated since the arrival of Mabel and was always pleased to see us. Pete seemed to enjoy these visits and always made a fuss of Mabel. I took that as a good sign, perhaps he would be happy for us to settle down soon and have a baby.

Occasionally at weekends we would all drive up the M40 and wander round the vineyard. I found the whole wine-making process completely fascinating, from the cultivation of the grapes to the picking and pressing, to the bottling and labelling and the marketing. It was clear that it was a well-run operation. Hugo put in the odd appearance in the office, but seemed to work mostly at the house. Sebastian showed us how the various processes were carried out and Colin let us have a go at operating the press and the bottling machine. Dorothy seemed to flit in and out, helping with this and that, but she was also surprisingly friendly.

Most of the wine was sold through specialised vintners or wine clubs and it was quite a lot more expensive than the stuff in the supermarkets, but it was gradually becoming well known in wine circles and, amazingly, English wine now had a certain cachet. People were prepared to pay a bit more for it.

This relaxed way of life changed six months later when I discovered I was pregnant. It was unplanned and Pete was visibly shocked when I told him. I hoped it was happy-shocked rather than horrified-shocked and we had our first serious row when I accused him of not wanting a baby with me. He said that wasn't true and, as the days passed, he seemed to get more accustomed to the idea. I didn't bring the subject up again, I so wanted to believe in us and our future as a family and I didn't want to ask any question to which I might not like the answer.

It was clear that we couldn't stay in the tiny flat in Victoria. It was really too small for both of us and babies require far more space than adults. After some frantic searching I found a two-bedroom flat in Pimlico. It was considerably more expensive than where we were living, but still affordable and only a very short distance to move. With a baby on the way, we needed the transition to be as easy as possible.

I carried on working through most of my pregnancy and stopped about three weeks before the due date. This meant that I could have the maximum amount of maternity leave to spend with the baby. My work colleagues gave me one of those giant cards and a very generous voucher for an expensive babywear shop. Effie brought me all her baby stuff and a whole slew of books detailing the gruesome minutiae of giving birth. I resolved not to read any of them.

Effie had suffered very few of the problems of pregnancy, apart from the tiredness, and had never looked pregnant. She reminded me of those cases of women who think they have indigestion and then suddenly give birth, without anybody having spotted that they were pregnant. I was very different. For some reason, my body was programmed to retain as much fluid as possible. When I woke up in the morning my legs looked normal. By 10 am they would be so swollen that I couldn't bend my knees. The only solution was to keep them up as much as possible. Going down to the swimming pool and just floating on my back brought instant relief. Between the fluid retention and the morning sickness, there was a whole period when I was conscious of little else besides the condition of my body. This is probably why I paid less attention than I should have done to Effie.

This is not to say that I paid no attention at all. It was becoming clear that her marriage was in trouble. She very rarely mentioned Hugo and when she did it was in disparaging terms. Her main source of happiness seemed to be Mabel and she claimed that Hugo had little interest in his daughter. I didn't understand how the relationship which she had entered into so enthusiastically had gone wrong so quickly and I was too self-absorbed at that time to ask the right questions. Whether I would have gotten the right answers is another matter.

About two weeks before my due date I hauled my distended body round to see Effie and found her in the company of an older woman who introduced herself as Kate Black. She had short hair cut in a smooth bob and the sort of slim figure that I was wondering if I would ever get back to and, as she smiled at me with her white teeth, I saw her taking in my unkempt appearance – or maybe I was imagining that. Most of the time I was too tired to fuss about personal maintenance – showering and remembering to put on a clean T-shirt was about as far as it went – and then I would meet a new person and become suddenly aware of my appearance. So it was with Kate. I had the feeling I had seen her somewhere before, but I couldn't think where. I asked her and she laughed and said wasn't it always that way in London? We'd probably been in the same shop or restaurant once, but she was sure she would have remembered me. We shook hands and as she moved away the scent of her remained. She smelled expensive. This would be Effie in twenty years' time I thought – still attractive, relaxed, stylish, prosperous. I was wrong about that.

Kate took her turn holding Mabel and began telling us about her two grown-up daughters. One was studying medicine and the other was working in advertising. They were twins, but not identical, although they did look a bit alike in some respects and they were the best thing in her life. (She actually said that. What had they done to deserve a mother like that?) It soon became clear that Kate and her daughters were wealthy, thanks to the death of her husband, who had apparently invested in the right things at the right time. So now it fell to Kate to protect her daughters (or their money at least) from fortune hunters. Sounds pretty Dickensian, but I guess the concept doesn't date.

Effie pronounced herself very much in favour of this approach, but I thought it was not a problem she would have to deal with in the immediate future in respect of Mabel. Then I wondered if she was thinking more of herself. Although Hugo, whatever his shortcomings, could not be accused of having married her for her money. While I was lost in these random thoughts, Effie was telling Kate all about her in-laws and Kate was letting her run on. Either she didn't like to interrupt, or she was just relaxing into it, as people often did when Effie got going. Or maybe she was really interested, but that didn't seem likely.

'Your father-in-law sounds a bit off-putting' I heard Kate say. Something in the way she said it snagged my attention. Or did it? Maybe this is just hindsight.

'Totally. He's the most unfatherly person you can imagine. So different to my dad. To be honest, I think he does like Mabel, but he acts like I don't exist. His gaze kind of passes over me without stopping.'

'That's not an experience she's used to,' I pointed out.

Kate laughed. 'No, I bet you're used to getting lots of attention, Effie.'

Effie smiled ruefully. 'Well, that was certainly the case before I got married. I think I've lost it a bit now.'

'But what about your mother-in-law?' said Kate. 'She must surely be interested in you and Mabel. I'm so looking forward to my daughters having babies.'

Effie refilled the glasses and sat back. 'Don't get me started on her.' People always say that, I've noticed, when they are totally planning to get started on some subject.

Effie put her glass down and set off. 'I don't think she relates to other people. She's certainly never bothered with me. I would say she doesn't even like her own kids most of the time. Hugo told me that when he was small his dad used to hit him a lot and she never tried to stop it. She's been on drugs all his life.'

'That sounds very sad,' said Kate, putting her glass back on the table. 'Something must have happened to make her like that.'

'I guess so. I think there may have been a few incidents, but I shouldn't gossip. She won't be having too much to do with Mabel, that's for sure.' Effie was right about that, of course. Verity wasn't going to have much to do with Mabel.

'Well Mabel is what matters' said Kate, looking down at the sleeping child in her arms.

I was thinking about Hugo. Maybe being beaten as a kid had made him the way he was. I would imagine it makes it hard to relax with other people. So he could blame his mother for that.

Kate left a few moments later and we watched her driving off in a smart black Lexus. As we moved away from the window I asked Effie how they had met. She smiled. 'We both tried to get into the same taxi outside Selfridges' she said. 'Then I suggested we share the ride.'

'First world problems again' I laughed. 'You don't get that problem on the bus.'

It would be some weeks before I saw Effie again, not that I realised it at the time.

A week later my waters broke just as I was about to get into bed and a white-faced Pete drove me to St Thomas's. He was driving too fast, while I doubled up and gasped next to him, and we overshot the hospital twice before finally making it into the car park. I had assumed that once the waters had broken everything would be well on the way, but not at all. Ben's arrival was long and painful, a lot more painful than I had expected (I should have paid more attention to Effie's magazines) and I did my share of screaming and swearing but I did at least avoid the emergency caesarean, if not the episiotomy. And when I looked into Ben's eyes, I knew that here at last was the person I would love forever.

Chapter Nine

I SPENT THE NEXT few months in the haze of new motherhood – breastfeeding problems, cracked nipples, discharges, aching episiotomy scar, delirious with tiredness, overcome with love. Whenever Ben slept, I was tempted to lie down and sleep too, which is of course the sensible thing to do. But then any period when he slept was also the only opportunity to clear up the mess made while he was awake. I was constantly fantasising about sleep, wondering if I could hire a babysitter for an evening and just go to bed, but I knew I'd be out of the bed as soon as I heard him cry. Effie came round sometimes and we would sit there surrounded by nappies and bottles, wondering how we had arrived so soon at this point in life.

It was really important to me that Ben would feel happy and loved. I wanted him to be able to look back on his childhood and think it was one of the best times of his life. Pete was just as besotted with Ben as I was and would often take him out in the pram at weekends so that I could get an extra sleep. Our relationship seemed to be back on track and we now had visits from Pete's parents who lived in Cambridge and were excited to meet their new grandson. They were too far away to do any babysitting, but I appreciated their support. Pete had probably told them something about my family, so they were tactful enough not to ask if my parents had been to visit.

This upheaval in our lives unfortunately coincided with Pete being put in charge of a new project with a crucial deadline. He was working late most evenings and I had to wonder if it was partly so that he could escape some of the chaos at home. I would also have preferred to be back in the office some of the time, to be sitting in an ergonomic chair, sipping coffee, thinking about something removed from the domestic. And our life was now disrupted in other ways. Ben was waking for feeds about four times a night and we realised pretty soon that there was no point both of us being awake half the night, so I was sleeping in our bed with Ben and Pete was sleeping upstairs in the attic room.

This probably explains why when, three months later, Effie called and said she was sure Hugo was trying to kill her, I thought I was just hearing things. What she was saying didn't compute. I knew extreme tiredness could lead to delusion, and here it was. She invited herself round and I expected her to march in and laugh and say, 'No Livy, you must have misheard, I never said that'.

I got a shock when I saw her. If she wasn't her best self at the christening, she was looking even more washed out when she walked heavily in and put Mabel down on the rug next to Ben. She was wearing a beige Burberry trench which seemed to suck all the colour out of her and the knot around her waist only emphasised her thinness. Her pale blonde hair looked dead and dull tied up on top of her head with a scrunchie and her cheekbones stood out darkly in her white face. I twisted the top off a bottle of wine and waited to hear what was going on.

She took her coat off and draped it over a chair then took the glass from me.

'He doesn't want me anymore' she said, without preamble. 'Oh, he wants me in *that* way of course, no getting away from him, but he doesn't want me as a person. The family have never liked me and that's never going to change. I think he wants to get rid of me. Not a divorce – he won't want me taking half his money – but some other way. I'm like a failed project.'

I forbore to remind her that she had always regarded Hugo as a project, so maybe it wasn't so surprising that he saw her in the same way. Just as I was having this thought, she pulled up the sleeve of her sweater and showed me the bruises. 'I'm afraid next time he'll go too far.'

I was shocked by the bruises. Some of them were turning yellow, all of them looked deep and vicious. Effie has the sort of pale translucent skin that will bruise easily, or at least show the bruises easily. There was no hiding them.

I tried to imagine what his hands were doing when he made those marks. And I was angry on her behalf. Effie is the ultimate 'moving on' girl. She's left a string of disappointed men in her wake. How can anybody think he can do this to her?

I started with the standard advice. 'You have to get away from him. Just walk out. Or tell him to get out and leave you and Mabel in the house. You're not going to be one of those women who stay with men who abuse them.'

She laughed and I relaxed. She wasn't going to turn into some downtrodden female. 'I'm not going to be staying with him because I still love him and think he can be reformed, that's for sure. But I'm not going without a decent settlement and I may have to take on the whole bloody family to get it.'

Of course. Hugo being rich does complicate things.

And then she sat back, topped up her wineglass and settled in to talk about the Finchams.

'There's something going on in the family that I don't understand' she said. 'It's like a hidden subtext. They all know about it but they don't discuss it and certainly not in front of an outsider like me.'

'But how do you know that it's even a thing Effie? They're not very outgoing people – maybe that's all it is.'

She shook her head. 'Oh no, it's definitely a thing. You know how most families have shared jokes, shared experiences, stuff they all remember, some way in which they relate together as a group? Well, there's none of that here.'

'Well to be honest' I pointed out, 'there was none of that in my family either. Not all families are happy families.'

'Yes, that's true, your case was another outlier. But me and my dad, although there was just the two of us and we had rows sometimes, we were comfortable with each other, we could relax in each other's company. I think that's what's missing. They're all on edge with each other. I don't think old Fincham even likes his kids much – or certainly not Hugo. And she – the mad mother – hardly ever appears. I saw her once or twice driving off in her Alfa Romeo, but she was on her own, she didn't take anybody with her. That's when she's not having one of her relapses and having to take to her bed. They all put on a good show in public – like they did for the wedding and the christening – but that's all it is – a show. They're just a bunch of separate individuals and I think if it wasn't for the business, they wouldn't have too much to do with each other, which would be a better thing. And I think the reason they're not comfortable in each other's company is because there's a secret there, there's something they're not talking about.'

'But lots of families have secrets.' I was definitely playing devil's advocate here. I thought she shouldn't get too carried away with this.

She took another swig of wine and put the glass down by her feet. 'Yes, they do. But most family secrets get kind of buried and people forget about them and life goes on. In this case, there's a secret that's travelling through time with them, it's not staying buried. And of course, they're a wealthy, high-profile family. The rich are different from us, just like Hemingway said – only they don't just have more money, they have more secrets, and they're more vulnerable to exposure. That's what I think anyway.'

'But you're part of the family Effie – you're one of the rich.'

'Well I may not be part of the family for much longer. And when it all unravels, I'll need some leverage. So I'm going to find out exactly what's going on. I'm not going to get a decent settlement out of them without a fight. And I want sole custody of Mabel.'

'But you're entitled to a settlement anyway Effie. You have Mabel, he has to support her.'

She shook her head. 'We haven't been married very long. I can't exactly claim half his income. They have tame lawyers. I wouldn't be able to afford legal representation. They'd just run down the clock on me. I'll get whatever they're obliged to pay for Mabel and they'll probably give me a payoff. That will be it.'

'In that case, you'd be better off killing him. You'd do better as a widow.' It was the sort of thing you shouldn't say, even in fun, but we laughed it off.

Pete arrived home in the middle of this. Recently he hadn't seemed to have much patience with Effie, brushing off any discussion of her, and the way he rolled his eyes at me when Effie repeated her tale of woe suggested he thought she was dramatising as usual.

Effie got out her phone to summon an Uber and Pete offered her a lift home, as it wasn't far. I told him to take my car, but he said his was closer to the house. I could see Effie was grateful – she looked exhausted and Mabel had already dropped off.

'Just come in quietly' I said to Pete. 'Try not to wake us up.' He nodded.

Chapter Ten

At about six am there was a loud banging at the front door, followed by a further banging at the door of our flat. I was in the middle of a dream and immediately began to tell my antagonist that there was no point throwing those rocks. After a few seconds I woke up and realised it was happening in the real world. I was out of bed, down the hall and opening the door in my dressing gown before I'd even begun to wonder who it might be.

It was the police of course, who else would it be at that time?

They flashed their badges and I invited them in, wishing for some mad reason that I'd tidied up Ben's things before going to bed. Pete managed to drag some clothes on before coming down, which gave me a chance to run back to the bedroom and dress. Ben had now woken up so I brought him with me. Neither of us really knew what we were doing.

The middle-aged woman was called Murphy and she was a Detective Inspector and the young guy was a Detective Constable Wilcox. So she was the senior one. Her hair was purple. His hair was neatly cut and definitely not purple.

They wanted to know about Effie. When had we last seen her? Hugo had told them she was coming here last night and they wanted to know when she left and how she got home.

It was at this point that I asked if something had happened to Effie, but they weren't answering that question.

Pete had turned white. 'What's happened?' he demanded. 'I drove Effie home last night. She was fine when I left.'

That was it. They immediately split us up, no conferring. Pete was taken to the police station by the senior woman and DC Wilcox settled in to get my version of events. He wasn't going to help me out. He looked like the sort of guy you could tell a joke to and if it wasn't funny, he wouldn't laugh. He wouldn't humour you. He sat on a straight-backed chair and got out his notebook. There's something about somebody sitting in front of you ready to write stuff down that makes you feel guilty whether you've done anything or not. I spent a few seconds focussing on his large and very well-polished shoes and their exact placement on my carpet, then the knife-edge creases in his trousers, and then worked my way up to his face which carried an expression that told me he was waiting for me to begin, and would wait as long as it took. It was hard to breathe. I took a shallow breath and started.

I told him about Effie's visit, what time she arrived, how she looked (not great), what we talked about (her not great marriage) and what time she left with Pete. And the question he seemed most interested in – what time did Pete get back? I didn't have a ready answer to that. I did a quick calculation, allowed an hour for him to get there and back and said eleven o'clock. Was I still up when he came in? No, but I heard him

'What's happened to Effie?' I said. 'I want to know, Effie's my friend.'

He told me Effie had been found dead. Just like that. Efie's dead. A great wave of sadness seemed to hit me in the diaphragm and I bent forward to absorb it. I guess I had known as soon as they turned up and started asking questions, but I was somehow hoping that it was just some kind of mistake, that nothing had really happened. She'd turn up somewhere. Then I had another thought.

'What about Mabel? What's happening to her?'

'I think one of the family members is looking after her.'

I pressed him for details but that was all he would tell me. Or maybe he hadn't got any details either.

It was now sinking in that Pete was a suspect. Effie was dead and Pete was a suspect. That was why they had taken him away. Driving her home last night had put him right at the scene. There wasn't much I could usefully do. I would have asked to go and see Pete, but that probably wouldn't be allowed at this stage, and anyway I had to feed Ben who was properly awake now and gathering his strength for a big scream.

Another police officer arrived with a warrant to search the place. DC Wilcox asked if I wanted to leave but I opted to stay. I thought that might persuade them to get through it a bit quicker and leave me and Ben alone. After a bit I realised that that was a mistake. I think it's the gloves that do it. Watching them opening cupboards in surgical gloves, as if the place was contaminated. Thinking of those same gloves rooting through my underwear drawer and lifting out the sticky bottles of ketchup and soy sauce in my kitchen cupboards. After a few minutes I bundled Ben up and we went to sit it out in Starbucks.

And all the time I was thinking about Pete. What possible reason could Pete have for killing Effie? None at all. So the police would realise that. As he didn't do it, they wouldn't find any evidence that he did, so there was actually nothing to worry about. But that didn't stop me worrying – we've all seen TV dramas where the wrong person is convicted.

Maybe it was odd that I was thinking about Pete, who was facing temporary disruption to his life, rather than Effie, who was facing eternity. Thinking about Effie was just too difficult. I knew I was avoiding it. She'd just always been there, always with an opinion on everything, usually a disgraceful opinion, the person I had been closest to for so long, the person who would always tell me how it was, with no regard for tact or socially acceptable truths. There was a big hole there now and it would never be filled.

Then I thought about Effie's dad – Bernie – and how he must be feeling. It occurred to me that of all the people in her life who would be affected by her death, Bernie's loss would be the cleanest, his grief the least sullied by any self-serving considerations. I was glad he had Albert.

Later it turned out that the information I'd given the police about what time Pete returned was fairly accurate, or at least agreed with the sighting of his car by the camera on the high street. That was a relief because I didn't actually hear him come in.

But, as far as I could tell, it didn't seem to have taken him off the suspect list.

PART TWO

Chapter Eleven

DI MIRANDA MURPHY CALLED up a squad car and arranged for Pete Grantham to be taken to the station ('and give the poor bugger a cup of tea'). Then she got in her car and set off back to Cheyne Walk. She had been up since three o'clock that morning, awakened from a dream of herself holidaying on a Greek island, with a handsome Greek (as if) by a call from the station. She had thrown on some clothes and run for her car, belatedly aware that she had left the house keys in the house. Hopefully the lodgers would be around tonight to let her back in. What she would really like now was a shower and a cup of coffee, but the crime scene was unlikely to provide either of these requirements. Time to put bodily discomforts to one side.

It had been some time since she had had a major case and she was eager to get on with it. She knew she had only been given this case because DI Wellesley had sustained a broken leg in a rugby match at the weekend. The DCI, a woman-hater named Bellweather, would never have let her loose on it if there was any alternative and she certainly wouldn't have made DI on his watch.

It had always been clear to Murphy that Kevin Wilcox had been assigned to her in order to keep her in her place or, even better, keep her on edge. Wilcox had come through the graduate recruitment stream and arrived in the division fresh from basic training, sporting an immaculate suit, naked ambition and a fixed, dedicated glare. Murphy had seen Bellweather licking his lips as he sized him up and known that she was destined to get him. Here was the person, she could see Bellweather thinking, who would report her if she didn't do things by the book, or if she made un-PC remarks, or got too familiar with members of the public, or failed to complete the necessary paperwork in the allotted time. Here was her nemesis and he, Bellweather, would enjoy running him. By Christmas she would have resigned or put in for a transfer. Well, Bellweather was still waiting and hoping, and Murphy didn't fancy his chances.

***

The police tape was already up around number 183 as she drove past, looking for a parking space, and Murphy thought she saw curtains moving in a few windows, but there were no obvious rubberneckers to disperse. People in Cheyne Walk wouldn't want to be seen gawping in the street. And maybe one or two of them wouldn't be too keen to attract the attention of the police. The accumulation of large amounts of personal wealth often required the employment of practices which were morally, if not legally, dubious. The door-to-door operation here would be interesting, that was for sure.

The officer on duty outside had changed and she showed her badge to his replacement, a frankly good-looking young man who put his feet together and straightened up at her appearance. She didn't envy him this shift. Standing around doing effectively nothing is the most tiring occupation imaginable.

'Anybody arrived?'

'The pathologist is inside and that lady over there just turned up. I told her she wouldn't be allowed in.' He indicated with a sideways nod of his head a woman leaning against the inside wall. Murphy looked across and then walked over to her and the woman drew herself up to her full height, putting her chin about level with Murphy's eyebrows. It was a strong chin, rounding off a well-chiselled face and large brown eyes. Not exactly pretty, but certainly arresting. Murphy decided she was probably older than she looked.

The woman held out her hand and seized Murphy's in a strong grip.

'Dorothy Hepple. I work for the family. Mr Fincham asked me to come and check on the house.'

'I'm DI Murphy Ms Hepple, and I'm afraid we can't let you into the house until we've completed our enquiries. By Mr Fincham, I take it you mean Mr Fincham senior.'

'Yes of course, Edward Fincham, not Hugo. Hugo called his father, but it was a very brief call. He told us Effie was dead, which has been a terrible shock. Can you tell us what happened?'

So here comes the real reason she's here, thought Murphy. She shook her head.

'I'm afraid I don't have any details at the moment. Mrs Fincham was found dead, her husband called the police and he is now helping us with our enquiries. As soon as we have any information to release, we will make sure that the family are informed first.'

Dorothy Hepple nodded. 'Certainly. I understand.' She gathered her coat more closely around her and Murphy, who prided herself on not being a clothes whore, was impressed nonetheless by the expensive swing of the toffee-coloured wool.

'As you're here, can I just ask you a few questions?'

Dorothy inclined her head. 'Of course'.

'I haven't been to see the family yet, the only one I've met is Hugo. So you are not a family member?'

'No, I'm an employee. I've worked for Edward Fincham for over twenty-five years. I used to be his children's nanny and now I'm his housekeeper.'

'He must be a good employer. And part of your job is to look after this house?'

'Yes. If anything needs fixing or replacing, I organise it.'

'Does that mean you have a key?'

Dorothy hesitated. Murphy could see her weighing up her answers and deciding there were really no options. 'Yes.'

'Did you come here yesterday at any time?'

Dorothy shook her head. 'No, I didn't.' Murphy stayed silent, wondering if anything else might follow this, but Dorothy Hepple was too smart for that. She simply hitched her bag higher on her shoulder. 'Is that all?'

'For now, yes. Thank you for your time.'

Dorothy nodded and walked out of the gate. Murphy followed a few seconds later and spotted her climbing into a navy blue BMW parked a few doors down. She memorised the number plate. Definitely a well-paid housekeeper.

Inside the house SOCO were padding around puffing powder and collecting samples and generally making themselves at home. One of them that she thought she recognised despite his plastic pantomime suit gave her a brief nod.

Death had occurred in the sitting room which now looked like nobody had dusted it in a year.

The toddler had been collected by Hugo Fincham's sister and the body was still in place. She lay spread out on the carpet in a pose that she would probably not have wanted to be seen in. She was wearing, or half wearing, a dark blue silk kimono embroidered with apple blossom. Very Japanese. Undoubtedly very expensive. The kimono had fallen open and it was clear that she was wearing nothing underneath it. It looked as if somebody had drawn the kimono across to cover her pubic area and Murphy knew that wouldn't have been the paramedics or the pathologist. Her husband perhaps? That would have been understandable. In spite of the bloated and distorted face, Effie looked young and vulnerable and Murphy was sure that if her eyes had not been closed (presumably by the paramedics) the expression in them would be one of utter surprise.

The pathologist, Linda Fleming, was still bent over the body and now stood up with a grimace. 'My bloody knees. I think the department should pay for replacements.' She brushed herself down. 'A very workmanlike job. It would have been very quick. I know that's not always true but, in this case, I think it is. So maybe that's some comfort for her relatives. She's very slight, a strong pair of hands round her throat and it wouldn't have taken long. No sign of any rope burns or anything like that, so no point looking about for weapons, silk scarves or whatever. This is manual strangulation. Death between 9pm and 1am, can't get any closer than that. We'll know more after the pm.'

Murphy looked at the hands. The nails were quite short, but well- manicured and painted dark blue. She remembered hearing something about nails continuing to grow after death, but, on reflection, that was probably rubbish and she wouldn't dare ask Linda about it. 'Anything under her fingernails?'

'Not that I can immediately see. She might not have had time to fight back. Bruises on the arms, but they're old. Although there are two sets of bruises on the shoulders – old ones and some new ones over the top. Pm tomorrow morning. Will you be there?'

Murphy nodded reluctantly. She hated post-mortems, as did everybody else, but they did serve to stiffen the determination to catch the perpetrator, if only because it was he/she who had created the circumstances in which Murphy had to stand in that freezing place for an hour witnessing something unspeakable.

Linda Fleming closed her bag and staggered off and Murphy signalled to the mortuary staff that the body could be removed. Now the clock was running. That crucial first twenty four hours in which they needed to get the evidence in. Time to get out of the way and let SOCO get on with it. They couldn't be rushed, much as she'd have liked to. But SOCO were mainly working on the ground floor, so she could probably seize the opportunity to have a quick look upstairs. By the time she had finished having this thought, she was on the top landing. Nobody had stopped her yet. A SOCO emerged from a bathroom and gave her a questioning look, satisfied himself that she was wearing gloves and then went back to what he was doing.

There would be more than one bathroom, Murphy thought, they probably had one each. She set about opening doors at random – four bedrooms, a nursery, what looked like an office. All four of the bedrooms contained beds and two of them appeared to be in use. One was obviously Effie's bedroom – a large closet crammed with clothes and shoes and more of each draped across the floor. Murphy counted thirty-two pairs of shoes. This was probably not useful information, but it did demonstrate that Hugo Fincham allowed his wife pretty free rein with the bank cards. She tried to imagine what it would be like to have thirty-two pairs of shoes and presumably at least thirty-two outfits (more, by the look of the rail). Didn't that just make life more difficult? How about those mornings when you got up and couldn't think what the hell to wear? Wouldn't it be worse when you had so many more options to choose from? The truth, of course, was that usually the people who had this amount of clothing to deal with were not the people who had to drag something on and dash off to work in the morning. They probably had hours at their disposal to select and discard outfits at leisure, to worry about what they'd already been seen in and to wonder what other people would be wearing. And of course, what would look good on their Instagram. It sounded bloody exhausting.

The bed was furnished in what she could see was high thread count Egyptian cotton. Murphy approved of this. It was one of her personal extravagances. It was rumpled as if somebody had recently risen from it. Which of course Effie probably did last night, when her caller arrived.

The dressing table had a triptych mirror, allowing the user to check their profile from all angles and the surface was littered with jars and bottles – day cream, night cream, under-eye cream, cleanser, toner and four different perfumes. A make-up bag held more of the same, plus paracetamol and a blister pack of what looked like contraceptive pills.

It was a woman's room, not a marital bedroom. Maybe Hugo had to arrange a visit to his wife's bedroom in order to obtain his conjugal rights.

The other occupied bedroom presumably belonged to Hugo and things here were much tidier. Suits neatly lined up in the wardrobe, each with a plastic cover over the shoulders. Shoes with shoe trees in (who the hell does that?) and a box with assorted brushes. A dozen shirts with laundry tags (presumably he knew better than to expect Effie to do washing and ironing). It looked like the bedroom of an older man – a fussy, particular older man. Murphy's memory of her son's bedroom into which she had occasionally ventured when the last of the cereal bowls had disappeared, seemed like a model of sanity and normality compared to this. She hoped he hadn't started putting plastic covers on his jackets and trees in his shoes. Twelve-hour shifts at the hospital probably took care of that.

The bed was made and had not been slept in. That would be because the cleaner had been in yesterday to make the beds and clean up and Hugo had not yet made it into his bed. The sleeping arrangements raised a number of questions and she was looking forward to asking them. Two suspects in the frame so far – the husband and the friend's husband (or were they married? Maybe not). Lots of questions to be answered.

Chapter Twelve

Hugo Fincham was not at his best. His shirt looked as if he had slept in it (which he had, briefly) and a shadow covered his lower jaw. He was only in his thirties but Murphy looked at him closely because his current appearance seemed like a foreshadowing of how he would look in his forties or fifties or even (perish the thought) sixties. Already there was a coating of bad temper over his features and that would deepen and harden with time, narrowing his eyes and fixing forever the set of his jaw. But right now he was thirty-four, according to the paperwork, still attractive and returning her stare with one of his own which said that he was affronted to be stuck in this ghastly room about to be questioned by a middle-aged woman who looked like she should be cleaning offices. He was right about the room. It had bottle green walls, a grey ceiling and a cement floor to which the tiles clung listlessly. It felt cold even in summer as the brick wall right outside the window prevented any heat or light from entering the space. It was generally acknowledged to be the most horrible interview room and Murphy always booked it for suspects that she felt would benefit from a bit of initial softening up.

Hugo sat next to the family solicitor, a rotund, wheezy man in a similarly crumpled suit, who looked as if he had been rudely dragged from his bed and really wished he was somewhere else. Murphy hoped he wouldn't complicate things by having a myocardial infarction while the interview was in progress.

Wilcox had returned from Pimlico and joined her in the interview. He was looking pretty good for somebody who'd been up all night. That was youth for you. She decided to let him start off and gave him a nod. Wilcox started the tape and intoned the preliminaries. When that was done, he turned to Hugo.

'We're sorry for your loss Mr Fincham.' Hugo rolled his eyes. Wilcox continued regardless. 'Now Mr Fincham can you tell us in your own words everything that happened yesterday from the moment when you left your place of employment.'

Hugo curled his lip at that 'place of employment'. 'I've explained all of that at least twice already.' He sighed. 'I left the vineyard at about ten in the evening, it was late because we had a meeting. I arrived home about midnight and found my wife unresponsive. I called the emergency services. That's it.'

Wilcox nodded as if at the reasonableness of this response, and then got going.

'So let's get some details here, Mr Fincham. You were at your place of employment from say six o'clock until ten o'clock and did not leave the premises at any time. Is that correct?'

'Yes. That's correct.' Hugo was keeping his annoyance under control.

'And this meeting, what time did that begin?'

'About eight o'clock.'

'Bit late to start a meeting, isn't it? What were you doing up to eight o'clock?'

The solicitor laid a hand on Hugo's arm and Murphy saw Hugo make a definite effort to control his breathing. He was obviously a man with a short fuse. His reply when it came was terse and mechanical.

'I was at work – my other 'place of employment' until about 5pm. I drove out to the vineyard. We had dinner from about 6.30 to 8 o'clock, then we had a meeting.'

Wilcox nodded understandingly. 'OK, that's good. So there will be minutes of this meeting?'

Hugo looked surprised at this question. 'Yes' he replied eventually, 'but they won't be typed up yet.'

'No problem. Who will be responsible for that?'

'Dorothy will.'

'That's your father's housekeeper?'

'Correct.'

'OK, we'll get a copy from her. So perhaps you can tell us what the agenda items were according to your recollection.'

Murphy knew that Wilcox was now enjoying this interview, although his expression remained completely deadpan. Hugo was finding it less enjoyable.

'This is ridiculous.'

'Well you see, sir, it does enable us to verify, to our satisfaction, that such a meeting did take place and that you were a participant. We have to establish your whereabouts for the evening, so this meeting is really quite a fortunate event. If you had spent the evening on your own at the cinema, there would be a lot more investigation needed.'

Wilcox continued to dig with commendable persistence into the minutiae of Hugo's movements during the relevant two hours and for a moment Murphy thought they were going to be rewarded with an eruption, but it was averted by a swift glance from the solicitor.

Wilcox moved on.

'Did you touch your wife's body at all?'

'I felt her wrist to see if there was a pulse. There wasn't. I couldn't see her chest moving, so she wasn't breathing. I sat and waited for the ambulance.'

'Did you adjust your wife's clothing?'

Hugo narrowed his eyes. 'What do you mean?'

Wilcox consulted his notes 'Did you adjust her dressing gown (he was no way going to say kimono) to cover parts of her body?'

Hugo hesitated. 'I may have done.'

'So you would have ascertained' Wilcox continued 'that she was naked underneath it – the dressing gown.'

'Yes.' He waved a hand. 'That wouldn't have been unusual.'

'Did your wife normally sleep naked?'

'Why is this relevant?' The solicitor opened his mouth to join in this protest, but Wilcox carried on.

'Just answer the question please.'

Hugo's nostrils were flaring now. 'Yes, my wife often slept naked.'

'Did you share a bedroom with your wife?'

Hugo slammed a fist down on the table. 'OK that's it. No comment.'

'OK, we'll move on' said Wilcox. 'You suggested when we arrived that a burglary had taken place. At what point did you become aware that items were missing?'

'While I was waiting for the ambulance. I noticed that the mantelpiece was empty. I've already given a description of the items in question.'

It was becoming clear that this initial interview was not going to yield much. Hugo's position seemed to be that it was all very tiresome. He was the victim here, and now he was being treated like a perpetrator.

Murphy sat forward and locked eyes with him. 'Does your organisation often have meetings that go on until ten at night? That sounds like serious overtime to me.'

He glared back at her. 'The organisation is my family. I was at work in the City until 5pm. I left early and drove out to Windsor. We had dinner and then a business meeting.'

'Who exactly was present?'

'My father, my brother, our housekeeper and myself.'

'So all of those people will be able to vouch for your presence up to 10 pm?'

'Of course, but I strongly resent the inference that they should have to.'

'Well here's the thing' said Murphy. 'You stayed out until late at night when you have a young wife and baby at home. A lot of married men in your position would have suggested that the meeting take place earlier so that they could go home to see their family. It's not like you've been married for thirty years, is it? And, of course, grief affects different people in different ways, but your performance as a grieving widower leaves a lot to be desired. You're not even making an effort. Now we're grateful that you're not sitting there sobbing, but at the same time it does make us wonder what's going on. Perhaps you'd like to tell us a bit about your relationship with your wife.'

Hugo's nostrils flared slightly. 'No comment'

'And the other point I'd like to put to you' Murphy continued 'is the bruises.' She gave this a second to sink in. 'We found some serious bruising on your wife's arms. Care to explain about that?'

The solicitor looked shocked at this. He turned to his client and shook his head.

'No comment' said Hugo.

'You are probably also aware' said Wilcox, 'that there was no evidence of forced entry to your house. Which rather calls into question the idea of a burglary. Either somebody had a key or your wife let them in, wouldn't you say?'

Hugo nodded and added 'yes' for the tape.

'What seems odd to me' said Wilcox, 'is that a young woman at home alone with a young child would open the door late at night to somebody she didn't know. Doesn't seem very sensible, does it?'

'No, of course not' said Hugo, 'but Effie was not always sensible.'

'What does that mean?'

'No comment.'

When Hugo had been taken out of the room, Murphy listened back to the tape and thought it was good enough for a preliminary skirmish. Hugo didn't seem like a man bereaved, so there was definitely more to discover about their relationship. Perhaps his laptop would tell them something, but they'd have to charge him to get their hands on it. They'd have to collect a lot more information before they got down to the serious questioning. At the moment they had nothing to hold him on.

***

Murphy thought Pete Grantham was pretty good-looking. Clean shaven, good strong face, muscular body. Scar over his eyebrow, but that did not detract from the overall effect. Probably lots of girls fancied him. Did that include Effie Fincham?

He'd been kept waiting for many hours, which probably contributed to the dishevelled look and the general air of defeat. He'd had a canteen breakfast, which wouldn't have helped. Sitting next to him was the duty solicitor, who was young and keen and probably thought she was there to prevent a miscarriage of justice. Grantham was ignoring her.

Wilcox performed the preliminaries and Murphy began the questioning.

'We know that you drove Effie Fincham home last night' she said. 'That's not in dispute. The problem we have is that there's quite a gap between when you left home and when you arrived back. Even if you were driving at ten miles an hour, which I'm sure you weren't, that wouldn't account for it. So how long did you stay with Effie Fincham?'

He shrugged. 'About half an hour.'

'Why?'

He was silent for a moment and then raised his head to look at her. 'Why not? I saw her safely in and then she put Mabel to bed and we chatted for a few minutes.'

'About what?'

'How do I know? I can't remember. She probably talked about Hugo and the family. I think she found them pretty hard going.'

Murphy stretched her legs. 'Which ones did she find hard going?'

He gnawed at his thumb. 'Hugo, her father-in-law, Dorothy. They all seemed to disapprove of her.'

'Well that's not very specific is it? What did she say about Hugo?'

'She said they were not getting on. She wanted a divorce, but she wanted sole custody of Mabel.'

'And were you able to give her any advice about this?'

'Of course not. She wasn't asking for my advice. She just needed to talk.'

'I think you're hiding something Mr Grantham. Did you have a relationship with Effie Fincham?'

Pete stared at his hands and Murphy stared at him. Then he looked up and shook his head.

'She was a friend. I'd known her for years. That's all. What's happening to Mabel?'

'Mabel is fine. The family are looking after her. Now here's what I don't understand' Murphy leaned closer. 'Effie Fincham was your partner's friend, not particularly your friend. You offer her a lift home, out of the goodness of your heart, I'm sure. And then I would expect that, job done, you would want to get home to your bed. But no, you stay around, longer than half an hour I'm sure, because we've timed your journey – just chatting. I would expect that to be a significant chat because you're staying up at night to have it, after working all evening. But now you tell me that you can't remember what it was about. I imagine that Effie had already unburdened herself about Hugo and his family to Olivia. In that case, would she really be interested in explaining it all over again to you? You see my problem. So we need to know what happened between the two of you.'

'Exactly what I've told you. We sat and talked.'

Murphy rose. 'OK. We'll leave you to have a bit more of a think about it. Just bear in mind that you were probably the last person to see her alive. That's an awkward position to be in.'

***

Kevin Wilcox stood in the queue at Pret wrestling with a bout of last-minute indecision. The avocado wrap or the grilled tofu salad? At the moment he was clutching the wrap, but still in pole position to make a switch without losing his place. The queue seemed to be moving unusually fast. Go with the wrap. Easier to eat discreetly at his desk. He wasn't feeling up for the ribbing he'd get from the other DCs if they spotted him forking up tofu. He knew that this was his problem rather than theirs. DI Murphy also didn't eat meat, but if anybody made a comment to her, she'd just laugh and tell them to piss off. It was a level of social skill that he hoped to eventually acquire. Kevin took his health seriously, that and the planet of course, while Murphy's reasoning seemed to be more to do with animals, but the upshot for both of them was that they never went near the canteen – and the canteen didn't forgive. Those who are not patrons of the canteen soon become the butt of canteen jokes.

He tapped his card on the reader and made his way out. The sun had suddenly come out and he spotted an empty park bench. Sitting down and stretching his legs, he thought suddenly of Hugo Fincham and Pete Grantham who would even now be taking delivery of canteen lunches. He hoped they weren't being given the lasagne. There was bad food and then there was awful food and then there was canteen lasagne. For Hugo Fincham certainly, station food would be a shock to the digestive system. At the moment both of these men were getting the same treatment, but it was important to bear in mind that one of them was innocent. One of them didn't deserve the lasagne. Only one of them, Kevin was certain of that. In most murder cases it was the husband, wife or lover. Let's face it, who else cared enough about somebody to kill them? But the problem in this case was that they both had means and opportunity, motive was not really clear and they were both hiding something. Hugo Fincham was not a likeable character but Wilcox was determined not to let that cloud his judgement. It all had to rest on the evidence. But what if there was no evidence? If both suspects stuck with 'no comment' and there was no compelling evidence against either of them, the CPS would throw it out. It would be an unsolved case, which was good for nobody. And the brutal murder of a young woman was not a good case to leave unsolved. Something would have to turn up, or be turned up. He finished his wrap, threw his wrapper in the bin and made his way back inside.

Chapter Thirteen

'When Crossrail opens it will be quicker to get here by train' said Wilcox. 'Although it's not usually a bad drive.'

'Well I'm glad about that' said Murphy. 'Hold that thought.'

They were sitting in a stationary pile of traffic (the word 'queue' didn't really cover it) on the M25, where a lorry, trying too hard to overtake another lorry on an uphill bit, had toppled sideways and shed its load, blocking two lanes. The driver appeared unhurt and was pacing backwards and forwards shouting into his phone, so the incident was not so far tragic, but the carriageway was covered in a thick film of what looked like cooking oil.

The cars which had so far ventured onto the outside lane had in some cases slid past sideways with panicked faces at the wheel and could be seen up ahead veering precariously from side to side. The queue to get onto the outside lane was building exponentially and there was an increasing amount of nudging, edging and horn blasting. Murphy had called the fire brigade, but they would have some trouble getting through. They were in it for the long haul.

'Pity we're not in a police car' said Wilcox.

She sighed. 'Well we could hardly claim we're on our way to an emergency. I just hope there are no ambulances stuck back there.'

Wilcox was doing his fair share of edging and nudging and half an hour later they were practically at the front of the line when, with a triumphant burst of sirens, a fire engine appeared and everybody had to swerve aside to let them through. After the fire engine had gone past, the motorists regrouped and the more desperate, or selfish, ones had seized their chance to scoot in front. Wilcox swore with a fluency which Murphy had not heard from him before, and of which she thoroughly approved.

'Grace under pressure' she laughed. 'That's what one's supposed to exhibit in these situations. But sometimes it's bloody hard.

The lorry driver now sprang forward to meet the fire crew, with the air of a man proposing to direct operations. A few seconds later he withdrew and hovered by his upturned cab. Murphy hoped they'd told him to piss off. The fire brigade were now spraying the carriageway with some kind of detergent and after another half hour they were on their way.

'I'm glad you're driving' said Murphy. 'I'm exhausted from just sitting here.'

Once they had escaped the M25, the rest of the journey was without incident and the sat nav, previously bamboozled by the delay, now recovered and guided them to an unnervingly quiet residential area.

Hugo Fincham had identified his wife's body, which meant her father had been spared the ordeal. The local police in Maidenhead had already informed him of Effie's death and when Murphy and Wilcox knocked on the door of his bungalow, he opened the door and waved them in without saying anything.

Murphy was interested to see the house in which Effie Fincham had grown up, but she soon realised that this could not be it. From the chime of the bell, belting out *Greensleeves*, to the embossed wallpaper, fitted carpets and white and beige colour scheme this place screamed 'retirement'. Murphy had always promised herself she would never live in a place like this. Better to have a heart attack running up and down the stairs, or collapse at work with a stroke. Effie's dad must have moved down here to be near his daughter – that decision wouldn't seem so good now.

Bernard Watson had the reddened nose and protruding midriff of the habitual drinker but managed to look insubstantial with it. Murphy guessed that he was probably not in good health and now it was compounded by grief. Here at last was somebody who genuinely loved Effie and was feeling the loss. He sat down in an armchair and gestured to them to do the same. A large black dog came over and rested its muzzle forlornly in his lap. Did even the dog know what had happened? Murphy asked herself. No, that was stupid, it was merely reflecting the mood of its owner.

Watson looked hesitant and ill at ease in his surroundings, as if he had not yet figured the place out. He offered tea and Murphy suggested they move to the kitchen while he made it. When he banged the teapot down on the table, she was glad to see it. He was entitled to feel angry and that made it more likely that he would tell them what he knew.

'I'll be mother' she said and picked up the teapot while he rummaged in the fridge for milk. She gestured to Wilcox and they sat at the kitchen table. Better than the beige sitting room with the insipid prints on the wall.

'We're very sorry for your loss Mr Watson' Wilcox began. 'I'm sure you understand how important it is for us to gather any information we can in order to find the person who did this.'

Watson nodded and Murphy could see the effort it cost him to maintain control. His hands were clenching and unclenching and he was controlling his breathing with an effort.

'We're hoping you can tell us a bit about Elizabeth – Effie – and what was going on in her life' said Murphy. 'Otherwise, the only viewpoint we get is that of her in-laws.'

He took out a large handkerchief and blew his nose loudly. 'Effie's mother left us when she was young' he said. 'She met another man, there was nothing I could do about that. After that it was just us – her and me. And we did fine. We had a cleaner who came in but we did everything else. She was a clever girl, worked hard at school, she could have done anything. Oh, she wasn't perfect' he added, seeing Murphy's raised eyebrows. 'Once she got into her teens, there was all the usual boyfriend trouble. And I suppose that was when she would have benefitted from having a mother. I concentrated on just seeing them all off, all the boyfriends, that was what I could do, but I'm sure she got up to lots of stuff I didn't know about. She always came home at night, bit later than we had agreed sometimes, but she knew I would wait up for her. Then she got into university and I was so proud of her. I don't understand why she was doing History of Art, that wasn't even a subject in my day. I told her she should do law, something that would lead to a good job, but she wasn't having it. Anyway, off she went. And after that I was able to relax a bit. It's a funny thing. When your kids are living at home, and you're waiting for them to come home at night, you're always worried, imagining all sorts of things. Once they've left home, they could be getting up to all sorts, but you don't worry anymore.'

'Yes, it was exactly the same for me' said Murphy. 'And when they came back in the holidays, I'd start worrying again. Did you ever visit Effie at university?'

He shook his head. 'No way. I don't think she'd have thanked me for that. She knew where I was and she visited when she wanted to.'

'And after she left university, did she tell you much about what was going on?'

He refilled his cup. 'She told me about this posh job, working in an art gallery, meeting rich people. I never brought her up to think rich people were anything special, where did she get that idea?'

Murphy shrugged. 'I think that idea's spread around mostly by social media. Can you think of anybody who would have wanted to harm Effie, Mr Watson?'

His shoulders slumped and Murphy could see the effort he was making to control the tremors.

'I don't understand why anybody would want to hurt her. What could she have done to anybody? My girl. She was all I had left, her and the baby.' He looked up suddenly. 'What's happened to her? Where's Mabel?'

'Mabel's fine, Mr Watson,' said Murphy. 'She's with her father and his family are looking after her.'

He glared at her. 'I don't want that bloody family looking after her. That's my granddaughter.' His shoulders had suddenly straightened.

'Why do you not want them looking after her?'

He shook his head slowly. 'She should never have married into that family. They're not people like us.'

Murphy put her cup down. 'In what way?'

He shook his head. 'They're all bound up in each other and they look down on anybody else. They looked down on Effie, I'm sure of it. She was clever and beautiful, but she wasn't one of them. That husband of hers - cold fish - and the father – High Court judge with his alky wife. And as for the other brother – well what can you say about him? Something strange there.'

Murphy found this interesting. 'Strange in what way?'

He frowned. 'It's not easy to explain, but he's like an actor playing a part. What you see is not what you get. That's what struck me about him anyway. Although I've only seen him twice.'

'Was that how Effie felt about them all? Or did you get the chance to make your own assessment?'

'I only saw them at the wedding and then at the christening. And I have to acknowledge that they paid for both of those. I couldn't have afforded to. But really, for them they were just occasions to gather all their friends around, show off their wealth. Effie only had me. Her mum and I were both only children and her mum left us a long time ago. And so I only had Effie. But she was enough, I didn't need anybody else.'

'And how do you think she felt about her in-laws?'

'She told me they were a dysfunctional family. She said she kept away from the rest of them as much as possible. The father's miserable and repressed, the mother's on drugs, the sister didn't seem to want anything to do with Effie. Apart from that younger brother, she liked him, said he made her laugh. He didn't make me laugh. But she enjoyed having money, I can't deny that. And she loved Mabel. Do you think I can get custody of Mabel?'

Murphy stood up. 'I don't know Mr Watson. Might be best to leave her where she is until things are sorted. But you should contact the Finchams and tell them you want to see her. You are her grandfather after all.'

They walked out to the hall and Bernie Watson opened the front door. The sun had gone down and a black cloud was building overhead. It was going to be a trip back down the A4 in the rain. Perhaps they could skirt round the M25.

They both shook hands with Bernie Watson. 'Thank you for talking to us' said Murphy 'We'll let you know of any developments.'

'And I am now dying to meet these Finchams' she told Wilcox as they walked back to the car.

Chapter Fourteen

LINDA FLEMING WAS ALMOST unrecognisable in her scrubs and mask and Murphy thought she herself probably looked pretty much the same. Two middle-aged women who clearly spent insufficient time in the gym – that's really all an onlooker would be able to say about them. The onlooker would have no idea that Linda had an impressive academic record and was highly-regarded in the scientific community. In Murphy's judgement, the coroner's office was bloody lucky to have Linda. She could have had much better pay and conditions anywhere else, so Murphy concluded that there must be aspects of her job that she found interesting. As far as Murphy was concerned, no amount of interesting would have compensated for the gut-wrenching aspects of pathology, but maybe, if you were a pathologist, your guts didn't get wrenched that easily.

After the long day yesterday, Murphy had enjoyed a full night's sleep for which she felt grateful. She knew from experience that a murder case always entailed long hours and she might not be so lucky tonight, but it was easier to confront a post-mortem when you weren't dog-tired. And where did that expression come from? Most dogs she knew got far more sleep than she did.

The room was large and well-ventilated, but in spite of that, the air felt contaminated. No quantity of chemicals could disguise the more earthy smells that were generated here and the steel table with the channels for fluids to run off gave notice of what was about to take place. If this was her job she'd definitely be putting in for early retirement. But Linda, despite complaints about her knees and her back and various other bits of her anatomy, never seemed bothered by the nature of the job. Equally, thank God, she wasn't one of those annoying jokey pathologists that relished the discomfort of police observers.

Murphy sucked hard on a mint imperial, almost accidentally swallowing it in the process. That could have been bad. If it got stuck in her throat after things had gotten underway, Linda would have to give her the Heimlich manoeuvre with her gore-encrusted gloves on. She moved the mint to the inside of her cheek and forced herself to look at the body on the table. This was the perp's handiwork, it was important to confront it. She knew she would have to look away when the scalpel went in, but hopefully Linda wouldn't notice.

Ellie Fincham was pale and slim – almost too slim, Murphy thought. Something of an eating disorder there? Or maybe she was just one of those lucky people who didn't put on weight. Not so lucky now, of course. Either way, she didn't look that robust. It was a lovely, classically-proportioned face. That much was clear, although it was looking doughy in death and the eyes were closed. Her father had called her beautiful and he was probably right.

'Caesarian scar' said Linda. 'No other marks except for round the neck. Slightly under-nourished, maybe she was dieting.'

Then Linda picked up the scalpel and made the first incision. Murphy prided herself on never having vomited or left the room, but she spent the next half hour assessing the precise condition of the paintwork on the walls and ceiling and tracing where all the wires and pipes went. She did her best not to hear the sucking and sliding noises that accompanied whatever was taking place.

She was jerked back to attention when Linda announced, with unwanted cheerfulness 'Heart and liver healthy enough' and quickly looked away again as the organs in question were deposited in steel bowls. A few minutes later she risked a glance and saw Linda sewing up, while muttering that really she should have an assistant available to do this.

Murphy breathed in through her mouth, crunched down on her mint and approached the table. 'Can you confirm cause of death now?'

'Yes, definitely manual strangulation. The bruises on the neck are definitive and you can see what's happened with the eyelids.' Linda lifted one of the eyelids and Murphy could see the signs of petechial haemorrhage.

'There is also some bruising to the shoulders – fresh bruising, probably occurred at the same time as the bruises to the neck.'

'Like somebody shook her by the shoulders?'

'Yes, just like that. Maybe started by shaking her shoulders and then ended up constricting her neck. She died where she was found' Linda continued. 'The fluids have pooled where we would expect. The body wasn't moved.'

'And the timing?'

'Pretty much as I said at the scene. I think we can narrow it down a bit. i would say between 10.30pm and 12.30am.'

She waited while Murphy made a note of this.

'And one other thing. There are a few small tears in the vagina, some of them partially healed. So maybe rough sex.'

'Or sex in which she was not a willing participant?' said Murphy.

Linda nodded and dumped her instruments with a metallic clatter into a steel tray. 'Exactly. Or that.'

'How long ago would those tears have happened?'

'Probably about a fortnight.'

'So she's unlikely to have had intercourse over the last two weeks.'

'Very unlikely. That would have been quite painful.'

'Well at least she wasn't raped – or not on this occasion. So no prospect of any DNA?'

'I'm afraid not. I haven't found any useful deposits, such as hairs or dandruff. Whoever strangled her wore gloves.'

***

Wilcox looked up from his phone as she sat down next to him. She was about to ask if he was updating his profile, or something equally sarky, when she realised it wasn't his phone. It was Effie Fincham's.

'Wesley got it unlocked' he said, referring to the brightest of the technical staff. 'And the laptop's here.' He pointed to it, sitting on top of a pile of folders. 'The laptop wasn't even password-protected.' He shook his head and tutted.

'The poor girl's dead' said Murphy. 'Let's cut her some slack.'

Wilcox nodded. 'How was the pm?'

'Horrible as usual. I'm lining you up for the next one. Death by manual strangulation and, according to Doctor Fleming, it wouldn't have taken much to strangle her. She was very slim and small-boned.'

Wilcox raised his eyebrows. 'So a woman could have done it?'

'Yes, most women would probably be strong enough. There were also vaginal tears, which suggests abuse by a man. But of course, the two events could be unrelated – abused by one perpetrator, killed by another.'

'I'd say it fixes the frame more tightly around the husband.'

Murphy nodded. 'Yes, he's probably still the prime suspect, but what we need is evidence. There's no useful DNA evidence. We'll just have to keep digging.'

She took the laptop down and plugged it in. 'You won't be able to get into her Facebook', said Wilcox. Or Instagram. We've sent a request to Facebook and, in the circumstances, they'll probably comply, but it could take a few days. And we need co-operation from Google for the emails.'

Murphy wasn't sure she felt like looking at Facebook or Instagram just yet. The thought of trawling through all Effie's narrative of her wonderful life, full of posed studio shots and probably lots of happy mummy pictures with her baby, contrasted too baldly with the reality of the body on the slab that she had seen this morning.

'OK. Let's just note down all her contacts, all the numbers that she's exchanged texts or calls with, particularly in the last few weeks. That will give us a starting point. And maybe we should look at her photos. Here we are, she has files for the wedding and the christening.'

They scanned through the wedding photos, all in stylish black and white. 'These are definitely professional shots' said Wilcox. 'No blurring, no over-exposure.'

'She was certainly a beautiful bride' said Murphy. 'Even Hugo doesn't look bad. The photographer seems to have been roving around. There are lots of unposed shots, people he just happened to catch unawares. In fact there seem to be only two official wedding party photos. The rest are just whatever caught the photographer's eye. I think that's fashionable these days. Let's have a look at the christening. These are all unposed photos again, with lots of the same people. Here's Olivia, and Pete, and Effie, of course. And a few other people we haven't yet met. I want to go through these photos again when we've met a few more of the people involved, and talked to them. We'll learn more from them at that point.'

Chapter Fifteen

MURPHY WANTED TO GET some background before she interviewed His Honour (ret'd) Edward Fincham. Several of her colleagues had given evidence before him and described him variably as a miserable bastard, an arrogant sod and a stickler for the rules. Nothing wrong with that, of course, except that the rules sometimes got in the way of a conviction.

'Actually he was worse than that' said Tony Sherriff the desk sergeant. 'I remember young PCs terrified of having to give evidence in front of him. He could spot the inexperienced ones and he liked to see them scrabbling in their notes when he queried what they were saying. One young lass came out in tears. She'd done nothing wrong but he'd managed to make her feel like an idiot. So I used to tell them, take your time, make him wait, be polite but don't be scared of the bugger.'

'I think I must have come across him at some point' said Murphy, as she unwrapped her sandwich. 'That all sounds very familiar.'

'You'd remember if you'd given evidence in front of him,' said Tony. 'I used to wonder what his home life was like. Maybe his wife was beating him. Probably not though. I seem to remember hearing that his wife was generally not well. And how was he treating his kids? I was friendly with one of the barristers, I remember him telling me that Fincham never appeared at any of the dinners, he wasn't a man for glad-handing.'

'I wonder how Effie got on with him?' said Murphy. 'I think she was a girl who could generally get around men. He would probably have proved an exception.' But there was something else nagging at her memory as she headed into the CID room.

Wilcox was sitting at his desk consolidating the initial door-to-door reports. His typing speed was about what used to be expected of top secretaries in the days when such jobs existed and Murphy was always impressed to see that, unlike most men, he used at least six fingers, rather than two. Murphy perched on the edge of his desk and a bundle of files slipped off onto the floor. Wilcox tutted and bent to pick them up. As he came up, she flung out an arm and hit him in the eye.

'Yes!' She stood up. 'It's coming back to me. Fawcett Hall – that's his address, isn't it? Edward Fincham. Wasn't there something else that happened there years ago? That name's definitely familiar.'

Wilcox stopped rubbing his eye and looked up. 'Was there?'

She nodded. 'Probably before your time, but not before mine unfortunately.'

Wilcox straightened his chair and rattled his keyboard. It didn't take long.

'Suspicious drowning' he said. 2004. Billy Jukes, aged 16. Drowned in the pond. He couldn't swim, bit unusual for a 16-year-old. And apparently the pond is very deep. Let me see... Happened in the early hours, the kids had friends round, he was one of them.' He scrolled down a few more screens. 'They were all sleeping in some barn, after drinking copious amounts of alcohol and probably other stuff. The other stuff was what the investigating officer surmised – they owned up to the alcohol. And this lad decided to go for an early morning swim. There were some bruises on one of his arms, but nothing conclusive. All the others claimed to be asleep all night, and most of the morning. Police had nothing to go on. Eventually recorded as 'misadventure'.

'Interesting. I wonder how thorough that police investigation was. Another arm with bruises..' she broke off at the sound of a measured tread coming steadily up behind her.

'OK, so all wrapped up is it?' Bellweather switched on his famous menacing smile, exposing flashing white veneers. All around them faces were glued to screens. All heads below the parapet. Nobody wanted to catch his eye.

Murphy waited for Bellweather's jaws to return to their normal position. She often amused herself by imagining the state of his teeth before the expensive dental work. Maybe brown stumps with lots of gaps.

'Not yet sir, but we're making some progress. Most of the door-to-door is yet to report back and we've initially questioned two suspects.'

Bellweather rubbed his hands together. 'The two men in her life, eh? Which one are we going to charge?'

'Neither of them at the moment. We need more evidence. I'm going to release them both pending further enquiries.'

'Release them? Why on earth would you do that? Pending further enquiries' he repeated with another flash of the teeth. 'What further enquiries? And are you sure they've been *fully* interrogated?'

Murphy knew exactly what the 'fully' meant. 'We haven't begun the waterboarding yet sir, but we are now about to visit his honour Edward Fincham, in pursuance of our enquiries.'

Bellweather's reaction to the first part of that sentence was swallowed up in his reaction to the second. His eyes widened and his mouth fell open for a second.

'You can't go harassing the judiciary like that.'

'We'll make sure he's *fully* interrogated sir, and anyway he's retired.'

Both of them were out of the door before Bellweather had summoned up his reply.

'You're going to blight my career' said Wilcox as they clattered down the stairs. 'Him and Fincham are probably at the same golf club, rotary club, whatever.'

'Freemasons even' said Murphy. 'Don't worry. It's me he can't stand and if he manages to get rid of me, he'll have to promote you. You'll be fine. Now, is this upstanding ex-member of the judiciary expecting us?'

'Yes. Ten'oclock.'

'OK, let's take your car. It will probably fit in better up there.' Wilcox didn't argue, probably happy to tag a few more miles onto this month's expense claim.

Chapter Sixteen

Murphy hadn't heard of Bellingbury and a google search hadn't turned up much. After a blessedly uneventful trip out on the M4, passing Slough and Windsor, and then a bit of doubling back and arguing over which way the signposts were actually pointing, they entered the village and it was definitely a 'blink and you miss it' experience. No village green, no duck pond and no thatched cottages, just one pub and a post office cum general stores. There was a small row of what looked like 1960s council houses, another row of what would have been nineteenth century farm labourers' cottages, now surely fetching prices beyond the means of any farm labourer, and the rest of the dwellings were detached with expensive vehicles outside.

'Very nice' pronounced Murphy, 'but it wouldn't do for me. Too quiet, too far away from everywhere. I'd go nuts.'

'Be alright if you had one of those expensive motors' said Wilcox. 'One hour into London if you had a clear run. And if you were shut away out here nobody would notice that you were nuts.'

Fawcett Hall was just outside the village, the weatherbeaten sign so faded that they initially drove straight past. The drive was long and tarmacked.

'Thank God for that' said Wilcox. 'I thought it might be one of those awful rutted tracks that destroy your suspension.'

'I would guess' said Murphy, 'that Hugo Fincham, whose car is far more expensive than yours, has due regard to his suspension.'

The farmyard gave access to two large barns and a site office. The only sign of life was a couple of geese that wandered over and hissed at them.

'Pretend you haven't seen them' said Murphy. 'Don't engage.'

A short path led off to the main house and fields beyond. It was flagged with lupins and hollyhocks and shaded further out by mature trees. The house itself was a double-fronted two-story stone structure with a basement. 'Queen Anne' pronounced Wilcox. The front of the house was almost obscured by a deep red Virginia creeper, making it look a bit New England. Obviously, they had a good gardener.

Murphy was determined not to be impressed. She marched up the path and rang the bell hard. 'Police' she said crisply, showing her badge to the short woman in an apron and trainers who answered the door. They were admitted to a marble-floored hall with a wide, graceful staircase. The woman in the apron and trainers melted away as Dorothy Hepple appeared as if from nowhere and closed the front door behind them.

'Good morning DI Murphy. Wait here please'. She turned on her heel and walked down the hall. Murphy looked around at the high ceiling, the decorative plasterwork and the paintings mounting up the stairwell. Were any of them valuable? Probably. But would you really want to sink your wealth into paintings and then leave them hanging on the walls in plain sight? Maybe they were all worthless.

After a few moments Dorothy reappeared and led them into a room at the back of the house. It had floor to ceiling bookshelves, all glassed-in to keep the dust out. The French windows had threadbare velvet curtains and the view they framed was all greenery and sky – not another building to be seen. Edward Fincham was probably getting on for sixty, but in pretty good shape. Nothing baggy round the jaw, a good head of hair and his original teeth, as far as Murphy could tell. No veneers here. But it was a bad-tempered face, like he had permanent acid indigestion. She revised her earlier assertion. She probably hadn't come across him before. She would have remembered. He was seated behind a large leather-topped desk with decorative scrolls around the edge, and two chairs were drawn up in front of it. Murphy recognised this ploy. And yes, the visitors' chairs were slightly lower. Well, let him have his advantage for the time being.

'Thank you, Dorothy' said Fincham. Murphy sat down gingerly and hoped nobody else heard her knees creaking.

Fincham was a tall man, as far as Murphy could gather by seeing the top half of him. He could of course have short legs, but she doubted it. He wore a charcoal suit, an immaculate white shirt and what was probably a public school tie. So standards were being maintained. Murphy was glad that she was wearing one of her scruffier outfits, but Wilcox was as usual letting the side down. Why couldn't he wear jeans and worn leather jackets like TV cops?

Fincham pursed his lips and laid his elbows on the desk as if preparing to listen to their address to the bench.

'As you will know' Murphy began, 'your son has been released pending further enquiries.'

'Quite right too. He has no case to answer. It was obviously a robbery gone wrong.'

'Well, we can't be sure of that yet. I don't like to proceed in advance of the evidence.' Murphy saw Edward Fincham's lips tighten. 'I'd like to begin by asking you to tell us about your movements on Tuesday evening.'

'I was here as you very well know. Hugo will have explained all that to you already. I can't see that my version will tell you anything else.'

'We appreciate that Mr Fincham, but we'd still like to hear it from you.'

He laid his palms flat on the desk and drew a deep breath. 'Very well. I was here with Dorothy and my wife and my two sons. We had dinner together at about six thirty, maybe seven o'clock and then at about eight o'clock my wife retired to her sitting room and we had a meeting until about ten o'clock, at which point I went to bed.'

'Do you and your wife share a bedroom?'

'That's none of your business and I fail to see how it's relevant.'

'It's relevant only insofar as it confirms, or fails to confirm, the whereabouts of you and your wife after ten o'clock.'

'Very well.' He glared at Murphy. It was probably the same expression he used in court. 'No, we do not share a bedroom. My wife has trouble sleeping.'

'Thank you, sir. I'd like you to tell us what you can about your daughter-in-law. How did your son meet her?'

'Really, all this is irrelevant.'

'Anything to do with your son and his wife and their relationship is very relevant. And we will be questioning everybody who knew them. Any information you give us will reduce the time we have to spend questioning other people'. She laid stress on the last two words and knew he would get the message. The response was immediate.

'I am not prepared to have my wife questioned. She's in very poor health and this would be very bad for her nerves.'

'Does she know her daughter-in-law is dead?'

He was silent for a moment. 'No, not yet. I will break it to her at the right time.'

'What is actually wrong with your wife, sir?' Wilcox took over. Murphy found his tactlessness invaluable at times like this.

Fincham shot him a look of pure hatred which Wilcox affected not to notice. He turned a page in his notebook and took the top off his pen.

'My wife had a nervous breakdown about ten years ago. She has never really recovered and still gets bouts of depression. I try to spare her any stress.'

'OK, that's understood' Murphy said. 'So, in the interests of not disturbing your wife, perhaps you can answer our questions.'

He sighed. 'Yes, go ahead.'

'How did your son meet his wife?'

'I understand they met at an art gallery' he began, as if at pains to distance himself from the event. 'He had apparently gone to buy a painting and she was working there. It was quite a sudden thing, I think. He was very taken with her, wanted to get married quickly.'

'So they were very much in love?' Murphy couldn't easily associate 'in love' with what she'd seen of Hugo Fincham, but she was interested to see how his father would react.

Fincham's expression suggested that he would not have described it like that, but eventually he nodded. 'Yes, I suppose they must have been.'

'And how did you feel about that? Were you happy about the match?'

He was clearly taking time to choose his words. 'If I'm honest, I have to say that I didn't think she was entirely suitable, but the decision was Hugo's to make. Before you ask, I thought she was very pretty and not unintelligent, but she seemed to me to be a girl – woman – who relied on her looks and had never really done much. That said, she was a good mother and I'm very sorry she's dead.'

It was an admirable summing up, Murphy had to admit, but it wasn't going to stop them poking around further.

'Were you aware of any problems in the marriage?' she asked. 'We found a number of bruises on her arms.'

His eyes widened. 'Are you suggesting...?'

'We're just telling you what we found. Can you tell us anything about that?'

'Absolutely not. Hugo would never have done anything like that.'

'So would you have any other explanation to offer?'

'None whatsoever. I can only surmise that she had an accident of some sort.'

'There was a death here about ten years ago.' said Wilcox. 'Boy named Billy Jukes. What can you tell us about that?'

Fincham's face registered shock for the first time. 'That was all investigated at the time. It was a tragic accident.'

'It does just seem odd that a boy who couldn't swim, and who everybody knew couldn't swim, should have decided to go swimming by himself in the early hours in the pond.'

Fincham attempted a Gallic shrug. It didn't quite come off. 'We never found any explanation for that. Maybe he wanted to see if he could swim if nobody else was around.

It had been a hot night. Maybe he just wanted to cool off. We don't know. It was a tragedy.'

Chapter Seventeen

ARRIVING HOME JUST BEFORE nine o'clock, Murphy was mainly thinking about a shower and bed, but was also uncomfortably aware, mainly in the region of her stomach, that she had eaten nothing since the largely unsatisfactory sandwich at midday.

But she was about to be saved by the lodgers. She flung off her coat and kicked off her shoes. The smell of cooking drew her into the kitchen. She dropped the car keys into a bowl and sat down at the table.

James was stirring a frying pan and Clive was chopping herbs. Clive gave her shoulder a squeeze.

'Stay there Murph, you look bushed. We are cooking tonight – eggplant and cavalo nero with za'aatar and sumac and all sorts of other stuff and there's plenty for three. Just what you need. Our Middle Eastern phase is lasting quite a long time. We'll be moving onto Vietnamese next I think. And what you need first is probably some of this.'

He picked up a bottle of red wine and poured her a glass. Murphy took a few sips and felt better. That was probably bad, it was probably at least one of the intermediate stages of alcoholism.

James put a lid over the pan and they both joined her at the table.

'So have you got a big case? Do tell.'

Murphy had some time ago decided that James and Clive were not really her lodgers – they were more like her wives. They both worked from home in some sort of online business – website design or some such – so they were always available to do the shopping and cooking – in fact, they actually enjoyed it. And she liked having somebody there when she came in at night. Either of her now ex-husbands would have been there alright, but bristling with ill-disguised resentment that she wasn't at home and nor was their dinner. Her break-up with Jack had followed hard on the heels of her promotion to DI, when he had realised that she was never going to give it up and devote her attention to him. The fact that he was shagging Tracey was also probably something to do with it. The period following his departure had been so unexpectedly restful that Murphy decided they should have done it years ago. This allayed any feelings of resentment towards either Jack or Tracey, who she now considered to have done her a favour. Replacing Jack with James and Clive had been good for everybody.

She was just lifting a forkful of aubergine to her mouth when her phone buzzed and she pulled it out of her bag. The message was short but problematic.

'Susannah. Wants me to go round' she announced. She sighed. 'Too late now.'

'Tell her you'll go tomorrow' said Clive, topping up the glasses. 'I guess she's still upset about Simon and Felicity.'

'I'm afraid so' said Murphy, tapping out a message. 'I'm sure the moment will come when she arrives at the conclusion that she's better off without him, but I'm afraid that moment is not yet here.'

Chapter Eighteen

NETFLIX WAS A WONDERFUL thing, Susannah thought, as she poured herself a careful half glass of wine and tightened the cap on the bottle. Drinking alone was not good, but allowable in small amounts. And *House of Cards*, once the girls were in bed, gave her a whole hour's escape every evening.

Clare Underwood, Lady Macbeth for the twenty-first century, wasn't morally much of a role model, but Clare Underwood would be dealing with Susannah's situation a lot better than she, Susannah, was dealing with it. No doubt about that. Clare would not be fazed by her husband running off with the nanny. She'd have more important things to deal with. Because Claire Underwood had a game plan and the husband was just part of it.

And if she could just get herself round to that way of thinking, Susannah decided, she'd be fine. Hard as nails, that was the way to go. Maybe it was easier when you had the clothes. She had the running gear at least. The disdainful expression was certainly something to aim for. And the game plan. What could that be? The only game plan she'd ever had was for the game she had just been kicked out of.

Miranda would make a better fist of this. She'd been through two husbands and didn't seem to have been traumatised by any of it. Miranda would make a better Clare

Underwood. No actually, that wasn't right. Despite her tough exterior, Miranda loved children and animals. She didn't even eat meat. And some of the people she had to deal with must be pretty hard to love. Having Miranda around had allowed Susannah to be the baby of the family. Miranda had done all the rebelling, so she didn't have to.

But Susannah was a different person, with different weaknesses. She very much wanted to hate Simon or, better still, be indifferent to him, but she couldn't seem to get there. She would have hated him to know, hated anybody to know, that she still cried in private, but it was true. She was waiting for it to stop but it was taking a long time and there were so many triggers – old friends, old photographs, familiar restaurants, stuff he'd left behind, songs she remembered from the happy part of her marriage, things the kids said. It was like a long process of desensitisation and it refused to be rushed.

She had two things that gave her some relief from the pressure. One was work. She had hired a nanny so that she could go back to work, so this was where it had all started, but best not to think about that. However much self-respect she had abandoned in her personal life, work had given some of it back to her. She had never intended to be an accountant, but Maths and French at university had channelled her in that direction and she found working with numbers surprisingly absorbing. In fact, the forensic work that she was doing now was so absorbing that she forgot all of her problems for hours at a time. The other escape was running. She'd probably never run another marathon, but when she stepped out of the house in her trainers she felt like a different person, a strong person, and after half an hour she was aware of nothing but the condition of her legs and lungs.

So it was important to be positive. She still had the children – and the house. She had a decent job. All she'd lost was the relationship that underpinned everything. She would just have to carry on without it. And it was pointless thinking that she could have done something to prevent what had happened. It was always sitting there in future time. Dad had been right. Men who scanned every woman who crossed their path would eventually find another one that more exactly mirrored their requirements.

That was the best thing about children. You would always be their mother. They wouldn't trade you in for a new model. Trying to explain to Katy and Alice why their father only appeared at weekends had been hard and she was not sure she had made a very good job of it, but they didn't seem to think it was her fault. Obviously, she didn't want to convey that it was his fault either. Just one of those things. When they were older, they'd understand only too well.

***

Kevin Wilcox stopped at Safeway on the way home. He didn't approve of ready meals but sometimes, when he'd had a long day, anything else was too much effort. He grabbed a mushroom risotto and a bag of salad leaves (also not good, used a lot of water and the bags were filled with gas, but for once, never mind) and made his way to the checkout. Everybody in the self-service queue was like him – young, tired, clutching a ready meal. He made his way out to his car, just in time to avoid a ticket. The warden had spotted potential prey and was advancing in a determined fashion. Kevin got there first and slid into the driver's seat with an apologetic smile. He wished he was on his bike, head down, dodging between the snarled-up vehicles, rather than forced to join them. The journey north to Finsbury Park was a matter of minutes if you were a crow, but a frustrating three quarters of an hour if you were a Renault Clio. He wasn't of course obliged to bring a car into work, he could be using his bike, but that would mean having to be driven everywhere by DI Murphy, and he didn't think his nerves could stand it.

Opening the front door of the house he could hear voices from the first floor. Crap! That was Simon's girlfriend. Josie was actually a decent person and he liked her in lots of ways, but she had a laugh that sounded like a mechanical digger and it had travelled through the wall and down the stairs to meet him. He padded upstairs to meet it head-on. Just as well he'd bought a ready meal – three minutes in the microwave and he'd be done.

Simon and Josie were watching a rerun of Friends. Kevin tossed the salad into the fridge, heated up his risotto and sat with them to watch the rest of it. It wasn't that funny but it was more restful than making conversation. Simon was a programmer, which meant there was never much to say about his day job. Kevin could have told lots of stories about his, but soon realised that the problem of deciding what he could and couldn't tell people was best resolved by saying nothing. This left them with conversational topics limited to football, cars and the perfidy of the landlord. Fortunately, Josie was a nurse. She had plenty of stories and no compunction about telling them to anybody who would listen. After Friends had finished, she told them in graphic detail about one of the visitors to A&E that day who had injured himself with a piece of plumbing equipment in a sensitive place.

When they had exhausted all the possible jokes arising from that scenario, Kevin went off to take a shower and head for bed, hoping he'd be asleep before the creakings and squeakings in the next room got going. Sometimes he thought he really needed his own place, but financially it just wasn't possible. Also, he was honest enough to admit that, if he had a girlfriend, the situation would feel fine, they'd just be two couples. And he was uncomfortably afraid that if he lived on his own, he'd get too used to his own company and be in danger of turning into the sort of fussy, repressed man that DI Murphy would probably laugh at.

Chapter Nineteen

THE INQUEST ON EFFIE Fincham was held a week after her death. Murphy didn't expect any breakthrough to come as a result of the inquest, but it was an opportunity to observe all the various players and she hoped most of them would decide to turn up. Hugo Fincham was directed to appear and give evidence about finding the body and probably other members of the family would want to be there and support him. He had been released from custody pending further enquiries. Wilcox would be giving evidence concerning the police investigation, so she could sit back and observe.

The coroner's court was a tasteless modern building and the room booked for the inquest had windows which were almost no more than horizontal slits set up close to the low ceiling, presumably to prevent any nosey parkers outside from spying on the august proceedings. The windows also effectively stopped too much light from penetrating into the room, necessitating the use of electric lighting, even in daytime. The overall effect was uncomfortable, claustrophobic and oppressive, far removed from the wood-panelled magnificence of old courtroom dramas. As a means of encouraging people to spit out their evidence smartly and make their escape, it couldn't be beat.

Murphy spotted Effie's father sitting alone near the front and went down to sit next to him. She would normally sit at the back, the better to observe everybody else, but on this occasion, she left Wilcox to do the back row observation. Bernard Watson was the person who most needed support. He had dressed for the occasion in what was probably the smartest suit he possessed, but his hands were shaking and she could see a fragment of tissue stuck to his jaw where he had evidently cut himself shaving. She informed him in a whisper of this and then handed him a mirror to deal with it.

Several members of the press were also occupying the back rows. Effie had been wealthy and pretty and the daughter-in-law of a retired judge and it was a violent death, so this case ticked a lot of boxes for them. Murphy was hoping that they would find the proceedings very boring and not worth writing about. At the moment, any publicity was bad publicity. The coroner was a fussy little man she had encountered before. He could at least be relied upon to leave no nit unpicked, so she was counting on him here.

Hugo Fincham arrived at that moment, accompanied by Dorothy, Olivia and a stylish-looking young man that must be Sebastian. It was perhaps unsurprising that Edward Fincham would not want to be seen here and his wife had of course to be protected from anything upsetting. Hugo would probably feel most reassured by the presence of Dorothy – the closest he came to having a parent. Sebastian was dressed completely in black, which suited him, setting off his blond hair nicely. Dorothy was wearing a dark green suit and her attention seemed to be mostly focussed on Hugo, as if she was worried that he wouldn't be able to cope. Olivia was wearing unremarkable clothes and looked very upset. No sign of Pete.

The proceedings got underway and Hugo was summoned to the stand, looking like a boy being ordered to the headmaster's study. He rattled out his evidence as if wishing only to get it over with. It was fascinating to Murphy that after a privileged upbringing, which should have given him masses of self-confidence, Hugo was still so unsure of himself. It made her wonder if he had been abused as a child and she made a mental note to check whether he had been to boarding school. Hugo was followed by the attending paramedic and then Wilcox was summoned to give evidence about the police investigation, evidence which they had carefully rehearsed the day before. There were details which weren't going to be aired in a public forum. Wilcox didn't exhibit nerves like Hugo, but made it sound like he was reading the shipping forecast – hopefully that would have a soporific effect on the press pack. There was a bit of a stirring in the back row when the pathologist was called but Linda Fleming was not going to get their pulses racing, either by her appearance or by her evidence, which was dry, technical and included lots of words they probably had trouble spelling. When she mentioned the bruises, Bernie emitted a low growl directed at Hugo Fincham, but that was probably the only surprising detail. The upshot of her evidence was death by manual strangulation.

The result was a foregone conclusion – murder by person or persons unknown. The inquest was adjourned to allow the police to continue their investigation.

Chapter Twenty

Reggie Yates, formerly DI Reginald Yates, lived in a retirement village on the outskirts of Croydon. 'What is it with all this bloody retirement stuff all of a sudden?' said Murphy, swinging the steering wheel viciously. 'It's like it's ambushing me at every corner.'

'Baader-Meinhof phenomenon' pronounced Wilcox, who was bracing himself against the dashboard. 'Also called the frequency illusion.'

'What are you talking about? You're not even old enough to remember Baader-Meinhof. Unlike me' she added sadly.

'It's actually got nothing to do with the Baader-Meinhof gang itself' Wilcox told her. 'Some guy called it that because once he'd heard about the Baader-Meinhof gang, he kept seeing the name everywhere.'

'You should be writing bloody encyclopedias' said Murphy.

'Well I have sent a couple of contributions to Wikipedia, but...'

'Alright. Enough.' They swerved haphazardly through the pristine entrance to Celestial Apartments (*luxury retirement redefined*) and Murphy parked right in front of the reception. She stopped the car with a screech of brakes. Wilcox opened his mouth, no doubt to say something about worn brake shoes or the need for servicing. She held up a hand. 'Not a word.'

The block in which Reggie Yates lived was three-stories of Cotswold stone, surrounded by lawns with regimental mower stripes. 'You see?' said Murphy. 'The poor buggers who live here don't even get to mow their own lawn, which is probably the one thing that would do them the most good.'

'The poor buggers who live here are probably quite rich' said Wilcox. 'These apartments cost more than you'd pay on the open market and the service charges are hefty.'

'Is that so?' said Murphy as she rang the bell. 'So our Reggie has done well for himself.'

The door was opened with a welcoming smile by a plump man in corduroy slacks and a polo shirt. He held the door as they eased their way in past golf clubs and a bicycle, into a sitting room where a large picture window looked out onto more manicured lawns. Mrs Yates, as she presumably was, hovered in the open-plan kitchen, ready to provide the beverages. Both had an air of robust good health. In fact, Murphy had to acknowledge that Mrs Yates ('call me Brenda') looked like she had access to a much better hairdresser than Murphy did.

They accepted the offer of coffee and Brenda fired up the capsule machine. Once coffee was served, she left (tennis), which was a blessing. Murphy had been afraid she'd hang about and the whole thing would be difficult. Coffee was good, though.

'So Reggie' she began, as the door shut 'Fawcett Hall 2004. You were the investigating officer. What can you tell us about that?'

He stretched back in his armchair. 'Fawcett Hall' he repeated, in what all police officers were taught was a gambit employed by suspects to buy themselves time to think. 'That was a very odd incident.'

'Certainly was' said Murphy. 'Suspicious death.'

'The thing was' said Reggie, 'we had nothing to go on. Victim was already out of the water, had probably been already dead when they got him out, everybody had been working him over, obviously, trying for some spark of life, so there was no available forensic evidence.'

Wilcox was busy taking notes. 'Did you find the location from which he'd gone into the water?'

Reggie shook his head. 'There was no way of telling. People had been running in and out of that pond all the previous day. A lot of the grass was trampled. They had dogs as well and a couple of the sheep had apparently gotten out of their field the day before, so the scene was just mud.'

'How was he dressed? Was he wearing shoes?'

'He had jeans on but nothing on top. And he had one trainer on when we saw him, and it wasn't laced up. The other one was probably in the pond.'

'Did you attempt to find it?' Wilcox was getting into his stride now.

Reggie shifted in his chair. 'No, we didn't. There didn't seem to be any point.'

'You say 'we' said Murphy. Who else was with you?'

Reggie scratched his head, raking the remaining patches of stubble. 'Let me see...'

'It's no problem' said Wilcox. 'We can look it up.'

'DC Brian Ferris' announced Reggie. 'Good lad. Went to Doncaster I think.'

'Excellent' said Murphy. 'We can get onto him, see what he remembers.'

Reggie was looking a bit less cheerful now.

'Now tell us' she continued, 'all about the Finchams.'

Reggie crossed and uncrossed his legs a few times then took a deep breath. 'His lordship was still on the bench at that time of course, and very shocked to have something like this happen at his home. His wife was very distressed. She'd pulled the boy out, kept saying if only she'd come out earlier, she could have saved him. There was another woman, housekeeper of some sort. She'd apparently been attempting CPR before the paramedics arrived, but it was too late. There were a number of teenagers staggering around looking the worse for wear. The wife was getting hysterical so the husband nodded to the housekeeper and she took her off. I definitely remember that.'

'We looked at the records of the interviews you carried out' said Murphy. 'Nobody seemed to have seen anything and nobody had any information to offer.'

'Exactly. There was no witness to what actually happened, according to what we were told anyway.'

'Did you have any reason to think that anybody – either one of the adults or one of the children – knew more than they were telling you?'

Reggie thought for a moment. 'I did wonder about that housekeeper woman.'

'Why?'

'No reason. She just seemed a bit less devastated by it than the others.'

'OK. What did you think of Mrs Fincham?'

'Bit highly-strung. We interviewed her briefly, because she was the first to see the body, but she was unable to say very much. It had probably been too much for her. His lordship didn't want us to upset her.'

'Had you encountered his lordship on a professional basis prior to this?'

'Yes, once or maybe twice. I'd given evidence in court before him.'

'What did you think of him?'

Reggie smiled. 'He was a stickler wasn't he? You had to have your facts all in order.'

'How did you feel investigating an incident involving his family?'

'Well it was maybe a bit awkward, but I didn't let it stop me from doing my job.' He let out a breath as if well satisfied with this declaration.

'Very good' said Murphy. 'Now tell us about the various teenagers.'

'Not sure that I can remember them all.'

'Well maybe just the family, the young Finchams, you can remember them? Hugo, Sebastian and Phoebe.'

'Oh yes, the kids with the posh names. I remember them. Hugo was the older one. He was very shocked because he was the one who had invited this boy Billy to stay. He kept saying about Billy's parents, how awful it would be for them. The other boy was maybe a bit less bothered, but still pretty upset. All of them looked a bit hungover anyway, I'm not sure how much grasp they had of it all. And the daughter, pretty little thing, she was crying.'

'Alright Reggie, this has been very helpful' said Murphy. 'If you look back on it now, is there anything else that occurs to you?'

He shook his head. 'No, I've thought about it quite a bit over the years, but it just seems like a tragic accident – that or suicide.'

***

'Useless, lazy bugger' said Murphy as she reversed too fast out of the space. 'Frightened off by Fincham. Didn't dredge the pond. Didn't properly interview Verity Fincham. Didn't query the bruises on his arm. Probably happy to close it off. Inquest recorded death by misadventure. Job done.'

'But the result he arrived at may still have been the correct one' said Wilcox, wishing he was the one driving.

'Yes, but even so it would have been arrived at in the wrong way, with lots of stones unturned, so we can't rely on it. I liked the way he drew attention to the housekeeper – the non-family member. If he had to point the finger at anybody, he'd like it to be her.'

'Do you think suicide is a viable explanation?'

'No, I don't. There was no suggestion that he had suicidal tendencies or was under any kind of stress. This was before social media started driving teenagers towards suicide. And with all the available drugs around, why the hell would he drown himself in a pond? There were no drug residues found in his bloodstream. What a traumatic, difficult way to die. I'm not buying that.'

'The thing is' said Wilcox, 'it's impossible to imagine why anybody would want to kill this young lad. He had no involvement with anything criminal, he wasn't part of any gang. And anyway, it wasn't a street crime. It happened in a domestic environment. There's no motive anywhere. It really looks like an accident.'

'There's no motive that we've yet uncovered' said Murphy. 'If you were sleeping in a barn, what would lead you to pull clothes on and go out in the early morning?'

'If I needed a pee' said Wilcox. 'I'd have to pull some clothes on in case there was somebody about. Maybe just jeans, maybe I'd have slept in my underpants, but I wouldn't wander out in them, in case I saw somebody. And I'd put something on my feet, because it would be dirty, muddy underfoot. This was when they still had sheep.'

'That's right' said Murphy. 'You wouldn't bother lacing up your trainers, because you'd be taking them off again as soon as you got back in, probably settling down for another sleep.'

'And if I was going for a dip in the pond, I'd take off my trainers and my jeans' said Wilcox. 'Denim is the worst thing to try and swim in, everybody knows that, even people who don't swim.'

'So the idea that he wandered into the pond of his own accord, for a self-administered swimming lesson starts to look like bullshit' said Murphy.

'I would say so' said Wilcox.

They were on the outskirts of London now.

'I think a more extensive chat with Pete's girlfriend would be a good use of our time at this point' said Murphy, and she took the turning for the Finchley Road.

Chapter Twenty-One

Olivia Atwell was feeding the baby when Murphy and Wilcox arrived and opened the door still clutching him to her breast

The flat was mostly white – 'builder's finish', as Murphy had heard it described – but brightened up with cushions and throws in deep colours. The walls had posters on – arty prints rather than art. The effect was colourful and cheerful. A bit of thought and effort had gone into this place, she thought, in contrast to the Cheyne Walk interior, which spoke of money and indifference.

Olivia had quite striking Celtic looks – dark hair, pale skin and deep blue eyes. Less head-turning than Effie Fincham probably, but they would have been an attractive pair. Now she was looking tired, dark smudges under her eyes. Wilcox closed the door behind them so that she could go and sit down with her burden.

'Sorry to interrupt his feed' said Murphy, sitting opposite her. 'Is it a him?'

'Yes, it's Ben and we've only just started, I'm afraid. To be honest, if you hadn't said 'police' I wouldn't have opened the door.'

'I can understand that' said Murphy. 'Baby feeding's pretty full-on. Is your mum around to help you?'

Olivia laughed briefly. It didn't sound like a happy laugh. 'Sorry' she said, 'but it is kind of funny. My mother is the last person I'd ever let near my child.'

'Really? That bad?'

Olivia nodded, momentarily disturbing the baby. 'Well she was never much of a mother, too much of a narcissist, or that's what she became when my dad walked out, so I don't think she'd score too highly as a grandmother.'

'You'll appreciate that we're questioning everybody who knew Elizabeth – Effie – Fincham.'

'Of course. Do you really suspect Pete?'

'We've released him for the time being, as you know, but we may need to speak to him again.'

'He would never have hurt Effie, or anybody else.'

Murphy nodded her acknowledgement of this statement. There wasn't much else to say about it.

'You had known Effie for a long time.'

Olivia nodded. 'Yes, since we were nineteen.'

'What was she like?'

Olivia shifted the baby to the other side and gave him a minute to latch on. Then she looked up at them. 'Effie lit up a room. I know that's a cliché, but she really did. People would congregate around her. Half the time she was talking rubbish, but everybody listened anyway. Obviously, we haven't seen each other every day over the last few years, but we've always been there for each other.'

'You must be missing her now.'

She nodded. 'Yes, very much. I can't believe she's not around any more.'

Murphy stood up and wandered over to look at the photos in a collage on the wall. 'Here you both are in this group shot. You had long hair.'

Olivia looked across. 'That was a bunch of people in our year. I'm not sure who took those photos – somebody with an SLR – and then we got prints done. Really old school, technically. Long hair was more fashionable then. Can't believe it took me so long to get it cut.'

'And this one of the rowing team? Looks like a rowing team. All in lifejackets, holding up your oars.'

'Yes, that's me. Effie got us both into the girls rowing team, because she said all the best blokes were rowers. I actually enjoyed rowing. I made the first team. Effie dropped out pretty quickly, but not before dating three of the rowers.'

Murphy resumed her seat. 'So she had lots of boyfriends?'

'Yes, of course. None of them lasted that long. Not until Hugo of course.'

'And your boyfriend, Peter Grantham, he was her boyfriend at one time?'

'Yes, he was, at university. It was pretty short-lived, just a few months.'

'And he's still friends with her?'

'Of course, but that's only because Effie's my friend. Their relationship is ancient history.' She put the baby over her shoulder and patted his back. 'It was years ago. We were all much younger.'

'He seems to have spent some time with her after driving her home that night. Do you have any thoughts about that?'

Olivia stood up and began walking, patting the baby on his back. She was rewarded with a burp. 'I can only think that he ended up listening to Effie's problems. She really needed a sympathetic hearing.'

'But she'd already had that from you.'

She stopped pacing for a moment. 'I don't know. Maybe she wanted to get a man's perspective on it – on the business with Hugo.'

Murphy waited for Olivia to sit down again. The baby was now asleep and she laid him carefully in a car seat.

'Have you asked Pete about that? About why he spent so long with Effie?'

Olivia shrugged. 'We haven't really talked about it. But I will ask him at some point. Not' she added, 'that I think there will be anything untoward about it. Pity he didn't stay longer, she might not have been attacked.'

Well that was an interesting viewpoint, thought Murphy.

'Is that what you think, that it was a random attack?'

'I can't see what else it can have been. She was no threat to anybody.'

'No threat to the Finchams?'

Olivia waved an arm as if to dismiss the suggestion. 'She seemed to think she would be, but really she'd be no match for Edward Fincham. They would just have paid her off.'

'I think you're probably right about that' said Murphy. 'So Effie's had a lot of relationships. People sometimes don't take it too well when relationships end. Can you think of anybody who would want to hurt her?'

Olivia shook her head slowly. 'No, nobody at all. She stayed friends with all the men she went out with. All the ones I knew about anyway. It doesn't make sense.'

'Tell me more about these Finchams. What is your impression of them? I gather you've visited that farm a few times.'

Olivia took a deep breath and stretched her arms. 'Yes, I've been there a few times with Effie and I've been made some trips up there since... she died...to help out with Mabel. Hugo's leaning quite heavily on Dorothy at the moment, but I think he'll soon have to get a nanny. So the Finchams... well the father's a bit scary – or that's what he likes to project. I think he loves his family, but he doesn't have much time for anybody else. I've never actually had a conversation with him. His wife is what people call 'troubled', and maybe a bit worse than that. Effie told me she was on a lot of drugs and never much of a mother.

The family has the vineyard as you probably know, it's not a livestock farm any more. It's doing quite well I think, they've won several international awards. Hugo and Sebastian run that and Dorothy does most of the admin side. Neither of the men are any good at that. Sebastian is not much of a grafter, he's the social side of the business. Very good when people come for tastings. Hugo's no good at the social stuff, he deals with the money. He has no talent for small talk. Phoebe is apparently the cleverest member of the family, she works in a science park, nothing to do with the family business, so I've never seen much of her. She's much closer to Sebastian than to Hugo, maybe because they're closer in age.'

'How about Dorothy Hepple. What do you know about her?'

'Dorothy is also a bit scary – no, that sounds pathetic – she's not scary, but she's very competent and expects everything to be done properly. She's probably the only person outside the family who is not overawed by Edward Fincham. I've even heard her arguing with him. I think he relies on her quite a lot, because she deals with all the people he doesn't want to waste his time on.' She thought for a moment. 'I think that includes most people, actually.'

'What did you think of Hugo Fincham when you first met him?'

'I thought he was good-looking, probably quite clever, but a bit dull and a bit socially awkward – he wasn't exactly amusing company. He did seem to be very much in love with Effie.'

'Was she in love with him?'

Wilcox had risen and was walking around the room. Prying into all this female emotional stuff was best left to Murphy.

Olivia took a moment to answer. 'I guess so. She never said she was, she claimed not to believe in love, but she certainly wanted to marry him.'

'She married him for money?'

Olivia shrugged. 'I think that may have been part of it.'

'Tell us again what happened last Tuesday.'

'She called me. I hadn't seen her for weeks, probably nearer a month. She said she thought Hugo was trying to kill her. She wanted to see me. She came round a few hours later.'

'So what did you take this to mean – that he was trying to kill her?'

'I thought that he was fed up with her, wanted her out of the way – or at least that's what I thought she meant.'

'So what did she mean?'

'She said her marriage was over, at least as far as she was concerned. She showed me the bruises. I realised then what she was referring to, that he was beating her up. She said she was afraid next time he'd go too far. I said she should leave him. She said she would leave when she had negotiated a good settlement.'

‘Was this the first you knew of the problems?’

‘No, she had told me before that she was fed up with Hugo, she didn’t want to sleep with him. She liked the house and the money, but she didn’t like him anymore.’

‘That wouldn’t have made him very happy. Did she have somebody else in mind?’

‘Not that she ever told me about.’

‘And this negotiated settlement. Did she say any more about that?’

‘She said she wanted to keep Mabel and the house and have a good income. She said she had leverage. She‘d already had one conversation with Hugo’s dad about it.’

‘What did she mean about leverage?’

‘She didn’t want to go into details, but she said the Finchams had a secret that they didn’t want known. That’s all she told me.’

‘And do you have any idea what that was?’

‘No. None at all. I don’t think Effie knew what it was, but she was convinced it existed, if that makes sense.’

‘Was there anybody else she may have confided in?’

‘No. Well maybe. There was a woman called Kate - Kate Black - that Effie met at least once while I was there. She may have met her again after that. I was out of it with the baby, so I don’t know.’

‘Do you have a name or number for her?’

‘No, I’m afraid not.’

‘No problem. We’ll find out.’

The baby was waking up. Murphy handed her a card. 'Call me if you think of anything else.’

***

'Narcissist' said Wilcox, looking at his phone. 'A person who thinks the world revolves around them. There's a lot of that on social media. It says here they can be arrogant, self-centred, manipulative and paranoid, and they like bullying and intimidating other people. And lots of other stuff besides. Olivia must have had a hard time growing up. I wouldn't have wanted my mum to be like that.'

'No, me neither. And most people love their children, however they feel about anybody else. So someone who exhibits those traits towards their kids is in really bad shape.'

'Do you think Edward Fincham's a narcissist?' said Wilcox.

'Well he's not a very likeable individual' said Murphy, 'but I wouldn't necessarily put him in that category. I don't think that would have gone undetected in the legal profession for all these years. Although I could be wrong about that, I don't know that empathy is a requirement for judges. He doesn't look like he'd have been a hands-on dad. Maybe these labels are not that useful.'

'How about Hugo Fincham?'

Murphy considered this. 'I'd say he's a bully. And he's bullied and physically abused a woman, and a woman who's much smaller and weaker than him. So that makes him a bad lot in my book. I can imagine him losing his temper and killing her without really meaning to, but I can't see him cold-bloodedly planning a murder. I don't think he has enough self-control for that.'

'But Effie's murder looks like that doesn't it – a spur of the moment job?'

'Yes, it does. Which makes Hugo a shoo-in. But we still have to find the evidence. Maybe Jackson will have some insights to offer.'

***

Jackson Welby's receptionist was young and multiply pierced – lip, tongue, eyebrow, nose, ears. Her neck was tattooed all around with some kind of leafy wreath. She wore mostly black apart from a piece of tartan tied around her impossibly red hair and she walked towards them on what looked like builders' boots but were probably Timberlands. It was impossible not to be impressed, although Murphy thought Wilcox was possibly a bit alarmed. A greater departure from the picture Effie would have presented was hard to imagine. Hugo Fincham would have kept his mind strictly on business if he had been dealing with this young woman.

Jackson himself sported paint-spattered jeans and a cashmere sweater with multiple holes. He welcomed them to a room upstairs which looked like part-office, part restoration studio. There were paintings and frames lining the walls and a faint but not unpleasant smell of turpentine. He shifted a pile of brochures off two chairs and they sat down. He himself perched on a stool next to a laptop. Murphy glanced at the screen and saw emails drifting in constantly, announcing themselves in bold type. Business was busy. He looked like a man used to multitasking, if that wasn't an oxymoron.

'You'll have gathered that we want to talk to you about Effie Fincham' Wilcox began.

He inclined his head. 'Of course.'

'Can you tell us the last time you saw her?'

He picked up his phone. 'I'll have to check. It was a long time ago, just after she got married. Yes, almost a year ago. I did intend to stay in touch and now I'm very sorry I didn't.'

'And where were you last Tuesday?'

He checked the phone again. 'See, even last week I can't remember. OK, that was a launch party for a sculptor called Janetta Bright held in a gallery in Deptford – all the best stuff is in the East End now. I was there for about two hours, with my partner, until about ten pm, then we got a taxi home to Marylebone.'

'Long way to come in a taxi' said Wilcox.

'Yes, it is, but we'd both been drinking, so no choice really.'

'What can you tell us about Hugo Fincham?' asked Murphy.

'Actually, I don't know Hugo that well' said Jackson. 'I've sold quite a bit of artwork to the family over the past few years, but most of my dealings have been with Dorothy, and then I would meet the family when I went to hang the pieces.'

'So what can you tell us about the family? It would be useful to have an outside perspective.'

'Let me see.' He pulled his sleeves up and crossed his arms. 'Fincham senior is a humourless old bugger – is this the sort of character sketch you want?'

'Absolutely' said Murphy. 'That's exactly what we want.'

'OK. Well he's a man devoid of charm, whatever his illustrious progress on the bench. His wife is– a woman who has no idea that other people even exist. I have had the odd artistic disagreement with her – why I bothered I don't know – which have on each occasion resulted in her having some sort of hysterical episode and having to retire to her bed to be ministered to with fans and smelling salts – or more likely, prescription drugs. They all seem to tiptoe round her. At least the kids have grown up and escaped – he's stuck with her for life.'

'Very interesting' said Murphy. 'Do you have any idea why she's like that?'

'I think it can only be to do with her relationship with him. I don't think she was ever that interested in the kids. That's why he had to get in Dorothy. And I think Dorothy is very well rewarded.'

'And how about the younger generation?'

Jackson exhaled noisily. 'I think they've been financially indulged but had no real parenting. I get the impression – just an impression, mind you – that Hugo is a bit scared of his father. Sebastian is not scared of anyone. I've even seen the mother deferring to his opinion on one occasion. So I'd say he's more indulged. The sister I don't know – I've hardly ever seen her.'

'So what did you think when Effie took up with Hugo?'

'I thought it would be disastrous for her. His previous girlfriend was an intelligent and attractive young woman, but she didn't last long. I did counsel Effie to take it a bit more slowly, but she couldn't be stopped. I didn't think it would go well once the initial excitement had worn off. Although obviously I didn't expect anything this bad.'

'In what way did you think it would be disastrous?'

He took his time to think, swivelling round on the stool.

'I thought it would be really bad for her being part of that family. I thought they would look down on her and give her no support, and I thought Hugo was not a man strong enough to defend her – which when you think about it is part of the marriage vow isn't it? 'Forsaking all other...etc'. I thought they'd crush the life out of her, and he would be useless.'

'Did you ever think that he might beat her?'

He stopped moving abruptly. 'Was he beating her?'

'We found bruises on her body.'

He shook his head. 'The bastard. No, I wasn't expecting that.'

'Can you think of any reason why somebody would want to kill her?'

He shook his head. 'None at all. I can't imagine it was anybody who knew her. Not even Hugo, even if he had abused her. He's an asshole but I can't see him killing anybody.'

'You think it's more likely to be just a random killer?'

'I just can't think of anything else.'

'Your current receptionist looks very different to Effie' said Murphy.

He smiled. 'She does, doesn't she? Elsa's a talented artist herself. Any rich man who tried to pick her up would get short shrift.'

Chapter Twenty-Two

SUSANNAH WAS ALREADY SITTING in the restaurant when Murphy arrived, wearing a long-sleeved black jersey dress and sipping a gin and tonic. Murphy had been exhorted to 'make an effort', so she had ditched the usual trousers and jacket in favour of a soft grey suit that she had bought for some long-forgotten occasion. When she had unearthed it from the wardrobe, she was so gratified to see that the moths had not yet got to work on it, that she decided to give it an airing.

'You're looking good Miranda. See, it's good to dress up once in a while, isn't it? After all, this place isn't cheap.'

Murphy snorted. 'If we're going to be paying a lot of money, we should be able to dress how we want.'

The waiter arrived at that moment and saved Susannah from having to think up a suitable reply. When they had ordered Murphy poured herself a glass of wine.

'Now tell me how it's going.'

Susannah studied her nails for a minute. 'It's going to be fine, I think. I'm letting him have the girls every second weekend and he's OK with that. I don't want them making friends with Felicity, but there's not much I can do about that. I make myself as scarce as possible when he turns up, because I still find it a bit upsetting to see him. He's not making any demands about the house. At the moment he seems happy to just live in Felicity's flat with her. Further down the line he'll probably want me to sell it and give him his share, but probably not while the girls are living at home.'

'That's not so bad' said Murphy. 'I mean, obviously it's bad and if I ran into him, he'd be left in no doubt about that, but logistics-wise it seems OK. And he was never exactly Mr man-about-the-house was he? In which case you won't be feeling his loss when there's a water leak or a shelf falls off the wall.'

'Absolutely not. I'd be the one putting the shelf back up even if he was there. But I don't care about the DIY aspect. I still love him and to be honest, if he turned up tomorrow, I'd take him back.'

'Maybe you just have to wait for that feeling to pass' said Murphy. 'And it does, for 99% of people. The other 1% we have to watch out for. Some people are so badly affected when their spouse walks out that they almost become a different person – or maybe they always were that person and now they no longer need to hide the worst traits of their character. I was interviewing a young woman earlier today who told me she wouldn't allow her mother anywhere near her baby – because when she was a child her father walked out and her mother became what she described as a narcissist. It's an interesting concept, but I would take the view that her mother was always a narcissist, and after her husband left, she no longer bothered keeping it under control.

In your case, you're not one of the 1%, you're not a narcissist and you love your kids, so in time your relationship with Simon will become just a part of the past and the whole situation will stop looming up at you in the present.'

Their food arrived at that point and Susannah picked up her fork.

'I know that's how it was for you, but I think it will take me a bit longer. Didn't you even miss Jack?'

Murphy nodded with her mouth full and then swallowed.

'Of course. But I think by the time he left we both knew it was drawing to a close. For the first few weeks I really wanted him to come back, but then I started to appreciate the peace and quiet. If the kids had still been at home, I wouldn't even have felt lonely. Then, of course, I found the boys.'

'Yes, the boys' Susannah laughed. 'You replaced him with two men. You were very lucky there.'

'Tell me about it. I've had other people try to tempt them away, you know. Offers of peppercorn rent, free Netflix, probably private health insurance, God knows what. I've had to reduce the rent, which was pretty low already, in order to beat off some woman who's moved in further down the road. She ran into them in the supermarket and decided they were the solution to all her problems. As far as I'm concerned, they're the solution to my problems, and she can sort her own out.'

'But don't you ever want a man you can have an actual .. relationship .. with?'

'About once every three months, in passing, with a few drinks inside me, otherwise no. It would just completely upend my domestic arrangements. If you met somebody else – which of course you will – you would be worrying about how the kids would feel about it. But the kids are young, so at least they can't up sticks and leave. I'd have to worry about how James and Clive would feel about it, and they have plenty of other options.'

'Maybe that's what I need' said Susannah. 'A lodger.'

Murphy speared a piece of broccoli. 'A lodger is a great idea. But let me vet them first. And not anybody off one of those dating sites.'

Chapter Twenty-Three

Sebastian Fincham was up to his elbows in machinery when they found him in the vineyard. He was wearing oil-stained jeans and a sweater that looked like it had seen better days, but still managed to look like he could step off the pages of a glossy magazine.

Wilcox waved a badge at him and he signalled agreement. They waited while he did something energetic with a wrench and then he jumped down off the platform and came towards them.

'I thought you were just the brains of the outfit' said Murphy. 'Front of house, so to speak.'

He wiped his hands on a rag and smiled. 'Would that it were so. Actually I've discovered a love for the physical process. Almost biblical don't you think? Turning grapes into wine.'

'And quite successful wine I hear?'

'Yes. We've been at it six years. It takes a few years before you get any return and you're always worrying about the weather, but now we're reaping the rewards. Mostly whites, as the soil here is quite chalky and the climate is of course cool. Including some sparkling whites. But if the climate gets warmer, we're looking at moving into some of the red varieties, maybe Grenache or Malbec. I'd like to grow red grapes, or the black ones that you need for a really dark Malbec. But black grapes can mean bad luck, so maybe we should hold off a bit on that.'

'Whose idea was it originally?'

'Mine actually. It's fifty acres of hillside and so it used to be sheep, but I persuaded the old man to terrace it and move into grapes. The whole sheep business is declining and it's a distasteful business anyway – sending lambs off to slaughter and all the rest of it. I wouldn't have wanted any part of it.'

He pointed to a pressure gauge. 'We were lucky to be late adopters. The equipment nowadays is so much more sophisticated. It's really important to exert exactly the right amount of pressure, enough to squeeze out the maximum amount of juice without crushing the seeds, which gives it too much tannin. It also has to be exactly the right pressure to avoid mashing the skins. So quite a delicate operation.'

Wilcox moved closer to have a look. Murphy was more interested in looking at Sebastian.

'Where were you on the night of 22 September?'

He smiled briefly. 'Ah, alibi time. Normally I'd have to tell you I don't have a clue, but I know that was the night we had a board meeting. Just as well in view of what happened.'

Murphy leaned against the platform. 'So tell me about the board meeting.'

'To begin with, it was preceded by dinner. Do you want to know about that?'

'Sure.'

'OK. We actually ate in the kitchen that night – Hugo and I, mum and dad and Dorothy. Mrs Parsons had made a really quite outstanding fish stew and we had a bottle of one of our own whites – a Sancerre – well obviously not a real Sancerre, and we don't dare describe it as such, but very similar if I do say so myself. Then mum went off to watch TV and I would have been very happy to join her, but instead we had the meeting to get through. You probably don't have board meetings in your line of work. Believe me, they are invariably long and tedious. Just when you think it's all wrapped up, some bugger brings up another point and it all starts off again. This time it was Hugo. We'd ploughed through the bloody agenda, all the way down to 'any other business'. At that point you're home and dry as long as everybody keeps their trap shut. Then Hugo starts in about maybe we should change our insurance policy because he thinks the current one doesn't cover us for volcanic explosions or bird strikes or something. Sorry, I'm being facetious here, but you know what I mean. Dad doesn't agree with him. Dorothy chips in something or other and before you know it, we're off again. Half an hour later Dad asks again if there's any other business and I've decided, in my half-asleep state, that if Hugo says a word I'm going to leap across the table and attack him. I think he got the message. So we split up about 10pm and I drove home. Before you ask, I'd only had one glass of wine, but I was bloody tired.'

'Well thank you for that' said Murphy. 'Now tell me, how did you get on with Effie?'

'Very well.' He leaned against the platform and crossed his feet. 'I liked her a lot. She was full of life, possibly a bit too full of life for Hugo.'

'What does that mean?'

He laughed. 'Hugo can be a bit of a dry stick. She'd want to stay up and party and he'd be looking forward to an early night.'

'Did you know he was beating her?'

He looked up sharply. 'I don't believe that.'

'Well somebody was. She's got the bruises.'

'I find it hard to believe that of Hugo. He may not be the life and soul of the party, but he's not violent.'

'How about if she told him she was leaving him?'

He looked up at the ceiling for a moment. 'That would be a matter of negotiation between them. It wouldn't cause him to start beating her. Why? Had she told him that?'

'It looks like it. Did either of them ever confide in you?'

'Believe me, Hugo would never confide in me. Effie would complain about him sometimes, but only in a light-hearted way. I had no reason to think there was anything wrong.'

'Complain about him how?'

'She would tell me that he was boring, he was too old – in attitudes, not actual age. But it was a joke, none of that was serious.'

Murphy looked at him more closely. 'Maybe she found you more attractive than him.'

'Now wait a minute' his expression darkened. 'There was nothing like that going on.'

Murphy had the distinct feeling that, when Sebastian was involved, there would always be something going on.

'When did you last see her?'

'A few weeks ago. She'd come to see Hugo about something. I don't know what. She came with Olivia. I think Pete was here too – Olivia's boyfriend.'

'Do you remember a lad called Billy Jukes?'

If he was taken aback by the change of subject, he didn't show it.

'Of course. Years ago. Schoolfriend of Hugo's. We had friends over for the weekend and he drowned in the pond. Awful.'

'Why do you think he went into the pond? Did he not know it was deep?'

'The pond is big and it's very deep at the middle. It was a hot afternoon and we were all swimming in it. Billy said he couldn't swim, so we made him stay near the edge. Bit odd not being able to swim. Mum had taught all of us when we were small. Billy would have known it was dangerous.'

'Who was there that weekend?'

'Us three, and we were allowed one guest each. Phoebe had a friend from school, as far as I remember her name was Juliet and my mate Barney and Billy. We had a barbecue, well some kind of makeshift one anyway, just a pile of rocks and we burned wood from some tree that had been pruned and Mum and Dorothy brought out stuff to incinerate and drinks. Probably Mum and Dad were pleased not to have us all making a commotion at the dinner table.'

'How was your mother that weekend?'

If Sebastian wondered how much they knew about his mother, and why it was their business to know, he didn't ask.

'She was actually OK, it was during one of her better periods. We often avoided bringing friends home because we didn't know how she would behave, but she was fine that weekend, took a lot of interest in our friends.'

'Do you have contact details for Juliet and Barney?'

Wilcox passed over his pad and biro and Sebastian scribbled.

'These are Barney's details. Phoebe might know about Juliet, if they're still in touch. But the police went into all this at the time.'

'OK, just going over the ground. What was Hugo like as a child?'

He laughed abruptly. 'What on earth has that got to do with anything?'

'He was older than you. How did you get on?'

'You're thinking maybe he has form are you? Perhaps he bullied me, so that means he bullied Effie?'

'Did he bully you?'

Sebastian sat on the edge of the platform and crossed his arms. 'I can't say he was the ideal big brother and we did scrap a bit. And I guess he was bigger than me, so I often came off worse. But that's all it was, just boys scrapping. It would be wrong to assume he's a violent person, or anything like that.'

'I'm not making any assumptions. I'm just curious. You had a high court judge for a dad. What was that like?'

He was silent for a moment.

'I don't think the word 'dad' covers it really. We never saw that much of him. Or I didn't. Apart from family outings or whatever, which were always organised down to the last detail. Everybody had to appear at the marshalling point with their kit in order. Well not really, but it felt like that. Because he couldn't stand time-wasting. If he was taking a whole day off to spend with us, it had to be properly organised and proceed without a hitch. He would never spend time with us just mucking about or having a laugh or watching rubbish TV. It was like living with a scout leader. There you are – I've probably told you too much already.'

'Did Hugo get on well with your father?'

He shrugged. 'I dunno. You'd have to ask him. I don't remember them being particularly close.'

'Would you say Hugo was scared of him?'

He was silent for a moment. 'Maybe.' He sighed. 'As I said before, our father was not a comfortable person to be around. Not a hands-on dad. And Hugo was the eldest so there may have been a heavier weight of expectation on him. But you should ask one of them.'

'I'll probably do that. How did your sister get on with Effie?'

He looked surprised. 'God, you're jumping all over the place on this, aren't you? Phoebe? I don't know. I don't think they saw much of each other'.

'They were two young women, roughly the same age, now related by marriage. You would think they would have had some kind of relationship.'

Sebastian shrugged. 'I really don't know. They may have been closer than I knew about.'

Murphy smiled. 'Oh, I think you have a pretty good idea what goes on.' She pulled a card out of her pocket and handed it to him. 'Give me a ring if you think of anything else.'

Chapter Twenty-Four

MARIA REPTON WAS A psychotherapist attached to the probation service. Her office was on the top floor of a Victorian building in Brixton, which had once been a private residence. The lower floors were occupied by various other organisations and the brass plates were lined up next to the front door. Maria's plate simply listed her qualifications, which made it clear that she had a private practice. What interested Kevin Wilcox was that she was also an ex-girlfriend of Hugo Fincham.

Wilcox announced himself via the intercom and climbed the expensively-carpeted stairs. As the door was opened, he was greeted by a serious of barks coming from underneath the desk. A thing that looked like a scrubbing brush on legs rushed out and sniffed him all over. Wilcox liked dogs.

'Irish wolfhound?' he said to the young woman who had opened the door.

'Correct' she said. 'This is Norman.'

Introductions made, Norman retired to his basket under the desk. The room had two big windows looking out onto the street and they had curtains, rather than blinds. Long sofas were backed up against two of the walls and behind them were large embroidered wall hangings. There were no official posters to be seen. Apart from the desk and chairs, the effect was of a comfortable sitting room rather than an office. Wilcox wondered how much Norman hankered after lying on the sofas.

Maria Repton waved Wilcox to a chair and resumed her seat behind the desk. She was a serious-looking young woman with dark hair tied up on top of her head and dark-rimmed glasses through which she peered intently.

Wilcox thought he had the measure of her when she suddenly smiled and all his carefully-prepared introduction and questions suddenly went out of his head. She came to his rescue.

'You wanted to talk to me about Hugo Fincham?'

Wilcox had gathered himself now. 'Yes, you probably know why.'

She nodded. 'I was very shocked when I realised it was Hugo's wife. I guess he's a suspect?'

'Well, we can't rule him out at the moment. So, it would be really helpful to hear anything you can tell us about him.'

She hesitated a moment.

'Can I start by asking how you found me?'

'Of course. A friend of the family remembered you and you were easy to track down once we had a name. We hoped you might be willing to help.' ('Friend of the family' didn't seem quite right but was the only way he could think of to describe Jackson.)

'Yes, I'm happy to help, not that I can tell you very much. Hugo was never a patient of mine, so there is no patient confidentiality to consider. But what this means is that I'm not giving you any kind of professional opinion. All I can tell you is what I observed as his girlfriend – which only lasted a few months.'

'Agreed.'

'OK. Hugo and I got together about two years ago. We met up at a friend's wedding. I hadn't had much to do with him at university, but we ended up sitting next to each other at the reception and he wasn't bad company. Also, he's pretty attractive and I had just broken up with someone, so I was probably looking for someone to fill that gap. Always a mistake, but I didn't know then what I know now.'

'How do you mean?'

'Well, I think when you split up with somebody, you have to get used to being on your own again. Then, when you're happy being single, you can think about meeting somebody else. Rushing into another relationship straight away is usually a bad idea – let's say your critical faculties are not at their best.'

Wilcox was tracking with this now. 'You're saying that you wouldn't in retrospect have taken up with Hugo?'

'No, I wouldn't. Simply because I was a bit vulnerable at the time. I don't think Hugo's a bad person, and I would find it hard to believe he could kill anybody, but I would classify him – not professionally, but personally - as damaged goods. That's just my personal opinion. I wouldn't want it to be repeated.'

He nodded. 'Understood. Damaged in what way?'

She hesitated and pushed her glasses further up the bridge of her nose. 'He's like a musical instrument that's been strung too tight. You feel like something could snap at any moment. He was never a relaxed person to be with and the couple of times when I met his father, I felt that he exacerbated it.'

'Why do you think that was?'

'I'd say he was scared of his father, even as an adult. That makes me wonder what it was like when he was a child.'

'You think he was beaten as a child?'

'It wouldn't surprise me. After all, it's not so long ago that people believed that parents were entitled to beat their children.'

'If he was beaten as a child, would that make him more likely to beat a woman?'

She hesitated for a moment. 'I think it's possible, if only because he lacks the empathy, social skills, whatever, to deal with a woman in a more grown-up way.'

'What did you think of his father?'

'Not a likeable man. He couldn't really be bothered speaking to me, which I thought was a bit of a snub to Hugo. And he wasn't a happy person. Happy people don't behave like that.'

'Did you ever meet his mother?'

She shook her head. 'I did make some suggestion at one point about how I'd like to meet his mother, but Hugo was aghast – that's the only word I can think of for it – so I gathered I wouldn't be granted an audience. I guess I was pretty naïve. I thought Hugo had decided I wasn't good enough to meet his parents. In fact, I've realised since, it was the parents he was worried about.'

Wilcox thought she'd certainly be good enough to meet his parents. He should be so lucky. He dragged his attention back to the matter in hand.

'How about Sebastian? Did you ever meet him?'

'Now it's funny you should say that.' She grinned suddenly. 'Hugo definitely didn't want me to meet Sebastian. When he realised Sebastian was on his way home, he whipped me off to the pub. And Sebastian was equally determined to get in on the act, so to speak. So Sebastian turned up at the pub and was very charming to me. Hugo was spitting nails, he knew Sebastian had done it on purpose. When Sebastian had succeeded in making Hugo mad, he took himself off. Job done. So there was some kind of games condition going on between them, probably had been for years.'

'Do you think maybe Hugo bullied Sebastian when they were kids.'

'Yes. That would explain it. Sebastian was getting his own back. I really decided after that visit that Hugo was not the man for me.'

Wilcox had run out of questions. He frantically scoured his brain but nothing was coming up. He'd have to wind it up.

'Well thank you very much for your time' he said. 'It's been very helpful.'

'No problem' she said. 'If you want to leave me a card, I'll call you if I think of anything else.'

He scrabbled furiously in his pockets, unearthing parking tickets, receipts and chewing gum wrappers, some of which fluttered to the floor. Norman scampered over to see if there was anything interesting. Then he remembered his wallet and yanked out a card.

'Yes, please do' he said, handing it to her. 'Quite often things come back to you after the event.'

'Yes, that's what I often find' she said and smiled up at him.

Wilcox extricated himself with as much dignity as possible and sat in the car for several minutes before starting the engine. Then he thought she might look out the window and he'd look like a wally, still sitting there. He slid into first gear and moved off with a lurch. Then he took off the handbrake.

Chapter Twenty-Five

BACK AT THE STATION, the door-to-door officers were coming back. None of them looked particularly enthusiastic, although one or two looked well-fed. Wilcox hung his jacket over the back of his chair and leafed through the reports, then took them over to Murphy who was trying to shift a mound of paperwork.

He took a seat opposite her desk and gave her the abbreviated version of his visit.

'Maria Repton described Hugo as 'damaged goods'. She can imagine him doing the beating, but not the murder. And she thinks he was beaten as a child and is still scared of his father.'

'Interesting. I'd say she's right about that. But it still doesn't give us any clearer pointer to whether or not he killed her. It was also interesting what Sebastian was saying about Hugo dragging out the board meeting – if that's what he was doing. That would make sense if he had arranged for his wife to be killed professionally and he wanted an airtight alibi. But that seems a bit far-fetched.'

She picked up the contents of her in-tray and dumped the lot in the recycling bin. 'Departmental memos' she explained to Wilcox, who was looking shocked. 'Waste of trees. OK, what do we have from the door-to-door?'

Wilcox had prepared a rough summary.

'No sightings of anybody seen entering or leaving the house. Maybe that's not so surprising. It was late on a cold night, so people wouldn't be hanging about. This is not a hanging about area. But it is of course an area where security is taken very seriously, so a lot of our officers seem to have been invited in. And these are much better places to be invited into than some of those we have to visit, so nobody's complaining particularly. In fact some of our officers have been given top-notch refreshments, but no useful information. Several reports of cars driving past between the relevant hours, but nobody paid any attention and it was dark so we don't even have the colours of any of these cars. Two of the cars we know about anyway – Pete Grantham's car and Hugo Fincham's. The neighbours on either side didn't hear any noises. And no reports of hearing taxis dropping anybody off, idling outside getting paid-off or whatever. Just a load of nothing.'

Murphy took a sip of her coffee. It was horrible. Brewed in the CID room. Should have gone to Costa. 'And we picked up Grantham and Fincham's cars on the ANPR?'

'Yes. Two cameras on the King's Road and one on Oakley Street. That means we can pinpoint them. Anybody else would have to have arrived in a car – or maybe a taxi?'

'If they came in a taxi they'd probably get dropped some way off – they wouldn't want the driver to remember dropping them off in Cheyne Walk. We'll put out a call for any taxi drop-offs in the area at that time.'

'Unless it was unpremeditated' said Wilcox. 'They may have come not with the intention of killing her. In that case they wouldn't be covering their tracks on the way in, just on the way out.'

'It was still an unholy hour to be making a social call, especially to a woman with a small child. Although I would have Effie down as a bit of a night bird.'

'It really does look like it has to be one of our two suspects' said Wilcox. 'There's nobody else in the frame. Maybe we should shake them down a bit harder.'

Murphy shook her head. 'You sound like Bellweather. What we need is evidence. What have we got from SOCO?'

'Prints identified belonging to Effie Fincham, Hugo Fincham, Dorothy Hepple, Pete Grantham, Olivia Atwell and Jane Belling – she's the cleaner. No unidentified prints. If her assailant wasn't one of these people, they wore gloves. If it was a burglary, they would probably wear gloves because they couldn't be sure we didn't have their prints on file, and most burglaries happen at night. It was a cold night anyway, so gloves wouldn't look out of place.'

Murphy wasn't convinced. 'Most burglars don't kill people. She was a vulnerable householder. A slight woman home alone with a small child. She would have represented no threat to a burglar. He/she could simply have shoved her into another room and told her to stay there and she would probably have complied, especially if her daughter was threatened.'

'How about if she started screaming and he/she wanted to shut her up?'

'That's a possible scenario, but he would only have needed to shut her up long enough to utter some very specific threats. That would have quietened her down. There was no need to actually kill her. And none of the neighbours heard any screams.'

'You're not liking this burglary theory are you?'

Murphy shook her head. 'No, not at all. I accept that some of the silverware is missing, or at least that Hugo Fincham told us that it was, but that doesn't seem like much of a haul. The pictures on the walls were probably far more valuable but none of those were taken – admittedly that would only be possible if he/she had a car outside. It would have taken too long to remove them from the frames, unless somebody had the right tools and knew what they were doing. There was no break-in, so Effie opened to door to whoever it was. Maybe a burglar rang the doorbell and forced his way in, but that's a pretty unusual modus operandum. And if I had killed Effie, I'd make off with a few trinkets just to make it look like a burglary. No brainer really.'

Wilcox sighed. 'We don't have any evidence for anything at the moment. Bellweather is going to start letting off steam anytime now. I walked past his office on the way to the bathroom and he narrowed his eyes at me, so he's coming up to the boil. And it's only a matter of time before the press pick up on it, warning women home alone to keep their doors locked and generally frightening people. All it needs is a slow news day. Once that circus starts up, there'll be bloody press conferences and they'll be following us around. Do we get these two chaps back in and push a bit harder?'

'Let's leave it a bit longer before we get into that. We're probably on thin ice but we haven't gone through yet. If we don't have any evidence, we would at least need to have some theories to shove at them. At the moment I don't see a clear motive for anybody to kill her. Maybe Hugo was beating her up and she was planning to leave him, but that's the sort of situation that can be resolved with negotiation and money. And Pete? He was happily settled down – as far as we can tell – with somebody else. Maybe he was having an affair with Effie, but we have no evidence for that. And even if he was, why kill her?

There's something else going on here. Two deaths connected to this family. And somebody got away with the first one. It doesn't look to me as if it was properly investigated. His Honour will have been on the bench at that time. Maybe the coroner felt his Honour's family couldn't be involved in any wrongdoing. After meeting Reggie I'd say the investigating officers were at least guilty of negligence, if nothing worse. Now we know that his Honour was possibly being economical with the truth. According to Olivia Atwell he did have a meeting with Effie. Was that when she told him she was leaving and wanted a settlement?'

'And why was she talking to Edward about it rather than Hugo?' added Wilcox.

'Exactly. Maybe her bargaining chip was something that concerned the family as a whole. Maybe she'd found out something. Olivia said Effie hinted at something she knew which gave her leverage. That suggests something the family would not want anybody to know. And how did Effie find out? That's the sort of question we can put to Hugo Fincham when we get him in again. Who is there left to speak to?'

'Phoebe and her husband, that housekeeper - Dorothy - and of course Mrs Fincham.'

'Mrs Fincham, yes. As his Lordship has withheld information from us, I think we are now entitled to ask to speak to her. Let's start with Phoebe, she seems to be keeping well out of the picture.'

Chapter Twenty-Six

Phoebe Fincham – or Barton, as she was now – was sitting on a sofa with a book and didn't get up when her husband showed them in and offered them seats. She gave off an air of calm, which may have been real or assumed. Either way, Murphy was pretty sure she wouldn't be easy to extract information from. Most young women these days had plenty to say for themselves. Oversharing, they called it. Phoebe didn't look like one of them.

'You're the only member of the family living in south London' Murphy remarked looking around the riverfront house in Barnes. It was a large modern house furnished in bright colours with a big picture window looking out over the water. The artwork was all slashes of colour and splatter patterns – probably valuable just the same.

'That was me' replied Andrew, coming in behind them. 'I thought a bit of distance would be a good thing. And we like it here.'

Murphy turned to look at him. A perceptive young man. 'That's interesting. And it's certainly beautiful here. Why did you want to be further away?'

'I guess I wanted Phoebe to myself a bit more. The family can be a bit overwhelming. Isn't that right darling?'

His wife smiled briefly but it looked like an effort. 'Yes, it's quieter down here. And we both have busy jobs so it's good to come home to a bit of peace.'

'You'll know that we're questioning everybody who knew Elizabeth Fincham' said Wilcox. 'Can we begin by asking you where you were on the night of the twenty second?'

It was Andrew who answered. 'Well, we've remembered that of course because it was the next day that we got the news. Hugo called and told us and we went over to collect Mabel. And it had been a fairly memorable evening anyway. Phoebe had been working late at the lab in Clerkenwell and I'm at a City firm in Moorgate. I picked her up about seven thirty and we went to have dinner with my parents. They live in Stepney.'

Murphy suddenly realised what she had been struggling to place about Andrew's accent. It was cockney overlaid with the result of a good education. He seemed to have read her thoughts.

'That's right' he smiled. 'I'm officially a cockney. I don't sound so much like it these days but my mum and dad certainly do.'

'So was it just the four of you?' said Wilcox.

'Oh no. It was my mum's birthday, so there was mum and dad, us two, my sister Beth and her husband and two kids, my brother Ben and his girlfriend, Tommy and Fred, they're teenagers my mum's been fostering, Mrs Caldwell and Jerry from next door and my nan – she's ninety now but still lives on her own. How many is that?'

'Fifteen' said Wilcox weakly.

'That would be right' said Andrew. 'We left at about eleven, got back here about eleven forty five, maybe a bit after. I hadn't drunk much' he added.

'Can you give us contact details for these people?' Wilcox passed over his pad.

'I can give you my parents and my brother and sister' said Andrew, scribbling 'and the Caldwells are just next-door. I'd like to keep my nan out of it.'

Wilcox nodded. 'Of course. No problem.'

'What did your parents think about you going into the City?' asked Murphy. 'Was it what they wanted for you?'

'My dad worked on the railways' said Andrew, 'and my mum worked in a laundry. As long as I didn't end up on the railways, they didn't mind what I did. All of us did well at school. Beth's a teacher and Ben's a vet – and vet college is a lot harder to get into than the City. My job seemed a bit less worthwhile – teachers and vets can explain much more easily how they've spent their day – but as long as we were all happy, they didn't mind. And as long as we didn't try to give them money. We've all tried to buy them houses, but they're still living in the one we were all brought up in.'

'What did you think of Effie Fincham?' Murphy asked Andrew.

'I didn't meet her until our wedding' he said. 'I guess we just hadn't spent much time with Phoebe's family. And I don't think we exchanged more than a few words, so I can't make much of a judgement. Very attractive of course, but she knew that. In fairness, she'd just had a baby, so she'd done well to come at all. I really don't know what to say about what's happened to her.'

'OK' said Murphy. 'How about you Phoebe?'

Phoebe took a moment to reply. 'What can I say? She was very pretty, lots of personality, very much life and soul of the party…' The recitation petered out and seemed to dry up.

'OK' said Murphy. 'So you didn't like her.'

'I didn't say that.'

Murphy leaned forward. 'Listen, there's nothing wrong with not liking someone – even if they're dead. There's quite a few people I don't like.' The image of Bellweather floated into her head. 'One of the problems we have is that death ennobles people. Everybody rushes to tell us how wonderful they were, even if they were a malevolent, scabrous old misanthrope. And all we want is the truth. To be honest, the only person we're likely to get it from is someone who is not prejudiced in favour of the deceased. So tell me why you didn't like her.'

Phoebe just looked at her for a moment, then seemed to make up her mind. 'OK.' She took a deep breath. 'She just didn't seem to me like somebody you could have a genuine relationship with. It was all about men, she flirted with everybody. I wouldn't have trusted her.'

'Did she flirt with Sebastian? Or was it him flirting with her?'

'Of course she flirted with Sebastian. And he was always up for that. I guess he's a bit like her. He likes women. But I don't think he was taken in by her. I thought it was a bit off though, when she was married to Hugo.'

'Do you think Hugo noticed her flirting with Sebastian?'

She shrugged. 'He could hardly have missed it. But it wasn't just Sebastian, it was any man. The men working in the vineyard, Hugo's friends, anybody. I don't know that Hugo was that bothered. He understood that she just was that way. And he would have known that Sebastian wasn't actually interested in her.'

'How would he have known that?'

'Well, he would have known that Sebastian wouldn't do that to him and anyway she's not Sebastian's type.'

'In what way was she not his type?'

'She was too ... obvious. There's nothing under the surface.'

Murphy thought this quite interesting. 'So Sebastian likes women who are more...enigmatic?'

'Yes, possibly, although I could be wrong. It's not really my business.'

'But you are his sister, and I gather you've always been very close.'

'Of course, when we were children.'

'What was your family like when you were children?'

Phoebe frowned. 'I fail to see what that has to do with Effie.'

Murphy sat back in her chair. 'Yes, I understand that. But somebody killed Effie and we need to understand as much as we can about the people closest to her. We've had pretty tight-lipped responses from your father and Hugo. That makes it look as if people are hiding something. Which they may not be. So humour me please.'

Phoebe stretched her arms above her head, yawned and then seemed to come to a decision. 'OK, what do you want to know?'

'Was it a happy family when you were growing up?'

'Not really. I guess it was OK, but my mother was never very happy. That created a certain amount of tension. We would all be watching her all the time, wondering if something was going to erupt. I used to love going to friends' houses, just to be able to relax.'

'Do you know why she was like that?'

'I didn't know why at the time but, looking back on it, I suppose things weren't too good between her and my father.'

'Do you think either of them was having an affair?'

'I don't know, you'd have to ask them. We were children. We wouldn't have known.' Her expression hardened. 'But why would they tell you? It's none of your business.'

'Agreed. We'll let that pass. Did you get a lot of attention from your parents?'

'No, we were pretty much left to ourselves. I think we were quite happy with that. We liked being able to do what we wanted. I guess when Dorothy arrived life became a bit more structured.'

'Did either of your parents have favourites?'

Phoebe hesitated. 'I don't think my father was that interested in any of us. He was always in his study – not to be disturbed.'

'And your mother?'

'Her favourite was Sebastian.' It was as if the words had come out of their own accord. Phoebe rested her forehead on her hand. 'Why am I telling you this? I've never told anybody.'

'You're telling me because I'm the person who bothered to ask the question' said Murphy. 'What was Hugo like as a child? Did you get on well with him?'

'Hugo was horrible. He used to pull my hair and kick me. He beat Sebastian around too.'

'Why do you think that was?'

'I think he resented us. Before we came along, he had all the attention.'

'So you two kind of banded together.'

'Yes, I suppose we did.'

'And your parents never noticed that he was beating you up?'

'No, or they never bothered to do anything about it. But listen, this was all kids' stuff. We're grown up now and Hugo doesn't behave like that anymore.'

Do you think he behaved like that with Effie?'

'Of course not. He was very fond of Effie. You surely can't think...'

'I'm keeping an open mind at the moment' said Murphy. There's one more thing I want to ask you about. What do you remember about that weekend when Billy Jukes drowned in the pond?'

Phoebe looked at the floor for a few seconds. Andrew moved protectively towards her. She lifted her head and wiped a hand across her eyes.

'It was awful. He was a lovely boy, really kind and funny. I wondered afterwards if it was my fault.'

'Why was that?'

'I think he was quite interested in me. I wasn't interested in him, not in that way, but I liked him. And I was the one who was most insistent, trying to get him to come into the water. I think I said I'd teach him to swim, or something stupid like that. So then, when it happened – I thought he'd gone in to try swimming because of me.'

Murphy shook her head. 'Don't think that. It's very unlikely to be true. You had a friend with you didn't you?'

'Yes, Juliet.'

'Do you still have a number for her?'

Phoebe nodded. Wilcox passed his notebook and pen over and she wrote it down.

'Thank you for your help' said Murphy. 'Please call us if you think of anything else.'

***

'That was interesting' said Wilcox as he negotiated a roundabout. 'Although I can't see that it takes us any further forward.'

'I tend to think' said Murphy 'that everything somebody tells us takes us a bit further forward. To be honest, if Andrew had told us his dad ran a pie and mash shop down the Old Kent Road, I would have thought he was a chancer. At that point I would have decided to disbelieve his salt-of-the-earth honest cockney schtick. But, as it is, my disbelief remains suspended. Maybe he's exactly what he appears, in which case I'd say Phoebe's done well for herself. But we'll find out. I think you should go round to his family and check out their joint alibi. I'm sure Andrew has a fast car, they could easily have slotted in a quick trip to Cheyne Walk. Can't see any motive, but we have to check everything. Maybe there'll be time tomorrow.'

Wilcox took an exit and put his foot down. 'They might all be lying of course.'

'Well that's the most interesting thing of all isn't it? That really tells us something. Did you think Phoebe was lying?'

'Maybe not, but I'm sure there was more she wasn't telling us.'

'Undoubtedly. There's definitely something she doesn't want us to know. But I think she told us more than she intended to. And that's always a good thing. She was a bit touchy about Sebastian, really rejected the suggestion that there could have been anything between Effie and Sebastian. It seems to me quite possible that Effie, not enjoying marriage to the grouchy older brother, might have set her sights on the more entertaining younger one. It's something to explore.'

'And it sounds like there was a lot of stuff going on between Fincham and the wife' said Wilcox.

'Yes' said Murphy. 'I really want to know more about that. What I would really like would be to sit down with Andrew and get his take on the rest of them – Hugo, Sebastian, Edward – maybe even Dorothy and Verity. Not possible really with Phoebe there, but I think his observations would be useful. Anyway, we have to check their alibi first. In the meantime, let's try the cleaner.'

***

Jane Belling agreed to meet Murphy at the house in Cheyne Walk that day ('it's my usual day, so that will be convenient').

'She made it sound like I was being granted an audience' said Murphy. 'Didn't want us coming round to her home address, lowering the tone of the neighbourhood or whatever. Still, I have to admire a woman who's made a career out of housework. Washing the kitchen floor is almost beyond my capabilities.'

The door was whipped open when they rang the bell and a large middle-aged woman stuffed into tight jeans looked them up and down.

'You'd better come in' she conceded and held the door open. She pointedly waited until they had wiped their feet on the mat and then led the way into the sitting room. No invitation to sit was forthcoming, so Murphy sat down anyway and motioned Wilcox to do the same.

'So Mrs Belling' she began, 'as I'm sure you know, we are investigating the death of Mrs Fincham which occurred here three days ago.'

The woman nodded with her lips clamped shut.

'Can you tell us what your schedule is for cleaning this house?'

'Tuesdays and Fridays.'

'And how long have you been coming here?'

'About five years.'

'So for most of that time Hugo Fincham would have been living here alone?'

'Yes.'

'How did you find him as an employer?'

'Alright. He paid on time. Is that what you want to know?'

Murphy narrowed her eyes. 'I'm more interested in how you found him as a person. Did you see much of him?'

'No. He was always at work when I was here.'

'And how about Mrs Fincham?'

'What about her?'

'How did you get on with her?'

'Alright. I came in and got on with my work. Sometimes she was here and sometimes she wasn't.'

'Do you remember a set of silver ornaments on the mantelpiece?'

'Yes. Took a lot of dusting.'

'Were they here when you cleaned the house on Tuesday?'

'As far as I remember.'

Murphy decided a change of tone was needed.

'You have a key to this house Mrs Belling?'

'Yes, of course.'

'Perhaps you can tell us how you spent Tuesday evening.'

'What do you mean?'

'I mean we have to check the whereabouts of anybody who has a key to the house.'

'I was at home, same as any other evening.'

'Were you alone?'

'No. I was with my husband.'

'So he will be able to confirm your whereabouts?'

'Of course, but this is ridiculous. Whatever happened here is nothing to do with me.'

'I'm sure that's right, Mrs Belling, but as you can appreciate, we have to check. It's just a formality. We'll send somebody from the uniform branch round to have a word with your husband.'

Jane Belling's jaw dropped. 'That's surely not necessary.'

Murphy rose. 'I'm afraid so, but don't let it worry you. We'll see ourselves out.'

'If I had to choose' she told Wilcox as they got back into the car, 'I'd like her to be the perpetrator. I could enjoy reading her rights to her. Unfortunately, it doesn't work like that.'

'No.' Wilcox appeared to be thinking. 'Perhaps she was having an affair with Hugo and they offed the wife.'

'Nice try, but I can't see it I'm afraid.'

'Why do you think she was so determined to be unhelpful?'

Murphy fastened her seatbelt. 'It's interesting isn't it? Most people who are innocent of any wrongdoing are happy to help the police, perhaps as a way of demonstrating that they have nothing to hide. But equally, there have been cases of very guilty people bending over backwards to assist an enquiry, if only to keep it deflected away from them. In her case I would say that she's somebody who 'knows her rights' and, leaving aside actual obstruction, knows she doesn't have to co-operate with us. She probably cleans a number of houses round here and wants people to know that she wouldn't talk about their business. Or maybe Hugo told her to say nothing to us. Not everybody wants to talk to the police. Or maybe she just didn't like the look of us. We won't take it to heart.'

Chapter Twenty-Seven

Audrey Street was a huddle of late-Victorian cottages backing onto Stepney Green Park in the area now known as Tower Hamlets. Much of the neighbouring housing was in tower blocks and all of the parking was in the grip of a controlled parking zone.

Kevin Wilcox managed to find a spot in the next street which he could pay for on his phone and made his way to number 65. He had arranged a meeting with Mrs Barton, who sounded refreshingly unfussed about receiving a visit from the police and now waved him inside as if he was an invited guest.

Two of the six chairs around the kitchen table were occupied by corpulent ginger cats, who each opened one eye, looked at him and closed it again, as if having decided that he was nobody important. The other occupant was a very old (really very old) woman who smiled gummily at him and went back to perusing the Financial Times.

Mrs Barton bustled over with a loaded tray and said 'This is the young man from the police, mum.'

The older woman put the paper down, took off her glasses, looked him over and said 'He's a bit skinny. Needs feeding up.'

Wilcox wasn't sure how to respond to this, but he was sure that this interview was about to get off on the wrong foot. It was time to reclaim the initiative, or whatever.

'Thank you for seeing me Mrs Barton.' He addressed the younger woman.

'You're welcome son. How do you have your tea?'

'White, no sugar please, and do you have soya milk, no never mind.'

She smiled and passed over a mug accompanied by a large slice of fruit cake. Both of the women seemed to be waiting for him to take a bite, so he did so, and managed to convey with his mouth full that it was very good, which it was. At this they both appeared to relax and the older woman put her glasses back on and went back to the paper.

'Don't mind Nan' said Mrs Barton. 'She's checking her shares. Andrew got her interested in it.'

Wilcox remembered uncomfortably that he had told Andrew that he wouldn't bother his nan. Perhaps if she stayed stuck in the paper she wouldn't hear anything.

'As you'll know, we're just checking the whereabouts of anybody who was connected to Effie Fincham and we just need to confirm that Andrew and Phoebe were with you that evening.'

'That's right, isn't it Nan? It was my birthday, remember?'

'Of course I remember' said the older woman, as if her memory was being impugned. 'Andrew came with that young wife of his. She's another skinny one, but I made sure she ate plenty. She needs somebody like him to take care of her. You should have seen her in that wedding dress. Looked like a waif.'

The wedding. Wilcox sat up straighter and accidentally kicked the chair next to him. The cat jerked awake, glared at him and went back to sleep.

'So you'll have seen Effie Fincham at Andrew's wedding' he said tentatively.

Both women opened their mouths, but Nan got in first.

'Certainly did' she said. 'She was the young woman with the new baby and the miserable-looking husband. No Doreen – he was. They left quite early – well she must have been tired. It's exhausting you know – breastfeeding.'

She seemed to be aiming this last assertion at Wilcox, who shifted uncomfortably.

'Was the wedding at Fawcett Hall?' he asked.

'No' said Mrs Barton. 'They offered of course, but Andrew and Phoebe didn't want it there. In fact Phoebe didn't want a church wedding at all. So we organised it here – St George's Town Hall. It was lovely. Phoebe's family came and we split the cost. They weren't happy about that, but my husband insisted.'

'Funny lot they were' interrupted the older woman. 'Her father gave her away of course and I think he was pleased she was getting married. Maybe he was afraid she'd end up on the shelf. After a few drinks he became almost sociable. The mother looked out of it. She wasn't allowed to drink because it would interfere with her drugs. I'd say she was well tranquilised. There was another woman who came with them, who was keeping an eye on the mother – making sure she didn't drink anything I suppose. The older brother was the miserable-looking one and there was the other brother who seemed very attached to his sister, but once he had a few drinks inside him he suddenly lightened up. We had a good laugh with him.'

Wilcox had finished his slab of cake and saw with a jolt that Mrs Barton had picked up the knife again. Time to get out. He closed his notebook and stood up carefully to avoid disturbing the cats any further.

'Thank you very much for talking to me' he said. 'It's been a great help.'

'That's alright, son' said Nan. 'Come and see us again. Find yourself a nice young woman and bring her along.'

Mrs Barton saw him to the door. 'Don't mind Nan' she said. 'She doesn't understand boundaries. You take care now.'

Wilcox exited with as much of his shredded dignity as he could muster and had arrived back at the car before he remembered about the Caldwells next door. He might have to drink more tea in there. Maybe that wouldn't be necessary. He got in and started the engine.

***

Barney Roberts was a junior doctor at Homerton Hospital and agreed to talk to them after his shift. They waited for him in the car park, watching the lights in the building go on and off. He came out a few minutes later, breathing deeply and smiling. It was wet and miserable but he didn't seem bothered by that.

'It's so great to get out into the air, any air, after twelve hours in the hospital.' He stretched his arms above his head and breathed deeply.

They sat in Wilcox's car with the doors open. Murphy was grateful for Wilcox's superior car cleaning. It wouldn't have been good to ask a doctor to sit in a squalid car.

'Thank you very much for agreeing to see us' she said. 'Especially when you're probably very tired.'

'No problem' he said. 'Tiredness is just part of the job.'

'As you'll have gathered, we are interested in whatever you can tell us about that weekend at Fawcett Hall.'

'Totally awful.' He shook his head. 'It had happened early in the morning. If I had woken up a bit earlier... I wasn't trained or qualified then of course, but I knew first aid. Sebastian's mother saw him first, I think she'd come out to feed the geese. She went in and pulled him out, but he was already dead. Drowning can happen so quickly.'

'Mrs Fincham seems a very different person now' said Wilcox. 'I don't get the impression of her as a person who would wade into a pond to save somebody.'

'From what I saw of her after the accident, I'd say that's true' said Barney. 'She may have retreated into herself after that. I'm sure she was badly affected by what happened. But probably not as badly as Billy's parents, poor people.'

'What were the sleeping arrangements in that barn?'

He took a deep breath and let it out. 'As I remember, it was a pretty big space. We all just spread out, with our sleeping bags. We were pretty tired, we'd been swimming, riding the farm bike around, chasing a couple of runaway sheep and all sorts of stuff, so I guess we fell asleep quite quickly. Although it was actually a bit hot for sleeping bags. I think I'd fought my way out of mine by the morning.'

'What was weekend like before Billy was found?' asked Murphy.

'It was really good fun. Everybody was enjoying it. We all drank rather too much. Sebastian is a very bad influence. And we had a barbecue. Pretty makeshift. These days I wouldn't touch meat as badly cooked as that. You know the sort of thing – black on the outside, raw in the middle. But we were young and I guess we had good immune systems.'

'And you and Sebastian ended up at the same university?'

'Yes, we were both at Durham. I did medicine of course and Seb did classics. Durham was definitely the place for classics. He was that sort of person, fancied himself as a Greek hero, full of quotations, especially when he'd had a bit to drink.'

'Did you see any of the rest of his family after that weekend?'

'No, the hospitality came to an end after that. Well, only Phoebe. She used to come up to visit Seb. He said she had some idea that she might come to Durham, so she wanted to get a feel for the place. I think she probably just wanted to have a break from home and hanging round the university was fun. In the end her dad persuaded her to go to Edinburgh. Maybe he thought it was better for science. Although they carried on visiting each other. Seb really liked Edinburgh, especially when the Fringe was on.'

'What do you remember about Hugo?' said Murphy.

'I think that weekend was the only time I met Hugo and he didn't make much of an impression. It looked to me like Sebastian and Phoebe were the wild kids and he tagged along, but he wasn't really part of it.'

'Did you think he had any propensity for violence?'

'Propensity for violence is something I see a lot of, every day. I didn't connect that with Hugo at the time, but I do remember Sebastian saying that Hugo used to bully him when they were small. Then Phoebe was born and after a few years the two of them together were able to outwit Hugo, he left Seb alone after that. But this is all very ancient history. I gather you're investigating the death of Hugo's wife, and she wasn't around at this time. She may not even have been born.'

'Some events cast long shadows' said Murphy.

Chapter Twenty-Eight

EDWARD FINCHAM RECEIVED THEM again in his study. His expression suggested that here was another tiresome intrusion which was going to sorely try his patience.

'Thank you for seeing us again, sir' said Wilcox. 'We are still looking at this unexplained death in 2004.'

Fincham glared at him 'Why? I thought you were supposed to be investigating a death last week. I can't see that there is any connection between the two. Are you deliberately harassing my family, raking over this upsetting incident all over again?'

Wilcox was admirably unruffled. 'No sir, there is no question of harassing your family, but I'm sure your honour will appreciate that we have to make sure that all avenues of investigation were correctly followed up. We owe this to the victim's family.'

Fincham had opened his mouth, apparently to protest, and now shut it again.

'We were informed' continued Wilcox, 'that it was your wife who found the body. We'd like to speak to her.'

'My wife is not...'

'We understand that she is not well, but we would still like to speak to her.'

'Very well. Stay here.'

He got up and left the room. Murphy gave Wilcox a nod. He was really good with antagonistic people because he simply didn't engage with them. She rose and walked over to the sideboard where family photos were displayed.

There they all were – the golden children. His honour tending the barbecue while they all romped around. Another of them all sitting in a boat in lifejackets, aged between about 8 and 10, Phoebe with her legs resting on Sebastian's knees, their two blonde heads together, Hugo further away looking out to sea.

She turned as the Finchams entered the room. Verity Fincham was wearing a dark polo neck sweater which seemed to emphasise her thin frame. She came in with a lift of the chin and a determined expression which suggested that she had just been given a pep talk.

'Thank you for seeing us Mrs Fincham' Wilcox began...her husband rolled his eyes...'I want to get your recollection of what happened on the morning when you found Billy Jukes.'

Verity looked at her husband and he nodded. She hesitated for a moment, then began to speak. 'It was quite early, about six in the morning. I had gone out to feed the geese and I saw him floating in the pond. I waded in and pulled him out.'

'So at that point he was in the shallows?' She nodded.

'Was he floating face down?'

'Yes, he was face down. I wasn't sure who it was until I got to him.'

'You didn't have to swim to get to him?'

She shook her head. 'I waded in. I got pretty wet, but I didn't have to swim.'

'And how did you get him to the edge? Did you drag him by his clothing?'

'I pulled him by the arm. Then I got him onto the bank and ran for help.'

'Who came first?'

'Dorothy. I yelled for Dorothy because she's a trained first-aider. She sent me off to call an ambulance while she attempted CPR, but it was too late.'

'How about the youngsters in the barn?'

'They didn't wake up until we woke them, or maybe when they heard the noise.'

'How do you think he ended up in the pond?'

'I don't know. Suicide maybe, or he was hot and wanted to cool down. I think he just forgot it was deep in the middle.'

'He surely wouldn't have been hot early in the morning' said Wilcox.

She shook her head. 'I don't know. Maybe not.'

'It must have been very upsetting for you' said Murphy.

'Yes, it was. It was a terrible shock.'

'Now if that's all Inspector..' Fincham cut in at this point.

'Yes, that will be all for the time being. Thank you for your help, Mrs Fincham. We'll let you know if we have any further questions.'

Fincham escorted them to the front door and shut it behind them.

'Nothing like being escorted off the premises' said Wilcox.

'You'd think' said Murphy, 'that a man of his experience would realise that the best way to put the police off the scent is to act nice and be co-operative. All this pent-up aggression just makes me wonder what they're hiding – and I'm going to find out.'

***

'We have an appointment to see Juliet Foster' said Wilcox on the way back to the station. 'She works on Cheapside. She'll meet us in her lunch hour. It will be easier on the tube.' Great. Murphy was quite happy to drive anywhere with Wilcox, but God save her from having to walk with him. Wilcox's performance as a pedestrian was just that – pedestrian. It drove Murphy mad.

Walking fast was one of Murphy's more useful accomplishments. People thought it was because she was really fit (in the original sense of the term). Nothing could have been further from the truth. Murphy walked fast because she could never see the point in getting somewhere slowly if she could get there fast. It was called having no patience and it hadn't done much to advance her career.

Getting around London threw up lots of dodges to annoy the likes of Murphy. People who walked on the escalators at less than half her speed, making it impossible for her to get past. People who wandered aimlessly in front of the doors as the tube was about to take off, making it impossible for her to take a flying leap. People who accompanied her places at a snail's pace, forcing her to do lots of doubling back manoeuvres (Wilcox, for a start). Once she had been in a hurry trying to exit Tottenham Court Road tube station and all movement in front of her suddenly ground to a halt. Weaving her way up the steps she finally discovered a teenager who had stopped on the top step to tap out a text message, while a queue of people waited beneath him. The temptation to kick him hard in the shins had been almost overwhelming.

Now, on the way to Cheapside, she concentrated on matching her pace to Wilcox's. It was really frustrating. 'No point you rushing ahead' he said complacently. 'You don't know where you're going.' Sometimes, Murphy thought, he seemed to forget that she was the senior officer.

Juliet Foster was already seated in Cafe Nero with a large Americano. She was slim with short dark hair and an enviable black linen trouser suit. 'I hope you don't mind' she said. 'I try to keep personal business away from the office.'

'No problem' said Murphy. 'We appreciate your agreeing to see us. We don't mind where.'

She ordered a flat white. Being able to have a cup of proper coffee and reclaim it on her expenses would be one of today's better moments.

'What we want to ask you about is what happened that weekend' she told Juliet. 'Just anything you can remember. I know it was quite a few years ago and you were interviewed at the time, but sometimes things become clearer after a bit of time has passed.'

Juliet nodded. 'I'll tell you what can. I don't know how useful it will be. I was a dumb sixteen-year-old. I was so excited that Phoebe had invited me – I hope this is confidential by the way...' Murphy nodded. 'I was so excited to be there because I really fancied her brother.'

'Hugo?'

'No, not Hugo. Sebastian.'

'Yes, of course. Sebastian. Did he fancy you?'

Juliet burst out laughing. 'No, not at all. You can see why I didn't tell the police any of this at the time. Obviously,

I wasn't that fanciable, but also I think...' she hesitated. 'I think Sebastian really only fancies himself.'

'Yes, that's the impression I get' said Murphy. 'How about Hugo? What did you think of him?'

'Well he was a bit older and I kind of felt he wasn't really interested in the rest of us. He just wasn't that friendly. Looking back on it, I think he was just socially awkward, not like Sebastian.'

'So he didn't make a pass at you?'

'Oh God no, definitely not. I wouldn't have known what to do if he had.'

'What were the sleeping arrangements in that barn.'

'As far as I remember Phoebe and I were in one corner and the guys were kind of spread around.'

'And did you wake at all in the night?'

'Once briefly. I think I heard some whispering. But then I fell asleep again. It had been a pretty active day, so we all slept well.'

'Who do you think was whispering?'

'I don't know.'

'Just think about it. Were you aware of where everybody else was?'

'I think at one point I woke up and Phoebe wasn't where I thought she was.'

'Could it have been Phoebe whispering?'

'Yes, probably with Sebastian. They were very close, lots of in-jokes between themselves. Hugo was pretty well out of their loop.'

'And what do you recall of the morning? '

'That was awful. We were woken up by the noise. Sebastian's mum was screaming and that Dorothy woman was doing chest compressions. They were both wet. Then the ambulance arrived and took Billy away. We could see it didn't look good.'

'When you heard the noise and woke up, where was everybody else?'

'I didn't see anybody else immediately. I dragged my trousers back on and ran out. I saw Hugo and Barney on the way and Phoebe and Sebastian were already outside. They must have been nearest to the door.'

'You didn't see or hear Billy leaving the barn?'

'No, not at all. He wouldn't have made much noise because the barn door was open all night. It was a hot night and we needed the air.'

'Thank you, Juliet. You've been a lot of help. If you think of anything else, give us a ring.'

'I did want to ask you about Effie. Have you found out who killed her?'

'Not yet. How did you know about it?'

'I phoned the house and Hugo answered. He told me she was dead. Such a shock.'

'What was your connection with Effie?'

'I didn't know her well, but I was actually at her wedding because I was going out with one of Hugo's friends at the time, so I was a plus-one. She contacted me a few weeks ago, one of the others must have given her my number.'

'What did she want?'

'She asked me the same questions you just did. She said Hugo was still haunted by what had happened and she wanted to understand a bit more about it, so that she could help him.'

'That's interesting. I wonder why she didn't talk to Phoebe if she wanted a female perspective on it?'

'I actually said that to her and she said she wanted to talk to somebody outside the family. I got the impression she wasn't very close to Phoebe.'

Chapter Twenty-Nine

Murphy and Wilcox were back at the station. It was generally a bad place to be, especially if the boss had had his ears burned by the Chief Constable, but sometimes it was good to check in and do some thinking away from the scene.

Murphy kicked off her shoes, rubbed her eyes and took a swig of coffee. 'I swear to God they're trying to poison us. Don't let me drink this again.' She put it to one side.

'OK. Let's see what we've got. So Effie Fincham told Olivia Atwell that she was going to take on the family. She told her that she had already had a meeting with Edward Fincham. He told us no such meeting had taken place. Let's park that discrepancy for the moment.

Juliet Foster told us that Effie sought her out and wanted to find out about this drowning. So what did Effie suspect? And did she tell anybody? Was she making demands based on something she had found out? She would have been entitled to a reasonable settlement anyway. Was she asking for more than that?'

'Maybe she threatened to publicise the fact that he was beating her' said Wilcox.

'I think that would have persuaded his honour to get Hugo to cut her loose fast. But the family weren't that fond of her anyway, so they would have been happy to see her go. In that case maybe she wanted more than they would be happy to give her. What can that have been? Sole custody, the house in Cheyne Walk and a substantial income for life? That might have gone beyond what they were prepared to exchange for her not mentioning the beating. And of course, once the bruises had faded, she'd have no evidence.'

'So we think she'd found out something about this episode ten years previously?'

'It looks that way doesn't it? That's most likely to be what she meant by leverage. Maybe she'd found some evidence that nobody else had access to, or maybe she'd somehow guessed the truth. Which of course we are not allowed to do – we have to have evidence. But there's definitely something more to be discovered. While we're at it, let's have another look at those wedding and christening photos, now that we've talked to most of the people involved.'

Wilcox opened the file and they looked through.

'Edward Fincham doesn't look overjoyed to be the gaining a daughter' said Wilcox 'or a granddaughter, for that matter. Effie doesn't look so good at the christening, maybe married life didn't agree with her.'

'She was getting over a caesarian' said Murphy, 'so not so bad considering. And that lilac outfit is lovely. Dorothy must have been running the show, she's appearing everywhere.'

'We haven't talked to Wonderwoman Dorothy yet' said Wilcox.

'That's right' said Murphy 'Let's see what she's got to say.'

***

The sun was setting over the vines and the first taste of spring was in the air as Murphy and Wilcox made their way across the field to where Dorothy was standing with a pair of secateurs. She was in agricultural worker attire this time – faded jeans and a red check shirt with the ends tied round her waist – but still managed to look expensively dressed. Murphy wasn't sure how that was achieved, but you had to admire it.

She was pruning the vines. Murphy watched as the woody stems came away with a satisfying crunch and fell to the ground. 'Those are quite tough stalks 'she observed.

'Yes, these are the older, woodier vines' said Dorothy. 'The grape yield isn't so high, but they produce the best wine. That means they're the most valuable plants. Pruning's not strictly my job, but I enjoy it, especially on a nice day with a bit of sun.'

'I gather you live here' said Murphy.

'Yes, I have a cottage on the estate. That sounds really feudal doesn't it? Both cottages were originally occupied by farm workers, people who worked with the sheep. They all left when the last sheep were sold and the vineyard was planted. Now I have one cottage and a couple who work in the vineyard have the other. Do you want to go indoors?'

Murphy rapidly weighed up the advantage of being able to get a look at Dorothy's living space over the pleasure of being outside.

'No, we're happy to just follow you round' she said.

'Do you mind if I wander over and have another look at the machinery?' said Wilcox.

'No, go ahead.' She pointed with the shears. 'The press is in the barn over there.'

Murphy kept pace with Dorothy, who was snipping as they went. 'How long have you been here?'

'Twenty five years' said Dorothy. 'Seems like an awful long time, but it went so fast. I never intended to stay so long, but here I am.'

'You started as the children's nanny?'

'That's right. Phoebe was about two at the time, Sebastian was four and Hugo must have been six.'

'Quite a handful.'

'They were. Very bright kids but not exactly obedient. They all knew what they wanted and sometimes that led to a lot of scrapping between them.'

'Did Hugo bully Sebastian?'

Dorothy sighed. 'I'm not sure how to answer that. The thing about bullies, as you know, is that they do it when nobody's looking. So I can't say I ever observed it. I did find Sebastian in tears a few times and I told Hugo off, but I don't know that it was anything worse than two boys fighting. And then Phoebe got big enough to join in and that altered the dynamic. Sebastian and Phoebe became a pair and they seemed to ignore Hugo a lot of the time. So then I was worrying on his behalf. But I guess they all grew up OK. And now I get to work in the vineyard, which is much more restful.'

'And Sebastian and Phoebe still seem to have a high level of affection for each other.'

Dorothy looked up quickly. 'Yes, I'd say they are still good friends.'

'So did you come here to help Mrs Fincham or were you solely in charge?'

'I came to help her but I did most of it. She has never been very – well.'

'In what way was she not well?'

Dorothy took a while to reply. 'She'd had some kind of breakdown – a nervous breakdown, I guess - before I arrived. I don't know what brought it about but I was told she was no longer able to cope and my job was basically to keep all stress away from her. She was on regular medication.'

'So she didn't have much to do with the kids?'

'I think she loved the kids, but if there were any problems, that was left to me.' They finished one row and moved on to the next. The sun was sinking in the sky and the breeze was cooling.

'Can you tell me what you remember of the tragedy ten years ago?'

'It seems like a long time ago now. I was woken up by Verity. She was screaming for help and banging on my door. She had managed to pull him out but I was pretty sure he was gone. I did CPR but there was no response and eventually the paramedics arrived, but they couldn't bring him back either. It was an awful thing to happen.'

'Did you notice any change in Mrs Fincham after that?'

'Yes, I guess it was a form of PTSD. She never quite got over it. Although, as I said, she had always been unstable, not really able to look after the children. After this she withdrew even more and I think she was prescribed stronger anti-depressants.'

'What do you think happened to Billy?'

'I think it was a tragic accident. I don't know why he entered the pond, but he probably didn't realise how deep it was.'

'Except apparently he'd been warned by the other kids' said Murphy.

'That's right. Maybe he was half-asleep. I don't know what else to think.'

'What did you think of Effie?'

The reply was prompt. 'I thought she was a troubled young woman.'

Murphy smiled. Troubled – such a useful euphemism. She waited to see if more was coming.

'It seemed to me that she was unstable. I was used to seeing that, dealing with Verity, but Effie was very different of course. I thought she could probably be ruthless. Whatever she had, she would want something else.'

'How do you think her marriage to Hugo was going?'

'It was none of my business of course but I got the impression they weren't that happy. Oh, they probably were in the beginning and Mabel was lovely, but there was definitely something going wrong.' Murphy raised her eyebrows but said nothing.

Dorothy moved onto the next row and wrestled with a particularly thick stem. It gave way with a crunch. 'I think Hugo wasn't exciting enough for Effie, maybe nobody would have been. She had tired of him. He was wealthy and good-looking but that was no longer enough. She was ready to move onto the next thing.'

'What gave you that impression?'

'I just never saw much affection between them and they spent a lot of time apart. He spends a lot of time here and she tended to stay away. I don't know what she did all day, maybe not much.'

'She had a lot of bruises on her arms. How would you explain that?'

Dorothy turned to look at her. 'I didn't know about that. That's awful. I can't believe it of Hugo.'

'She told Olivia Atwell that she was afraid Hugo was going to kill her.'

'That's absurd.'

'How about if Hugo just decided he'd had enough of her?'

'In that case they would have talked about it – come to some arrangement.'

'Some financial arrangement?'

'Yes, I would think so'.

'Did you know that Effie had already been to see Edward to discuss such an arrangement?'

She frowned. 'No, I didn't know that.'

'Would Edward have told you about it?'

'He may have done. He wouldn't have wanted to tell Verity, so if he felt the need to share it, he might have told me.'

'What I don't understand' said Murphy, 'is why she bypassed her husband and went straight to his father. Can you explain that?'

'I think she must have decided that it's Edward who makes the financial decisions, so she just went directly to him. If in fact she did so.'

'But here's my point. If she talked it over with Hugo and Hugo then talked to his father, that would be more like a correct procedure. Going directly to Edward shows either that she had no respect for Hugo or that there was pressure she felt she could bring to bear on Edward particularly. Or both. Can you think of anything she could have threatened Edward with?'

Dorothy straightened up. 'Absolutely not. Any threats she might have made would have been quite without foundation.'

They had arrived back at the main building. Wilcox came out of the barn and joined them.

'That was really fascinating' he said. He turned to Dorothy. 'We have a warrant to search the premises.

'Very well. I'll let you get on with it.' She walked back towards the field.

'So have you learned anything?' said Murphy

'Probably nothing specific, but I've certainly got a feel for the place. I had a chat with one of the chaps working here – that wine press is amazing. I know we had a brief look at it when we saw Sebastian but you should see it close up. It's a modern stainless steel version of the original vertical basket press – the container with a big screw that comes down, you can still see old wooden ones in France. Design goes back to Roman times apparently.'

'Well it's good to know they're not treading the stuff with their feet' said Murphy. 'Did you find out anything germane to our enquiry?'

'Colin – that's his name – reckons this family must have a lot of money. I guess old Fincham made plenty before he retired and Hugo's probably on a big salary. Colin says the vineyard isn't making much of a profit yet and might not do so for another couple of years. He says the sons don't really pull their weight – if they did, he'd probably be out of a job. And he says Dorothy is in charge of everything. The judge relies on her to make all the decisions. He says they never see Mrs Fincham – she's kind of kept under wraps. Never seen unaccompanied.'

'Interesting' said Murphy. 'Bit like in Jane Eyre.'

'Who?'

'The wife in the attic. Never mind. Let's get to work with this warrant. Where shall we start?'

'Let's have a look first at where they entertain the wine-tour punters' said Wilcox and they entered a glass-roofed building with a pale wood floor and two islands of the sort commonly seen in expensive modern kitchens. Each featured open cupboards full of glasses and stacks of glossy brochures were arranged on top. These gave the history of the vineyard, short as it was, a description of the process, a shot of the crop and a photo of the main men – Edward with his sons, all smiling as if they were best friends. Floor to ceiling wine racks carried stocks of the product, two large fridges presumably kept the white wine cold and the corner held a sink and dishwasher.

'Very nice' said Murphy, 'but I don't think it tells us much.'

'This might tell us something' said Wilcox, turning over the pages of a bound album. 'The visitors' book. Here's where the grateful punters provide free advertising copy.'

Murphy joined him and they worked through it. 'Here' said Murphy. 'Three weeks ago. Effie came and brought a friend, according to the friend. Kate Boswell Black. Says she had a lovely visit, loved the wines and the people. That's the woman we have on our list to interview – and here's her address and phone number. That's good of her, saves us tracking her down. We can go and see her when we finish here. So where's next?'

'How about the office?' Wilcox, who had carried out an efficient reconnaissance, led the way to a flight of steps and then up to what looked like a building site hut.

The office was unoccupied, which made things a lot easier. One wall was covered in charts with grape varieties, seasonal tasks, vintages and weather notes. There were three desks, each holding a laptop and nothing else. 'Clear desk policy' Wilcox noted approvingly.

Murphy snorted. She regarded the clear desk policy as just stuff dreamt up by people sitting on their arses with nothing else to do. A couple of weeks on traffic duty or door-to-door would handle that.

They pulled on gloves and set to work.

Murphy was never sure whether or not she liked doing this kind of search. On one hand it could feel a bit grubby and an invasion of people's privacy. On the other hand, sometimes the things that turned up were fascinating. She had once searched the home kitchen of a minor celebrity chef and discovered a cupboard crammed with Jammie Dodgers and Pot Noodles.

After half an hour Wilcox had made his way down to the bottom drawer of an unlocked filing cabinet and he gave a low whistle.

'Do you think these are the tea things?'

Murphy joined him and looked at the silver jugs and snuff boxes at the back of the drawer. She picked a couple up and looked more closely at them.

'OK, so we can now discount the robbery motive. No effort made to hide this stuff, so they weren't expecting a search. Who has access to this office? Let's ask Dorothy.'

She appeared a few minutes later, accompanied by Wilcox, and Murphy posed the question.

Dorothy was silent for a moment. 'Hugo, Sebastian, me, Colin or Dermot, Effie occasionally, Olivia occasionally, any member of the family of course. Anybody could wander in, obviously not anybody off the street, because we're on private land, but we don't run tight security. It never seemed necessary.'

'Pete?'

'Olivia's boyfriend? Yes, he's come in a few times this last week to collect Ben, when Olivia had him here with Mabel.' She pointed to the corner where a pair of fluffy ears drooped over a large cardboard box of plastic toys. 'They seem to like it better here than in the house.'

'And have you seen these items before?' Dorothy stepped forward to look.

'They look like Hugo's pieces. He picked them up at an auction. They were on the mantelpiece in his house...' Her voice trailed off.

'Can I ask you not to mention this to anybody else?' asked Murphy.

'Of course.' She nodded.

'And this office is now out of bounds until we have removed this stuff. Is there a key?'

Dorothy pointed to a bunch of keys hanging on the wall. Wilcox took it down and she showed him the office key.

They filed out, Wilcox locked the door and they went down the steps together.

'We'll be back later' Murphy told Dorothy as they walked back towards the car.

'She's bound to tell the others' said Wilcox.

'Of course she is, but that will tell us something too, won't it? Let's see if Hugo Fincham's around. Leave the car here and we'll try the house.'

***

They found Hugo in the house doing something on a laptop. Of course, thought Murphy. Much comfier place to work than the site-hut office.

'Not in the City today' said Murphy.

'No' he replied tersely. 'I'm on leave at the moment.'

'Can we ask you to come and look at something in the office?' she said.

He rose without a word and followed them out. It seemed to Murphy that he was looking a lot more stooped than last time she had seen him and while he was sitting, she had noticed a thinning patch on top of his head. Perhaps the stress was getting to him.

The surprise when he looked at the haul seemed genuine.

'But these are from the house' he said. 'How did they get here?'

'How do you think they got here?' said Murphy.

He sat down. 'I don't know.'

'Well somebody must have put them here. Who do you think that could have been?'

'Nobody would have done that.'

Murphy sat down opposite him. 'What I think is that they were put here by whoever killed your wife. Somebody who wanted to make it look as if she had been killed by a burglar.'

'And you think that I .. That's preposterous.'

'It's not preposterous really if you think about it. What explanation would you give?'

'I don't know. I have no explanation.'

'If you didn't put them here, who do you think did?'

He shook his head. 'I don't know. It makes no sense to me.'

'If your wife wasn't killed by a burglar, which I think we now know she wasn't' said Murphy, 'what do you think happened?'

He shook his head silently.

'While we're here', said Murphy, 'I'd like to ask you a bit more about your relationship with your wife.'

'There's nothing to tell.'

'Well I just think there might be. Did you ever suspect her of being unfaithful?'

'Of course not.'

'She told one of our witnesses that she no longer wanted to sleep with you. Is that true?'

'That's nobody else's business' he shouted.

'Normally I would agree, but when somebody is murdered all sorts of stuff becomes other people's business – specifically our business. So were you still sleeping with your wife?'

'I'm not answering that'. He folded his arms.

'Because that would be some sort of explanation for the bruises. You see, bruises on the arms like that, it makes me think of somebody being held down. When a man holds a woman down it's usually for one reason isn't it?'

'I don't know what you're talking about.'

'I think you do. The post mortem found vaginal tears. They signify rape or forcible sex. Sex which the woman didn't want. Marital rape, it's called. Effie told Olivia Atwell that she no longer wanted to sleep with you, so you forced yourself on her, didn't you?'

'These are appalling accusations. I'm not continuing this conversation without a lawyer present.'

He turned and walked out.

'Bingo' said Murphy. 'A reaction at last.'

Chapter Thirty

Kate Black lived in a new luxury flat with a river frontage in Putney. Murphy and Wilcox travelled by tube which meant, as she was with Wilcox, having to stand on the escalator. The alternative meant rushing down as usual and then having to wait for him at the bottom, which would have made her look like a wally.

'Very nice' said Murphy, looking at the pristine block, with its statement-designed glass and steelwork and the enormous plants filling up the atrium. 'I'm sure there's something non-optimal about visiting all these wealthy places. I'm afraid it will corrupt my soul.'

'Not to worry' said Wilcox. 'As soon as we've wrapped this up we'll be back to the muggings and knifings – good old street crime. These flats cost way more than a whole house in most areas of London and the service charges are a form of street crime. Once you're in, they put them up every year and you just have to pay. So' he added comfortingly, 'there are always downsides.'

The elevator whisked them soundlessly to the fifth floor and the door was opened by a woman that Murphy decided was probably about her own age, and looked like she would look if she had the necessary time and money to lavish upon herself. Well maybe not.

Kate Black had short blond hair tied up in some sort of scarf and she was wearing a boiler suit, probably a very expensive boiler suit. It was the here-I-am-looking-fabulous-while-wrestling-with-machinery look and it didn't come cheap.

She waved them in and offered coffee which Murphy immediately accepted. The coffee here would be good. While it was being brewed, she had a wander round, noted the polished floor, the kilim rugs, the glass doors opening onto a balcony with a patio heater.

'Not very ecologically sound, I know' said Kate, coming back in from the kitchen with a tray, 'but it's just so lovely, even on a cold evening, to sit out there and see the lights come on everywhere. I've given up driving to compensate. Not that there's any fun to be had any more in driving round London.'

'That's for sure' said Murphy. 'The congestion charge and the ultra-low emission zone have seen to that. Not to mention the parking.'

'What we want to ask you' Wilcox began when the coffee had been served 'is when you last saw Effie Fincham.'

Kate Black frowned and picked up her phone 'Let me check. OK, just over two weeks ago. We went out for lunch. River Café. Why? Has something happened?'

'I'm afraid so. She was found dead in her house ten days ago.'

Kate Black's face appeared to freeze. 'Effie? But that's awful. She was perfectly fine last time I saw her. What happened to her?'

'She was murdered. Strangled.'

Kate put a hand over her mouth. 'Oh my God. That's terrible. Do you know who did it?'

'Not yet, we're still making enquiries' said Wilcox. 'Can we begin by asking you where you were on the night of 22 September? It's just procedure. We're asking everybody.'

'Of course. As far as I remember, I would have been here, watching TV, and alone I'm afraid.'

'Did you see any of your neighbours, or anybody else at any point?'

'No, nobody. You don't often see the neighbours in this block. So no, not that I remember.'

'OK. Can you tell us how you knew Effie.'

She sighed. 'I hadn't known her very long, not much more than a couple of months. It was a stupid way to meet somebody, but we had a tussle over a taxi and then ended up sharing it. She is – was – a very friendly person and we became friends.'

'So how was she when you last saw her?'

'She was fine physically but mentally I'd say she was not in a good place. She was having some problems.'

'Problems with her husband?'

'Yes. They were not getting on well. She said to me that his family had never liked her and now her husband was becoming abusive.'

'Abusive in what way?'

'I got the impression he had hit her a few times and I guess they were probably verbally abusing each other.'

'Did you get any idea what may be behind this?'

'It seemed like he was fed up of her and she was fed up of him. So at least it was mutual. She was thinking in terms of divorce. But of course, she was very well provided for financially, so she wasn't going to just walk out. I told her she had to get a good lawyer. I don't know if she did that.'

'Did she tell you any more about her plans?'

'She said she thought the Finchams had skeletons in the closet, that was how she put it. She was looking for some leverage. She thought she would need that in order to get a decent settlement. I told her getting a good lawyer would be a better idea.'

'Did she say what she was going to do?'

'No, she didn't want to say any more about it. But I got the impression she had a plan of some sort.'

'And did you meet any member of the family?' said Murphy.

Kate nodded. 'Yes. Effie took me to one of the wine tastings. Maybe she wanted to get my take on them, I don't know. So I met Hugo, only briefly, and then the other brother – Sebastian. He showed us round and served the drinks. He was very – amenable. And a good salesman. I ended up buying a case of white. It's very good wine.'

'Did you meet Mr Fincham senior?'

'I saw what was probably him and his wife, but they didn't come over to speak to us.'

'What did you think of Hugo?'

'I thought he was a weak specimen to be honest. I guess that's true of any man who beats his wife. He didn't have a lot to say for himself and he disappeared fairly quickly.'

'And, apart from Hugo, do you have any ideas about who might have wanted to hurt Effie?'

'None at all, I'm afraid. Do you think it could have been a stranger?'

'It doesn't look that way', said Murphy. 'Thank you for your help.'

***

Bellweather was circling like a shark when they arrived back at the station and it was an immediate precision strike.

'My office. Now.'

They weren't given permission to sit, so Wilcox stood at attention and Murphy leaned against the bookshelf, which was swaying alarmingly.

'There's been a complaint.'

Murphy shrugged. 'His retired honour Judge Fincham?'

'That's right. I seem to remember telling you not to go harassing the judiciary.'

'What was he complaining about?'

'Harassment of his family, principally his wife, who is unwell.'

'You'd think' said Murphy, 'that he'd be concerned about his dead daughter-in-law. Most people in his position would want to help the police, not make their job more difficult.'

Bellweather seemed to give this some thought. 'OK, we need this wrapped up before he takes his complaints any higher. So where are we at?'

Pressure was obviously coming down the line. Murphy gave him a rundown on the case so far.

'But you have the person who was last seen with her. Why aren't you charging him?'

'Because we have no evidence against him.'

'Well you just need to look a bit bloody harder.'

'It's looking more likely that a member of Judge Fincham's family is involved – maybe even the judge himself' said Murphy, just for the hell of it.

Bellweather's eyebrows shot up and his face became suffused with colour. Murphy wondered if he was about to have a cardiac incident. She hadn't meant to go that far.

Bellweather regained control of himself. 'This stuff you've found – did our prime suspect have access to where it was found?'

'Yes, but so did our other prime suspect – Hugo Fincham' she clarified.

'Remind me why he's a prime suspect.'

'He was beating her up' said Murphy. 'Bruises on her arms. Suspected marital rape. That sort of thing often ends in murder, as we all know.'

Bellweather had had enough. 'OK. I want this sorted out fast. Go and get on with it.' He grabbed his coat from the back of the door and stalked out. Murphy stole a look at the planner on his desk. 'Lunch with the commissioner. Rather him than me.'

Murphy went and sat at her desk while Wilcox made the tea. She sipped gratefully.

'So whoever murdered Effie has access to that office' said Wilcox. 'Unfortunately that's everybody.'

'Yes. I don't think Kate Black – or Kate Boswell Black – told us anything we didn't already know.'

'She was married to George Black' said Wilcox, who was busy googling. 'He was a multi-millionaire. Mostly property, a bit of dabbling in renewables. Died about six months ago. Stroke. No wonder she has such a nice place.'

'I don't see her as a strangler' said Murphy 'and I don't think anybody killed Effie just to get out of paying alimony. The Finchams have plenty of money and that just doesn't make sense. What did she know and what had she found out? Something worth killing her for?'

'Seems to have been something to do with Billy – if we think about what Juliet told us.'

'Yes, it does look that way. A trip to Doncaster is called for. Let's go and see Brian Ferris tomorrow if he can fit us in.'

Chapter Thirty-One

Doncaster police station was a squat 60s building just off the A63. It looked like it had been designed, if that was the right word, by an architect who was confident they would never have to work in it.

'Looks like one of the buildings on the South Bank' said Murphy. 'Probably built on a bomb site.'

'Built in 1969' said Wilcox. 'A lot of these brutalist buildings are now getting preservation orders.'

Murphy sniffed. 'Well maybe it's nicer inside.'

Brian Ferris was now a DI and had his own office. He was a spare man and Murphy had no trouble imagining him as the young DC who had accompanied Reggie Yates to Fawcett Hall.

'Thank you for sparing us some of your time' said Wilcox. 'I'm sure you have lots going on.'

Ferris smiled. 'Of course. I expected it to be quieter here when I moved up, but not at all. Crime's increasing everywhere, it's just regional variations that you have to take into account.'

'As you know' said Murphy, 'we're taking another look at the events at Fawcett Hall in 2004, when you were accompanying DI Yates.'

'That's right. Reggie Yates.'

'You would have been pretty new then.'

'I was. I'd come through the graduate scheme, so I hadn't done long in uniform, and it was my first month in CID. I was a new DC. Reggie was teaching me everything he knew.' He paused. 'With what I know now, I can see that everything Reggie knew wasn't that much.'

'We've been to see Reggie and he's told us what he remembers' said Wilcox. 'He's now retired, so anything you tell us won't impact his career. Do you think the investigation was pursued with sufficient – vigour?'

He shook his head. 'No, definitely not. And I've always remembered this case – a textbook case of what can go wrong. It's always difficult to preserve the scene, of course, when the victim might not be dead. In this case the young man was taken off by the paramedics, by which time the whole place had been trampled over by a number of people, so that was the first problem. But it was pretty obvious by the time we arrived that he was dead, and we didn't take any steps to preserve what was left of the scene. That may or may not have yielded anything. We didn't search the pond to locate his other shoe. That may have told us nothing, but it should have been done. We did inspect the area where he had been sleeping and there were some articles of clothing there. I think they were bagged up, but I can't be sure. But the main shortcoming was in dealing with the witnesses. Of course, they were all upset, but there was no point leaving it until they had stopped being upset. The kids didn't seem to know anything, but we didn't question them individually right then and there. By the time we got round to it they had all had time to confer and they all told the same story. Maybe none of them were lying, but one of them could have been. And the biggest shortcoming was in not properly questioning the mother. She was the first person on the scene, she was the most important witness. But all we got out of her was a couple of sentences, then we were told that she was ill and she was whisked off.'

'Did you see Judge Fincham?'

'Yes, the judge. That was the problem, I think. Reggie had met Fincham before and was in awe of him somehow. So when the judge said we couldn't question the wife, that was the end of it.'

'Yes' said Murphy. 'We're definitely coming round to the view that she might have more to tell us.'

Chapter Thirty-Two

MURPHY WAS SITTING IN Susannah's kitchen when the call came in on her phone. They had almost finished supper and Katy and Alice were describing in detail the plot of their new school play, which seemed to centre around a riot in a dog's home. She picked the call up, hoping it wouldn't be something that would drag her back out into the cold. It was.

'I have to be off, girls.' She grabbed her bag and coat. Good job she hadn't drunk anything. 'Save me some of that pudding.' Susannah saw her to the door. It had started to rain. 'Take care.'

The traffic was stacked up in every direction. It was that peculiar phenomenon whereby whenever it started to rain all the people who had travelled to work on public transport miraculously sprouted cars to drive home in. Or that was how it always seemed to Murphy.

The police tape was already up when she arrived and a tent had been erected over the body. Murphy took a look inside. Kate Black looked smaller in death than she had in life. A pool of blood was spreading outwards from what was presumably a head wound. One side of her face was covered in blood but the other side was unmarked. Murphy thought that most of the damage would be internal. A fall like that would have broken a lot of bones.

Wilcox was already there, talking to a pair of high-pitched young women. A young uniformed policeman seemed to have been first on the scene and was looking very white. She ushered him further away. Please, no vomiting on the crime scene.

'Were you the first one here?'

'Yes. The call came over and I was just around the corner.'

'You did a good job of securing the scene. Was she dead when you arrived?'

He nodded. 'I know a bit of basic first aid and there was no pulse, no vital signs. The paramedics arrived soon afterwards and confirmed it. Poor lady.'

A car drew up just then and Linda Fleming emerged, wrestling with an umbrella. After it had blown inside out twice, she gave up and stomped over, hunched in her mackintosh, with her case clutched to her chest.

'Bloody thing. I hate umbrellas.' She disappeared inside the tent and Murphy went over to where Wilcox was standing.

'Fall from the balcony' he said. 'Nobody that I've spoken to so far witnessed it but a few of them heard a scream and came out to look.'

'It's only five floors' said Murphy. 'There wouldn't be much time to scream on the way down. If somebody pushed her off that balcony, that may have been the moment when she screamed.'

'It has to be that or suicide. We've seen that balcony. You wouldn't fall off it accidentally.'

Linda Fleming emerged at that point and came over, holding her hood over her head.

'Death was instantaneous. That head wound would be enough on its own. There will also be massive internal damage. At least there'll be no problem determining time of death in this case.'

She paused. 'Why is it you two again? Are you thinking this has anything to do with that death last week, or do they think you don't have enough to do?'

'Looks like there's a link' said Murphy. 'They were friends.'

'Nasty. Good luck with that. Pm on Thursday', said Linda. 'Would be earlier but I've got a few others stacked up. See you then.' She strode off back to her car and threw her case in the boot.

'She's right' said Murphy. 'It is definitely nasty.' The mortuary staff were in the tent, getting the body ready to move and a crowd of onlookers were straining for a look. 'Sooner we get this spectacle out of the way the better. Put in a call for a few more PCs to keep the public out of the way until SOCO have finished. I'm going to fetch a cup of coffee for that lone PC, he looks like he needs something. Then we'll head upstairs.'

***

The route up the stairs to the fifth floor was punctuated by doors opening and closing as people stuck their heads out for a look and then decided they didn't want to look like rubberneckers and hastily withdrew.

'Twenty flats in this block' said Wilcox. 'And twenty in the block facing us. The people in the block opposite are the people who had most opportunity to see what happened on Kate Black's balcony.'

'I want one team doing that block and one doing this block' said Murphy. 'Somebody in this block may have seen her visitor, if there was one, on the stairs or in the lift. They would have exited this building immediately after the fall and the exit is at the front, so they would have walked past the body. Then lots of people would have come running and they could just have joined all the shocked onlookers and then peeled off. So get them to ask anybody who came out here if they noticed anybody doing that.'

The door was closed when they arrived. Wilcox fished a key out of his pocket. 'Picked this spare up from the concierge' he said. Murphy smiled and clapped him on the shoulder.

They put on gloves, closed the door behind them and walked slowly into the room. Murphy had read lots of novels in which a space which has been the scene of a violent death has some kind of aura, a definite feel. She usually scoffed and remarked to herself that what it had was the feel of an awful lot of legwork coming up. But this time there was definitely an eerie feeling, despite the ultra-modern architecture and fittings. She remembered sitting on that sofa just a few days ago, when Kate Black was very much alive.

'We need to track down her daughters' she told Wilcox. 'They need to be told as soon as possible. If we're very lucky her phone may still be around.'

There was no sign of the phone anywhere in the room and they moved out to the balcony where an upended bottle of red wine dripped from the table to the floor and two glasses lay on the floor, one of them still intact.

'So they never got round to pouring it' said Murphy.

'That bottle could have been the weapon' said Wilcox, moving around to look at it from another angle. 'Hit her over the head hard and then grab the ankles and over the balcony.'

He looked down. 'And there's the phone.' He pointed to something flashing weakly in the bushes directly below. 'She was holding it when she fell.'

'Let's hope she was taking a selfie' said Murphy as they clattered back down the stairs.

Chapter Thirty-Three

It was a sunset, the time log on the picture matching the moment when the scream was heard. The phone had failed to lock, maybe due to the impact.

'So the perp is on the balcony with her' said Wilcox. 'She leans on the balustrade to take a photo of the sunset and he/she hits her over the head and tips her over the balcony. Fast, easy and pretty foolproof, as long as nobody is actually watching. And even if they are, they won't be close enough to make any kind of a positive ID.'

'Yes, it wouldn't take a huge amount of strength' said Murphy. 'Just enough to overbalance her, and gravity would do the rest. So we know how. Who and why is a different matter.'

She looked around the room. 'OK. SOCO will arrive here any minute and throw us out. Let's just see if there's anything else useful.'

Wilcox headed for the bathroom cabinet, Murphy looked at the magazines on the coffee table. Lifting one of them, she spotted that morning's *Times*, with the crossword half completed. The cryptic one. Murphy remembered her dad after his retirement, keeping his brain challenged with the *Observer* cryptic. So Kate Black wasn't just a rich woman, she was a clever rich woman. Did that mean she had discovered something that put her in danger?

Wilcox had drawn a blank in the bathroom. 'Lots of supplements and make-up. No sign of any prescription drugs.'

'So she didn't drug herself and then jump off the balcony' said Murphy. 'I think we can rule that out. If I was going to top myself I'd just do the drugs – jumping off the balcony is a bit *de trop*. Let's check the kitchen and bedroom.'

Wilcox tackled the kitchen cupboards and Murphy went through into the bedroom. The king-size bed was made and the closet doors were shut. Opening them she saw everything neatly lined up – suits, dresses, jackets, shoes. All expensive labels, all well cared-for, and the wearer would never get to wear any of them again. It was one of the ironies of sudden death. You could collect your favourite suit from the dry cleaners, not knowing that its next destination was the charity shop.

Wilcox had arrived behind her as she stood there gazing at a Chanel pencil-skirted suit in a deep charcoal with an ivory fleck and narrow lapels. He cleared his throat. 'Well she wasn't a messy person' he said as Murphy tore her attention away and shut the closet doors. 'Not much stuff in the kitchen cupboards, I don't think she did much cooking.'

Murphy considered this. 'I guess she had nobody to cook for, and maybe she ate out a lot. We need to find out a lot more about her. I think we're done here. I could really use some breakfast. Let's go home, have showers and then I'll meet you in the station. Hopefully we can still make it in before the boss.'

Chapter Thirty-Four

MURPHY SKIDDED INTO THE police station car park and narrowly missed scraping her offside rear wing. Not that another scrape would make a lot of difference, she thought. It wasn't as if there was much list price to take a hit.

In spite of her reckless and borderline illegal driving, she was too late. Bellweather's car was there and she cast around for the sleek Jag she had last seen the Chief Constable gliding around in. No sign so far, so that was something. She shot through the reception area, where the desk sergeant looked up from his sudoku, caught her eye and drew a finger meaningfully across his throat.

Inside the CID room there was definitely an atmosphere, composed of fear and excitement. Wilcox, bless him, was already at his desk. She hoped he hadn't been given too much flak in her absence.

Bellweather was pacing the floor, his hands linked behind his back like Sherlock Holmes. 'Inspector Murphy. Good of you to join us. Come this way.' He summoned them both into his office and pointedly left the door open.

'Remind me what you did with that suspect you had in custody.'

'You mean Justice Fincham's son?' asked Murphy, aware that she was flirting with danger.

'Not him' he roared. 'The other one.'

'We released him pending further investigation' Murphy replied, telling Bellweather nothing he didn't already know.

'And now you have another death, almost certainly related, am I right?'

'Yes, it does appear so. The two women knew each other. It's possible that they both knew something about what's going on in the Fincham family.'

Hi nostrils flared dangerously.

'What *is* this secret in the Fincham family? It's crap. There are no bloody secrets. You're making this up as you go along. You had a realistic suspect for the murder of Effie Fincham and you just let him go. Now another woman has been murdered. The likeliest scenario is that they were killed by the same person. Are you going to wait for number three? What am I going to tell the Chief Constable when he asks about this? More to the point, what is the Chief Constable going to say to the citizens of this borough once the press gets hold of this? Does two make a series, or should we hang on for a third?'

'I'm not expecting there to be a third – sir' said Murphy.

'Oh, aren't you? Well that's good isn't it? We can all relax. I'm planning to relax next week because that's when DI Wellesley will be back. I've told him I don't care if he's broken both legs and both arms, I want him back in to take over. In the meantime, you can sit down and fabricate a press release for the press conference I am no doubt going to be called upon to participate in before the day is out.'

They filed out in silence. The CID room was unnaturally quiet, all eyes fixed determinedly onto screens.

'He's going to miss his golf today' whispered Wilcox as she sat at his desk. 'That's why he's pissed off.'

'I think it's also press conferences' said Murphy, watching Bellweather exit the room. 'Last one he did, he still had false teeth and his top set dropped while he was talking. One of the photographers got the shot. It was hellish in here for months after that. So thank God for advanced dentistry – now he looks like he's a Hollywood extra.'

'I think we should point out that these cases may be related' said Wilcox. 'We don't want the press saying it's a random serial killer.'

'Yes, that's right. Just the usual stuff. Investigation still proceeding. And ask for anybody who observed anyone behaving suspiciously, or anything at all unusual in or around that block of flats in Putney early Tuesday evening to get in touch. That should do it. Will bring in all the usual helpful nutcases, but something useful may come in.'

***

Later that day they sat and watched as Bellweather and the Chief Constable sought to simultaneously reassure the public and fend off the press. It was a difficult balancing act and some members of the press were determined not to be fended off. Bellweather tried to explain, giving as little detail as possible, that the police considered the cases to be connected because the women had known each other, not because they were both victims of some random serial killer.

'But just because they had known each other doesn't mean it's not a series' pointed out one of the rising tabloid stars. 'What if another woman they both knew is killed? Will that make it a series? Should any woman who knew either of them now take extra precautions?'

The Chief Constable chipped in here and said gravely that the police did not have information to suggest that any other woman was at risk, that investigations were proceeding and that anybody who had information should get in touch on the number that was being publicised.

'He didn't come across too badly' said Wilcox. 'At least his teeth stayed in.'

Chapter Thirty-Five

TESSA AND BELLA BLACK were twins, but not identical. They had similar build and uncannily identical voices, but seemed to have strived to otherwise distinguish themselves from each other. Tessa had straight blonde hair and Bella had a mass of curly, almost frizzy, black hair. Whether any of that was natural or the result of trips to the salon was impossible to tell.

'We didn't want that situation where boyfriends thought we were interchangeable' said Tessa sadly.

They had both been visited by the uniform branch and informed that their mother was dead. They had also identified her body, so the worst of the crying was over. What they wanted now was answers.

Murphy and Wilcox were sitting with the twins in Bella's flat in a converted glue factory in Deptford. The windows were original, with small square panes and pre-war glass, the ceiling was a long way off and pipes still ran up the walls and across the ceiling, presumably positioned to carry off the noxious fumes. Relieved of their original function, they now looked like a design statement.

'What must it have been like to work here?' said Murphy.

'Horrible' said Bella. 'All those hooves boiling in vats.' She shuddered.

'You've been told now what we think happened to your mother' said Wilcox. 'Do you know of anybody who might want to hurt her.'

They both shook their heads. 'Absolutely not' said Tessa. 'It must have been some nutter.'

'And when was the last time you saw her?'

'About a week ago' said Tessa. 'We met for lunch. At the V&A.'

'And how did she seem?'

'She was fine, in great form. It took her a while to get over Dad dying, they were very close, but she was definitely getting there, and she seemed perfectly happy.'

'Did she ever mention Effie Fincham?'

'No... yes, she did say she'd made a new friend called Effie and we must meet her sometime. I gather she was actually closer to our age than Mum's.'

'She didn't tell you anything else about Effie?'

'She said Effie was married to somebody who wasn't very nice to her. She always told us we should stay single as long as possible, until we had enough experience to know exactly what we were getting into, and she said Effie was a prime example of that.'

Murphy nodded. 'She was probably right about that. What other relatives did your mother have?'

'Just Uncle Terry', said Tessa. 'He's her brother. Oh God, we should let him know.'

'Put his details in here' Wilcox passed over his notebook, 'and we'll get uniform branch round to see him.'

'How long was your mum married to your dad?' asked Murphy.

'Well we're twenty four' said Bella, 'so probably at least twenty five years. I think they'd have told us if we were born out of wedlock, or whatever. And they were very happy, she was very shocked when he died.'

'Do you think that shock could have made her contemplate suicide?'

The girls looked at each other and then both shook their heads. 'No way' said Tessa. 'She wouldn't do that to us, not after losing Dad, and anyway, she enjoyed life, she had plenty of money and she enjoyed spending it, she liked travelling and swimming and reading and seeing friends. She had lots to live for.'

'Do you know how your mum and dad met?'

'Bit shocking really' said Bella. 'She was his PA. So one of those getting-off-with-the-boss scenarios. Probably not as tacky as it sounds.'

'And has she had any other relationships that you know about since meeting your father?' asked Wilcox.

Bella stared at him. 'With men you mean? Of course not. They just loved each other. And by the time he died she was over fifty. Why would she be interested in men at that age?'

Wilcox was silent. He obviously felt that the question was way beyond his remit.

'I don't wish to shock you' said Murphy, 'but there have been cases of people over fifty having sex – even falling in love. Did you have any reason to believe that your mother may have met someone after your father died?'

The girls wrinkled their noses and Murphy forced herself not to laugh. If Kate Black was seeing anybody, she certainly wouldn't have told these two.

***

Wilcox led the way out of the building, down the iron staircase and round to the car park.

Murphy sighed. 'I'm not sure how much we learned there. If they knew anything I think they'd have told us. It's a bit of an inversion isn't it? When they were younger, they probably made sure that their mum didn't know too much about what they got up to. Now it's a case of she might have been getting up to stuff, but she wouldn't want them to know about it.'

'What do you think she might have been getting up to?'

'I don't know, maybe men friends, maybe toyboys, maybe nothing. She was an attractive woman with plenty of money. I can't believe she spent all her evenings sitting at home alone watching Netflix. OK, where to now? Let's do what Bellweather wants. We'll go and harass Pete Grantham. He might even know something.'

They set off up to Pimlico. 'I didn't particularly take against Pete Grantham' said Murphy, 'so I don't think we'll wreck his career by turning up at his office. He should be arriving home fairly soon.'

The door was opened by Olivia, who appeared to have just arrived home. 'We'll wait' said Murphy, as Olivia disappeared upstairs to change Ben's nappy.

She came down looking wary and offered to call Pete. 'I think you've already done that haven't you love?' said Murphy. 'No problem. We can talk to you while we're waiting. Do you remember telling us about a woman called Kate Black?'

'Yes' said Olivia immediately. 'I met her at Ellie's house. Oh no, is she the Kate Black that fell from a balcony? I saw it on the news.'

'That's right' said Murphy. 'So if you can tell us whatever you know about her, that will be very helpful.'

Olivia said nothing for a few seconds. 'That's awful.' Then she sat up straighter. 'OK, so I went round to Effie's house - she was expecting me - and this Kate Black was there. A very nice person, much older than Effie of course, but they seemed to get on really well together.'

'Do you know how they met?'

'Some tussle over a taxi and then Effie suggested they share the ride. And it carried on from there.'

'And what was talked about while you were there?'

'Mostly Effie's in-laws as far as I remember. Effie was describing them all, I guess it's always quite entertaining when she does that, and Kate was laughing. I don't remember anything else we talked about. Oh, I think Kate referred to her daughters, but she didn't tell us much about them.'

'And did you think that Kate was particularly interested in any member of the Fincham family?'

'Not really. Well Hugo maybe, because Effie was making it clear that he was not the dream husband she thought she was getting. And Kate was advising her, I guess, or something like that. I think Effie also talked about her parents-in-law. Kate said she was very protective about her daughters. They're quite wealthy because their dad left a lot of money. I suppose they'll be even wealthier now' she added.

'Undoubtedly' said Murphy. 'So, what was your impression of Kate Black?'

Olivia got up and deposited Ben in a playpen set up in the corner. 'I liked her' she said. 'She seemed like a woman who had a good life and enjoyed it. I thought it was slightly unusual that she wanted to spend time with Effie – I mean she was old enough to be Effie's mum – but they seemed to get along really well.' She was silent for a moment. 'I can't believe they're both dead.'

'Did you meet her on any other occasion?' asked Wilcox. Olivia shook her head. 'No, I thought for a moment there was something familiar about her, but we agreed I was probably mistaken.'

'And has Pete ever met her?'

'Of course not, I only met her that once. Pete would never have met her. Are you thinking these deaths are connected?'

'It's a possibility we have to consider' said Murphy. 'Can you tell us where you were yesterday between 6pm and 8pm?'

Olivia shrugged. 'I was here, feeding Ben and making dinner, then we watched some TV – well, Netflix actually.'

'And what time did Pete arrive home?'

She hesitated. 'About 6.30.'

'Did either of you go out again?'

'No, we were in all evening.'

The sound of the front door opening was succeeded by the entry of Pete Grantham, burdened with a rucksack and laptop bag. He didn't look pleased at the sight of the visitors.

'What the hell? What is it now?'

'Mr Grantham.' Murphy was on her feet. 'A word if you please. Perhaps we could have a little walk.'

Pete rolled his eyes at Olivia, said 'I won't be long' and followed them out.

'That your car?' asked Wilcox as they passed a Renault Passat parked outside.

'No, that's the neighbour's. Mine's over there.' He pointed to a gleaming Audi. 'Company car' he explained.

'Very nice' said Murphy. 'Well here's our company car, so we might as well sit in it out of the cold.'

'I imagine you appreciate' said Murphy 'that we moved this conversation out of doors for your sake rather than ours. You probably wouldn't like Olivia to hear what some of our suspicions are. And we have also spared you the indignity of being visited in your place of work. So, in recognition of the level of consideration which you have been shown, we expect you to be more forthcoming than you were last time we spoke.'

'I just don't have any more to tell you.'

'Well let me tell you instead' said Wilcox. 'You give her a lift home, your partner's friend, you've always fancied her and you think she fancies you too. You're old flames, after all. She asks you in for coffee, you think your luck's in. And then, just when you're getting going, she cools off, starts fighting you off. So you grab her by the shoulders and before you know what's happened your hands are around her neck. She has a very thin neck and suddenly she's on the floor. You didn't mean to kill her, but she's dead. It wasn't premeditated murder, the courts won't be too hard on you.'

'But it's just not true' said Pete. 'None of that happened.'

'I should tell you,' said Murphy, 'that our DCI – the Senior Investigating Officer – wants you brought in for this. He also likes you for the murder of Kate Black – have you heard of her?'

'Kate Black? I've never heard of her.'

'Kate Black was pushed off a balcony yesterday.'

'Oh God, yes, I heard about that. But what has that got to do with me?'

‘Kate Black was a friend of Effie Fincham,’ said Wilcox, ‘and your partner has also met her by the way. So there are really no degrees of separation between you and Kate Black. Our DCI considers these deaths to be related and he likes you for both of them.’

‘But I can’t help that. I can’t admit to something I didn’t do.’

‘Well you can start by telling us where you were yesterday between 6pm and 8pm.’

He sighed. ‘OK. I left work at about ten past six and I drove straight home. Probably got home around six thirty-five. Traffic was quite bad.’

‘OK, and now you can tell us what really happened between you and Effie Fincham.’

‘Nothing happened. I didn’t try to have sex with her. If you’d found any evidence of that you wouldn’t be asking me.’

‘What did she tell you about her husband.’

‘She said that he didn’t love her any more, he found her annoying, and she no longer wanted to sleep with him and he was abusing her – not exactly beating her, but something like that.’

‘So she wanted you to be her knight in shining armour and rescue her?’

‘Of course not. She was quite capable of rescuing herself. She was going to arrange for a divorce and she would have been entitled to a decent amount of maintenance. I don’t think she thought there would be any logistical problems, she just needed people to talk to about it.’

'And did you give her any advice?'

'No, I wasn't competent to advise her on whatever she wanted to do. I think I told her to get some legal advice, but that's all.'

'OK Mr Grantham.' Murphy came to a decision. 'That's all for now. If we find out that anything you have told us falls short of the absolute, unvarnished truth, we'll have you back in that unpleasant interview room.'

Pete Grantham climbed out of the car, slammed the door and walked off.

'We have nothing on him' said Wilcox. 'Massive dose of opportunity, not much means needed and we could hazard a guess at motive, if pushed – but no evidence.'

'No' said Murphy. 'I think we've done all we can do with him for the time being. Let's pay another visit to Hugo Fincham. He should be home by now.'

Chapter Thirty-Six

THE POLICE TAPE HAD gone from the front of 183 Cheyne Walk and the lights were on.

Hugo Fincham answered the door wearing jeans and a loose linen shirt. His feet were bare.

'Oh no', he said. 'I'm not talking to you without my solicitor present.'

'Why not?' said Wilcox. 'What have you got to hide? It's not a good look, you know, hiding behind lawyers.'

Hugo glared at him and then opened the door wider. 'OK, but just ten minutes. I have to go out.'

He led the way into the sitting room and Murphy glanced at the area of carpet where Effie Fincham had breathed her last. Probably been well shampooed by now.

Hugo dropped into an armchair and Murphy and Wilcox took the sofa. It was soft and deep and Murphy hoped she'd be able to get out of it with dignity when the time came.

'We're looking into the death of a woman called Kate Black. Do you know her.'

'No, never heard of her.'

'She was a friend of Effie's. Olivia Atwell met her here, in this room. Possibly sitting in that armchair you're currently occupying.'

Hugo squirmed slightly. Maybe she was getting him off balance. That was good.

'Can you tell us where you were last night. From about six pm.'

'Six pm I was still at the vineyard. I left about 7, came back here and I was in for the rest of the evening. I had my daughter to look after. I have a nanny looking after her during the day.'

'OK. Apparently, Effie told Kate Black all about how she wasn't happy with you' she continued. 'And then Kate's murdered, so obviously we're looking at a connection.'

'Just to be clear' Hugo began. 'I did not kill my wife and I have never heard of this other woman.'

'In fact there's another connection' said Wilcox. 'Kate Black came on one of your wine tours. Effie brought her, about a week ago. A woman with short blonde hair, early fifties. Ring any bells?'

'No, I don't have much to do with the wine tours. Sebastian may remember her.'

'Indeed he may' said Murphy. 'And we will be asking him. Now Effie told Kate Black, and we know this because we spoke to Kate, that you were beating her and that she wanted a divorce. So what's your response to that?'

'I don't need to make any response. These allegations are without foundation and you have no evidence.'

'Well somebody had been beating her – we've seen the bruises. Was she involved with some other man who could have been beating her?'

'That's an absurd suggestion. Nobody was beating her. She probably fell over.'

'So why would she tell people you were beating her?'

'I don't know. Some kind of bid for sympathy. Everything always had to be about her.'

'So things were not going too well between you?'

'We had our disagreements' he said stiffly.

'And had she asked you for a divorce?'

'No, not at all.'

'So let's go back to that night she died' said Wilcox. 'You came home. Maybe she was in bed. She came down, in her dressing gown, and started a row with you. She was being annoying. You got angry and shook her by the shoulders. Next thing you know, you're shaking her neck. She's very slight, it probably didn't take much. You didn't intend to kill her, but there she is, dead.'

'That's complete fantasy' said Hugo. 'I can't believe you came here just to spin something like that. And now I do have to go out.'

'Thank you for your help' said Murphy. 'If we think of anything else we'll be back. Don't leave London without letting us know.'

Hugo slammed the door and they walked slowly back to the car.

'Let's sit here for a bit, see if he goes out' said Wilcox. 'He certainly wasn't dressed for going out. Presumably his daughter's in the house, so he can't go out anyway.'

Twenty minutes later Murphy said 'OK we've established that he was lying about that, but it doesn't really get us anywhere. Let's call it a night, I've got the pm in the morning. I remember saying you should do the next one, but I've decided to let you off. You can go in and confront Bellweather. Not much to choose between those two options, is there?'

Chapter Thirty-Seven

THE FOLLOWING MORNING, AFTER an almost sleepless night and experiencing the jittery feeling that goes with it, Murphy found herself back in the hospital mortuary. She had woken several times with the question uttered by Bella Black going round in her head. Why would a woman over fifty be interested in men? It was a reasonable question and Murphy thought she had parried it quite efficiently, but it seemed to resonate with her on a personal level. If your parental ambitions had been achieved, which hers had, and she didn't need a man to provide for her, which she didn't, why would she need a man? It was a hard question to answer and she wondered if Kate Black had felt the same way. Kate had her beautiful daughters and plenty of money, but what if that wasn't enough? She probably missed her husband, so could she have sought to replace him? And maybe in that way she had come up against somebody dangerous? Somebody attracted to her money? She made a mental note to look into Kate Black's finances.

The body was now being wheeled out by the mortuary assistant and Murphy stood up straighter and checked her mask, not that they ever seemed to really fend off the smell. Linda Fleming was inspecting her equipment, flicking the lights on and off and testing the recording device. Then the assistant removed the sheet from the body and Murphy avoided looking at Kate Black's head by admiring her toned thighs and flat stomach, and the muscles of her upper arms and shoulders. Lots of trips to the gym.

Linda was now speaking into the microphone suspended on a bracket above the gurney. Murphy made out 'well nourished' and 'good condition'. She had to agree. Kate Black's legs were obviously waxed and her feet were pedicured, whatever the word for that was. Murphy tried not to think about the state of her own feet, but excused herself on the basis that she spent a lot of time standing on them. Kate's face, when she forced herself to raise her gaze to it, was partially destroyed. She must have landed with her head turned to one side and one of her cheekbones was shattered, with no doubt substantial damage to the eyeball. Thankfully her eyes were closed for the moment.

Because of the way death had occurred, Murphy knew there would be a lot of internal damage and was bracing herself for what would emerge when she was opened up. Linda made the long vertical incision and described the damage to the spleen, which Murphy gathered, shorn of clinical terms, was extensive. Then she listed the broken bones and damage to other organs. When the torso had been reassembled, the assistant helped her to turn the body over and peel back the scalp. The bruising at the back of the head was clearly visible. It was extensive but, according to Linda, not in itself fatal. The bottle was then produced and compared to the area of trauma. Linda's verdict agreed with Wilcox's. The victim had been hit on the back of the head with the bottle and then sustained fatal injuries due to the fall.

Prior to the fatal event, the body had been in good condition. No tumours or other possible causes of death. In good shape for her age, Linda pronounced.

'Recent sexual intercourse?' asked Murphy hopefully.

Linda shook her head. 'No sign of that.'

***

Wilcox was inputting data at a furious pace when Murphy arrived in the office. He looked up and then put his attention back on the screen.

'How was the pm?'

Murphy took her jacket off and sat down.

'No great surprises. Sizeable wound on the back of the head, but it was the fall that killed her – massive internal bleeding, spleen and all the rest of it. We know the time of death anyway. The bottle fits as the weapon of choice and she was otherwise healthy. So your assessment of what happened was correct. How are things going here?'

'Press conference is generally considered to have gone OK. No disasters anyway. There are some calls coming in, but nothing yet that looks useful. Bellweather's been out all morning, probably getting a bollocking, so he'll be in this afternoon passing it down the line. I've entered everything we've managed to get from the door-to-door. People in the flats opposite mostly didn't look across until they heard the scream and at that point everybody was looking at the body. They didn't even know which balcony she had fallen from. One person remembers seeing two people on the balcony, but they were too far away to recognise, and they went indoors to switch the oven off at the crucial moment. So we have no witness to the actual murder.'

'The way it looks' said Murphy 'the visitor was somebody she knew. They went out onto the balcony to share the bottle of wine and then the visitor hit her over the head with it. The last photo in the phone is a sunset shot, so while she was doing that, they took their chance. The only prints on the bottle belonged to Kate Black, so her assailant wore gloves. He or she hit her before she had a chance to pour the wine, because they could hardly accept a glass of wine with gloves on, and they didn't want to take them off and leave prints on the glass and the bottle. This was definitely a premeditated murder. Whoever did this needs to be stopped urgently. They could have somebody else in their sights. There was no sign of recent sexual intercourse, but she could have embarked upon a relationship which had not yet got that far. We need to get into her phone; she could have been signed up to one of those dating sites. Did you manage to access her bank accounts?'

Wilcox pulled some papers towards him. 'Yes. I printed out the last few months. She had three accounts – a current account, a savings account and a joint account, which still seems to be in operation. Sizeable balances in all of them. Income comes in from several funds and quite a lot of expenditure, but nothing that looks unusual. No payments to individuals or dodgy-looking companies.'

'So maybe it's nothing to do with money. Could she have represented a danger to somebody? Was there something that she knew? Seems to take us back to the Finchams. Let's go back to the vineyard, see what gives.'

Chapter Thirty-Eight

Dorothy was watching a large machine that was sticking labels on bottles. When the batch was finished, she clicked a switch and the belt stopped.

'Amazing' said Murphy. 'Seems like nothing in the world gets done by hand anymore.'

'That's just how it is' said Dorothy. 'Artisan products still need to be efficiently produced, or they can't compete in the marketplace.'

'Tell me', said Murphy 'have you met a woman called Kate Black?'

'I don't think so. Should I know her?'

'She was a friend of Effie's, she came on one of your wine tours, and now she's dead.'

'Dead how?'

'Pushed off a balcony.'

Dorothy looked up quickly. 'That's awful. I don't recall the name. I don't think I ever met her.'

'A good-looking woman in her early fifties. Short blond hair. You never met her at Cheyne Walk?'

'No, definitely not.'

'You see' said Murphy, 'her death coming right after Effie's makes it look like there must be a link. Apparently Effie told her that things were not going well with her in-laws, and with her husband. Then they're both dead, so that makes it look as if the Fincham family is the link.'

'I can see how it looks' said Dorothy, 'but I can't see how that can be true.'

'We're asking everybody where they were last night' said Wilcox.

'I was here until about six thirty' said Dorothy. 'Then I was just at home.'

'Who else was here until six thirty?'

She scratched her head. 'Hugo was around. I think Sebastian had left. Edward was at a formal dinner in London – something to do with helping pupil barristers. He doesn't often go to these things, but I think he felt obliged to show up for this one. The other vineyard staff had left about five thirty.'

'Did Mrs Fincham accompany her husband?'

'Not as far as I know. I don't think it was a function to which partners were invited.'

'But you didn't see her at all?'

'No, she doesn't come across here every day.'

'So she doesn't have any role here?'

'No, but she takes an interest, often comes and has a look around.'

'Do you know how Mr and Mrs Fincham met?' said Murphy.

Dorothy led the way outside and they followed. 'I don't see that that's any business of mine or yours.'

'When somebody is murdered' said Murphy, 'all sorts of previously private matters suddenly become our business. You wouldn't believe what we end up prying into.'

'Well I don't know how they met' said Dorothy. 'They had already been married for a number of years when I was engaged. Hugo was about six years old.'

'Was Mrs Fincham working?'

'No, she was just at home. She must have had a job earlier, but I don't know what it was.'

'So why did they need a nanny?'

'She was under a psychiatrist, having treatment. I was told she had to be protected from any kind of stress. Their relationship seemed under a bit of strain. But she did improve over the years, so things settled down.'

'So you were to a large extent responsible for bringing up these children.'

'Well my duties didn't extend quite that far, but in practice a lot of it was left to me.'

'What sort of a child was Phoebe?'

Dorothy stopped walking and they all stood. 'It's a bit difficult to say. Boys are very overt, but girls keep quite a lot hidden and Phoebe was like that. You never really knew what she was thinking. She was a child who liked to sort out her own problems rather than ask for help. I think she would have benefitted from having a proper mother, somebody she could talk to, who would understand.'

'But she was brighter than the boys' said Murphy.

'Yes, I think she was. She worked a lot harder than they did of course, but she also had a natural scientific aptitude. Most of the arts subjects, anybody can do them if they put in the work, that's what I think anyway, but for science you really have to have the brains. Looking back on it, I think she derived stability from school – the stability she didn't get at home.'

'And she had a strong bond with Sebastian.'

Dorothy nodded. 'Yes, they were the younger kids, ignored to some degree by their parents, so they went around together. Well, not really ignored, but I would say neither of their parents gave them that much attention.'

'Phoebe doesn't seem to have formed much of a bond with Effie' said Murphy.

Dorothy acknowledged this. 'To be honest I think it's a case of Effie was coming into the family at a time when Phoebe was probably intent on getting out. But they were also very different people. Effie was very outgoing and Phoebe kept her own counsel. I think she may have found Effie a bit intrusive.'

'Phoebe seems to have been badly affected by Billy's death.'

'Yes, that was awful. Mostly for that poor boy and his family of course, but Phoebe and Verity took it very badly.'

'Didn't you ever feel' said Murphy, 'that you would have liked a family of your own? You seem to have spent your life looking after theirs.'

'I did feel that, of course. And I have had a number of relationships, which could have resulted in children, but just didn't. I'm no Mrs Danvers, don't get that idea. But I'm well rewarded here and I never found anything else I really wanted to do.'

'You must have a strong sense of loyalty to the family' said Murphy.

'I do, but if you're asking whether I would lie to protect them, the answer is no, I wouldn't.'

Chapter Thirty-Nine

'YOU'VE TAKEN HIM BACK, haven't you?'

Susannah nodded reluctantly. 'I didn't intend to. I told him, if he was fed up with her, he could move into lodgings. So he did, he found himself an Airbnb, but then he came round to collect the girls and kind of made himself at home.'

'Made himself at home!' Murphy spluttered. 'What right did he have to make himself at home? Did he even bloody apologise?'

'Yes, he did apologise and he promised nothing like this would happen again. I didn't ask too many questions, I don't really want to know too much about it, but he said he'd made a mistake and he loves us. And of course, the girls were so happy to have him back. I know what you think, Miranda, and in principle I agree with you, but I guess I'm just not that strong.'

'Bollocks! Of course you are. You're free to make any decision you want and you're quite capable of carrying it out. I can see that this makes the girls happy and makes you happy in some ways. But if you're taking back this conniving cheat, then make sure it really is your decision, and not one you've been persuaded into. And don't take his promise too seriously – make sure you're mentally prepared for next time he wanders off.'

Susannah smiled wryly. 'Oh, don't worry. I think I've learnt a lot from this episode. I want him back for the girls, but I don't necessarily want him for keeps.'

'Well that's something. I guess you hadn't thrown all his stuff out like I told you to? Pity. Never mind, next time he misbehaves I'll come round and we'll do it together. We can have a garage sale.'

'And I've found a new nanny.'

'Great. Here we go again.'

'Maybe not. It's a chap.'

'Well that's different. Have you vetted him?'

'Yes, extensively. He comes highly recommended And he's very good-looking.'

'Even better. That should piss Simon off. The longer I stay in the job, the more I feel that people need to be able to let go of relationships. We all have to be able to stand on our own and move on when needed and not put more weight of expectation on a relationship than it is able to bear. So that's my advice, which I acknowledge you haven't asked for. Because the alternative can lead to some nasty results.'

Chapter Forty

Terry Boswell ran a used-car dealership in St Alban's, which appeared to specialise in Honda and Nissan. Wilcox occupied himself comparing some of the models on display to the online list prices, while Murphy watched with interest as Terry dealt with a woman agonising over whether or not her dog would be happy in the back of a Micra.

He was mopping his brow with a large handkerchief as he came over to them and Murphy made the introductions.

'We're sorry about your sister' she said. 'We don't yet know who was responsible, but we will find out.'

He nodded. 'Poor Kate. I should have stayed in touch a bit more, especially after George died. But she was very independent and she was doing fine. You just don't expect something like this to happen.'

He led the way into an office featuring a desk piled with papers and a variety of calendars on the walls. Murphy took the other available seat and Wilcox leaned against a rickety filing cabinet.

'When was the last time you saw her?' Wilcox dragged his attention from the forecourt.

Terry took a deep breath. 'About three weeks ago. I went to visit her. Beautiful flat, she had.'

'And where were you two nights ago? Between six pm and seven pm? We have to ask everybody this.'

'I was here until just after six, then I went home. My house is about a ten-minute drive from here.'

'Was anybody here with you?'

'My mechanic was here until about five-thirty. The dealership shuts at six. My wife was at home. You don't seriously think..'

'No, we don't. This is just standard procedure. But we'll check with both of them.'

'Can you think of anybody who would want to hurt your sister?' said Murphy.

He shook his head. 'I don't know all her friends and acquaintances, not anymore, but there's nobody I can think of. Why would they? She never harmed anybody.'

'Was it just the two of you?'

'Yes, me and Kate. She was two years younger than me, but she had the brains. Or different sort of brains I suppose. I was into engines, motorbikes, cars. She was more academic.'

'University?'

'Yes, law at Sussex. Then further training of some sort, but she dropped out of her course. She had a break, then she came back as a PA. Don't think they call them that these days, do they? Anyway, that was how she met George. And they were very happy together, until he died. That was a terrible shock, heart attack, but she seemed to be coping quite well.'

'Did you know many of her friends?'

He laughed shortly. 'I didn't know any of them to be honest. We moved in different circles. She would come up here to visit me, but I didn't usually go to visit her. They had a circle of wealthy friends, her and George, and that wasn't my sort of crowd.'

'Do you know who inherits her assets?'

He shrugged. 'Tessa and Bella, I should think. I think they are both quite well off anyway, and they both have good careers, as far as I know. They're very upset. I don't think any inheritance is going to make up for losing their mum.'

'Your sister was a wealthy woman. Did she ever invest money in your business?'

'I wouldn't let her' he said. 'She was always offering, and George too, and maybe, if I'd been about to go under, I would have accepted money from her, just temporarily, but it didn't happen. I didn't want to be bailed out by family – always leads to grief.'

'Did Kate ever mention a woman called Effie Fincham to you?'

He frowned. 'I don't think so, although there is something familiar about it. Was there something in the paper about her?'

'Yes, she was killed a week before your sister and they knew each other. We haven't yet established any link between their deaths, but it looks like there may be one.'

'You mean like some nutter killing women?'

'No, more like somebody who knew both of them. And not necessarily a man.'

He shook his head. 'They'd still have to be a nutter. Man or woman.'

***

‘He’s right of course’ said Murphy, as they headed towards the station. ‘Whoever did this might not be legally insane, in the sense that we can’t prosecute them, but you still have to be seriously disturbed, or at least temporarily insane, in order to kill someone. Effie Fincham’s killing could have been a spur-of-the-moment thing, but Kate Black’s murder was coldly premeditated. That’s a really dangerous person.’

‘Talking of which’ said Wilcox, ‘let’s hope he’s not in the building.’

‘He is’ said Murphy, as they entered the car park. ‘I can see him at the window. Drive straight out again. He’ll just waste our time. Park round the corner and we’ll check Terry Boswell’s alibi.’

Wilcox got his phone out and made the calls while Murphy leaned against the car and stretched her legs. She really ought to be doing something to keep fit. Maybe she should go running with Susannah. The thought made her feel weak. She got back in the car.

‘Some of those cars he’s selling are way below list price, but they may have things wrong with them’ said Wilcox. ‘Either way, that’s a sign of a business in need of cash. Wife and mechanic both confirm what he said. Of course, he’s had time to brief them both, but it would have taken him a while to make that drive even if he’d left at five-thirty. That’s the middle of the rush hour.

‘Yes, he’s not top of my list of suspects’ said Murphy. ‘Have we heard from her solicitor yet?’

‘Yes, he’s going to email us about her will.’

Wilcox’s phone buzzed. ‘Hi Sandra. Well we had a few other things to do. That’s interesting, give me the number. Thanks.’

He finished scribbling and looked up. 'We were spotted circling the car park, but not by the DCI, so no problem. A friend of Kate's got in touch, Martina Wells, wants us to call her.'

Wilcox made an appointment to see Martina Wells and Geraldine Masters at Martina's flat in Clapham and they drove over there. Murphy stood and looked around as Wilcox locked the car. Many of the houses looked newly-decorated and the high street had coffee shops, an artisan bakery and some species of supposedly upmarket butchers.

'I used to live round here' she said. 'It was the first flat I owned in London and it was a cheap area to live in. Most of the shops were cheap corner shops.'

'Well it's not a cheap area now, said Wilcox. 'One of my mates is renting a flat in Clapham for £1,000 a month – and not a posh flat either.'

'Like everywhere else' said Murphy. 'Colonised by the rich. OK, enough of the politics of envy. Where are we going?'

Wilcox led the way using his location app and they found themselves outside a modern block that had been grafted onto an original large detached Victorian house. It was tastefully done and the promo photos for the unsold flats featured young people in sports clothing running round the block, rather than old people playing golf. The prices were eye-watering.

Murphy brightened. 'It's not a retirement block. Thank God for that. They're using young people to advertise it, but probably only older people can afford it. Or maybe young people with lucrative Instagram careers or trust funds.'

The lift glided soundlessly up to the third floor and the door to number 35 was opened by a well-upholstered woman in a colourful kaftan and Birkenstocks. Her hair was dark brown and ballooned around her head in an unruly mass that could only be natural. Murphy introduced them and showed her warrant card. The woman glanced at it momentarily.

'Thank you for coming. I'm Martina. Come in and meet Geraldine.'

Geraldine rose to greet them with a taut smile. She was a totally different body shape to Martina – whip thin with short, spiky blonde hair, wearing what appeared to be her running clothes.

'Thank you for coming to see us' she said. 'We are so shocked, heartbroken really, about what's happened to Kate.'

'We're glad you got in touch' said Murphy, taking her coat off and sitting in an armchair. 'Can we start by asking where you both were on Tuesday night? Just to get that out of the way.'

'No problem' said Martina. 'I was here and my son and his girlfriend came round. They came around six and stayed till about nine. I'll give you their details.'

'I was home alone, I'm afraid' said Geraldine. 'I live in Camden. I went for a run about six, then I was just at home. I don't think I saw anybody.'

'OK, we'll leave that for now' said Murphy. 'What was your relationship to Kate?'

'We were just friends' said Martina. 'We'd been friends since our children were born. Since we were pregnant in fact. We met at NCT, the dreaded antenatal classes. So many years ago now.'

'And when was the last time either of you saw her?'

'Last Thursday' said Geraldine. 'We had lunch, just the three of us, in Soho. Do you want to know the name of the restaurant?.

'No, that's OK' said Wilcox. 'We know she was alive for five days after that.'

'Obviously you know the basic facts about the incident' said Murphy. 'Do you have information for us concerning what happened to Kate?'

They both nodded sadly.

'We're afraid it might be our fault' said Martina.

Chapter Forty-One

'To begin at the beginning' said Geraldine, 'about a year ago I fell victim to one of those romance scams. It was my own stupid fault. I'd split up with my husband, I was lonely, I went online and met a man called Matt. He was apparently divorced, living in New York, we exchanged loads of messages and I guess you could say he groomed me. I ended up sending him $5,000 for his medical bills. Then he needed more money, for some operation, at which point I told Kate and Martina and they told me it was a scam.'

'She refused to believe us at first' said Martina. 'But we did a reverse image search on google and there he was – only his name was Paolo and he lived in Verona. And of course, Paolo knew nothing about this – somebody had stolen his image.'

'Well I obviously wasn't going to get my $5,000 back' said Geraldine, 'but I was just grateful it wasn't more. And I guess I was kind of angry that I'd been made a fool of.'

'We looked into the whole romance scam thing, and it's huge' said Martina. 'Men fall prey to it as well as women and some people lose huge sums – six figures. So we wondered if we could get our own back on Matt – or whoever he was. We're older, unattached women so we're the right demographic for these scammers. Except we know they're scammers, so we thought maybe we can at least confuse them a bit, mess with their heads, like they do to other people.'

'So we joined Tinder' said Geraldine, 'and another site called seniorsingles. Just to see what we could pull in. We have a Whatsapp group, just us three, called 'mature sexy women'. That's how we advertise ourselves on the sites.'

They were both looking pretty shamefaced now.

'OK' said Murphy, who was actually finding this fascinating. 'So what happened?'

'We all managed to lure at least a couple of men' said Martina. 'Then we'd do the reverse image searches. We'd discard anybody who didn't come up as a scammer, but we'd just have fun with the ones who were. We'd declare our affection and promise to send the money and then lead them on with all sorts of excuses, the system was down at the bank, we need to go into the bank in person, and now we've got flu, we'll go in and send the money when we're better. Then we'd say we'd like to chat on Zoom first, that winds them up, they can't agree to that. So we were having fun with it, because we knew we weren't going to send them any money, and while they're snarled up with us they have less time to scam somebody else.'

'Did any of them turn nasty?' said Wilcox.

'One of them did' said Martina. 'It was one of mine, not one of Kate's. He swore at me, threatened to come and find me. But he has no way of doing that. I'd told him I lived in Maastricht, so I wasn't worried.'

'How about Kate?' said Murphy.

'That's what we're afraid of' said Geraldine. 'Kate was communicating with a guy called Richard, who said he lived in Cornwall. He wasn't coming up as a scammer and he wasn't asking for money, so we told her to get rid of him. She said she would, but she was letting it drag on a bit, she said he was an interesting guy and he wanted to come up and see her. I told her to google him and she said she would, but I don't know if she did.'

'And you think he might have come up from Cornwall and murdered her?'

'I know it seems far-fetched' said Martina, 'but the idea that anybody would kill her is completely far-fetched anyway.'

'So you want us to check this guy out?'

They both nodded. 'He's probably got nothing to do with it' said Martina, 'but we had to let you know about him.'

'We can look into him' said Wilcox. 'We have her devices. We're working on getting into her emails and Whatsapp. Do you have any other details about this person?'

'She said he was an artist. No, a musician.'

***

'That sounds too much like a stereotype' said Murphy. 'Probably lives in St Ives – I don't think.'

They walked slowly back to the car. 'The trouble is' she said, 'I feel now like it's all getting away from us. Every step forward seems to add a new complication. Nothing's actually getting any clearer.'

Wilcox unlocked the doors. 'Once we get into her Whatsapp, we should be able to track him down. And eliminate him if necessary. Wesley is onto it.'

'It's hard to imagine what motive he could have had for harming her. He'd have nothing to gain from it. Even if he knew she was wealthy, killing her wouldn't get him any money. Unless she had already sent him money and she didn't tell the others. But she didn't strike me as a gullible, needy woman.'

'No' said Wilcox. 'She wouldn't have been taken in by one of the romance scammers. But this guy might have been more sophisticated than that. He might have been playing a longer game. He might not know she's dead.'

'Yes' said Murphy. 'He might even be a genuine person. OK, let's leave him for the moment. We'll carry on pursuing the other lines. I think we should move onto Sebastian. He made an impression on Kate Black, maybe she did the same for him, and I have a theory I want to put to him.'

Chapter Forty-Two

Sebastian Fincham had a flat in Maida Vale, close to St John's Wood Road.

'This place will cost a bit' said Wilcox, surveying the mansion block. 'I wonder how much the brothers pay themselves? Plenty, I'm sure.'

Somebody was coming out of the building at that point, so Wilcox flashed his badge and they got in the front door.

'No point giving the suspect advance warning' he remarked with satisfaction.

'In case he heads for the fire escape you mean?' Murphy led the way up the stairs, which were wide with a graceful wrought iron balustrade.

Sebastian opened the door and his face fell momentarily, before he recovered himself and stepped aside with a flourish. 'Well this is a surprise. I was expecting Amazon.'

He was wearing a crumpled linen shirt and threadbare cargo pants and his feet were bare. Murphy was sure she could see dark roots in his blonde hair. Good to know he had to work at it.

'We thought it was time we had a proper chat' said Murphy. She had tried to make sure the last two words sound menacing, but the effect seemed to have been lost on Sebastian.

'Welcome. Come on in.'

He led the way into a huge, sparsely-furnished room with a high ceiling and ornate cornicing.

'As you can see, I don't go in for a lot of *stuff*, but do grab one of the few seats.'

'Thank you.' Murphy settled into an armchair. 'It's a bit different to your brother's place.'

He waved an arm. 'Well of course. Cheyne Walk.' He rolled his eyes. 'Lots of money, no taste. Fifty or a hundred years ago it was inhabited by people who would have been worth knowing. Now it's mostly a haven for those with money but no talent or imagination. The insides of some of those places have probably not been redecorated since the seventies, the rest have been given the standard interior designer look. And of course, some of them have been kitted out for people with more vulgar taste – gold bath taps and the like.' He was silent for a moment. 'Not that I'm putting Hugo into that no talent or imagination category you understand.'

'Understood' said Murphy. 'Do you live here alone?'

'Most of the time, unfortunately, yes.'

'I would have expected you to have plenty of women in your life.'

'In some ways, yes I do. But none of them that I'd actually want to live with.'

'Does the name Kate Black mean anything to you?' asked Wilcox.

'I don't think so. Should it?'

'She came on one of your wine tours, about a fortnight ago. Effie brought her along.'

'Good-looking woman? Short blonde hair?'

'Yes, that will be her.'

'I do remember seeing her, but I didn't recall her name.'

'Have you seen her on any other occasion?'

'No, I'm sure I haven't. Why? Has something happened?'

'She was murdered two days ago' said Murphy. 'Coming so soon after Effie's murder, it raises a lot of questions.'

Sebastian scratched his head and then shook it. 'I can see that. That's really shocking, but I don't think I can help.'

'Where were you on Tuesday evening?' said Wilcox. 'Between six pm and seven pm?'

'I probably left the vineyard about six. I usually do. Then I would just have been here – alone and unvouched for, I'm afraid.'

'OK' said Murphy, 'We'll leave that for the time being. We've been looking again at this incident that happened ten years ago, and there may be a few points you can help us with.'

Sebastian's leg gave an involuntary twitch, which revealed an ankle with a fish tattoo.

'Sure. Go ahead.'

'We've asked a few people about the sleeping arrangements in that barn, and now I'd like to hear what you remember of it.'

He shrugged. 'There weren't any sleeping arrangements. We all just bunked down anywhere.'

'OK, so can you tell us where everybody was, from your recollection.'

'Let me see.' He paused. 'It was a hot night, I remember that. I bagged a spot near the door, just to have the air. The girls were up in the back corner and I can't remember where the other guys were.'

'So anybody leaving the barn would have walked past you?'

'Yes, but I was asleep, so I wouldn't have noticed. Not unless they tripped over me.'

'When the alarm sounded and you got woken up, where did you find yourself?'

'In the same place, by the door.'

'Were you alone?'

'Yes, of course.' Murphy noted with interest that the leg was now twitching harder. It reminded her of her foot on the clutch at a particularly disastrous stage of her first driving test.

'How about your sister? Was she somewhere near you?'

'I don't know. I don't remember seeing her. I was too busy dragging on some clothes and running outside.'

'Why do you think Billy left the barn?'

'To have a pee is the obvious answer.'

'I think that's right. He got up to have a pee. He pulled on his jeans and his trainers and made for the door. And maybe he saw something on his way out of the barn that shocked him. Do you think that's possible?'

He laughed. 'Like what? A couple of chickens roosting in the hay bales?'

Murphy sat forward and looked closely at him.

'Like you and Phoebe maybe? Tangled up together asleep. Somebody said the only person you really fancy is yourself. I think that's probably true. But the nearest you can get to yourself is your sister. The Greek heroes did the same didn't they? Like Zeus marrying his sister. Their sisters were the only women they considered equal to themselves.'

‘That’s an appalling accusation.’

‘Yes, it is appalling, but it’s less appalling than murder. Did it start when you were young?’

He stared at the wall for a few moments. ‘I loved her from the moment she was born. She was beautiful. I knew we would be best friends. Then at some point during the teenage years we – started experimenting, I guess.’

‘Is it still going on?’

‘No, absolutely not, not for several years.’

‘Does Andrew know?’

He hesitated a moment. ‘I think so. He tends to blank me and they stay away from the family as far as possible, so I think she must have told him.’

‘He’s a good man’ Murphy observed.

Sebastian nodded. ‘Yes, he is. He’s what she needed.’

‘Incest is illegal in this country‘ said Murphy ‘but it’s not what we are investigating right now. However I do think you should take some responsibility for having corrupted your sister and you should consider the effect that may have had on her life – and possibly other peoples’ lives too. And maybe with fatal results.' She rose from the armchair in one smooth movement. That was good. Nothing creaking today. 'We’ll see ourselves out.’

Chapter Forty-Three

THEY ARRIVED AT FAWCETT Hall and then had to reverse back out of the drive to clear a path for an ambulance which was just leaving. Dorothy Hepple was standing by the side of the house watching it drive away. Wilcox parked the car and Murphy went over to Dorothy.

'What's been happening?'

Dorothy seemed to be in shock. Her face was white and Murphy could see a faint tremor going through her arms. 'Overdose' she murmured.

'Mrs Fincham?'

Dorothy seemed to spring back to life. 'No, not her. Edward.' A tear was forming balanced on her bottom eyelid. As Murphy watched, the surface tension broke and it rolled down her cheek.

'Was he in his study?' Dorothy nodded and Murphy signalled to Wilcox who entered the house through the open back door.

Murphy took Dorothy by the arm. 'Let's get you inside.'

Dorothy allowed herself to be led back through the yard towards her cottage. Murphy waited while she unlocked the door then followed her inside and told her to sit on the sofa while she put the kettle on.

'Or would you prefer something stronger?'

'No. Tea's fine. Black no sugar.'

'Yes, I would definitely have pitched you as a black no sugar woman' said Murphy a few moments later, putting a mug down in front of her and looking with interest at her surroundings. They were certainly interesting. From the outside, the building was a farm worker's cottage. The inside was sleekly modern. Painted floorboards, chalky white walls and large works of modern art – stripes and splashes and examples of what Murphy thought was called pointillism – or maybe that was something else – in a riot of colours. They all looked valuable, not that she would know. A large window at the back of the sitting room – clearly not an original window – gave a view directly onto the vineyard.

She returned her attention to Dorothy, who was watching her with a bemused expression.

'So tell me what happened.'

'I went to see him in his study. There was some new artwork for the brochure that I wanted him to approve. I was supposed to have left for the day, but I had stayed behind to finish it. I'd seen him go in there half an hour earlier, but the door was locked. He never locks the door. So I ran round and looked in the window and I could see him slumped over the desk. I couldn't break the door down on my own so I ran to fetch Colin – he was the only person I could find – and we broke in. I called for an ambulance – or maybe I'd already done that, I don't know. I couldn't find a pulse. I thought it could be a heart attack, but there was an empty bottle of Valium. So I guess that's what it was. I tried CPR, but it wasn't going anywhere.'

'Did the paramedics get him breathing again?'

'I think so. They carried on the CPR and then put him on oxygen and took him to the hospital. I don't suppose there'll be any news yet.'

'Probably not' said Murphy. 'He must have been very unhappy.'

Dorothy nodded. 'Yes, I suppose he was.'

'So tell me about it. Was it the wife? He didn't seem too upset about the death of his daughter-in-law, so I don't think that was the problem. Unless he was worrying about who might be responsible?'

Dorothy sat back and rubbed her eyes. 'Yes, I guess it was Verity mainly. She's never been an easy person.'

'So that was why he got you in at the beginning?'

'Yes. He really needed help when the children were small.'

'Why didn't he leave her?'

'He felt he couldn't. I think he had tried once, in the early days, and she had threatened him with everything she had. She would commit suicide and take the baby with her, she'd tell her story to the tabloids, or whatever story she chose to make up. He was a barrister at that time, the notoriety would have killed his career. When he became a judge, he was even more vulnerable to that kind of blackmail.'

'So you've been his support all these years.'

She sighed. 'I guess so.'

'And you stayed because you were in love with him.'

'I think I may have been, for a while. But as you get older, these feelings sort of diminish.'

'Tell me about it' said Murphy. 'So you ended up like an older married couple, just getting along together.'

'Yes, I guess we did. There was never anything between us, no relationship. He was never in love with me. But we understood each other and he relied on me.'

'And because he couldn't offer you any sort of relationship, he gave you money and security.'

'That's right. I have this lovely house and a very good salary, and shares in the vineyard.'

'Now' said Murphy, 'given that Edward Fincham has lived with this non-optimum marriage for all these years, what do you think has suddenly driven him to attempt suicide? Why now?'

Dorothy shook her head. 'I don't know. That's what I've been wondering. I've always known what was going on, but this must have been something he couldn't share with me.'

***

'The paramedics must have taken the empty bottle with them' said Wilcox, as they headed back down the drive. 'Makes sense, I suppose. I didn't see anything else useful. No papers lying around, no note. Door was definitely locked from the inside, lots of damage where they had to break the lock.'

'Dorothy was supposed to have left' said Murphy. 'That and the locked door makes it clear he didn't want to be found. He genuinely wanted to die.'

'But why. Do you think he killed Effie?'

'It just doesn't look that way to me. I think if she was threatening to tell family secrets, he'd have taken her on. He has all the legal heft he needs and she could probably have been paid off and tied up in non-disclosure agreements or whatever. I don't think he would have been fazed by Effie. He would have been a lot more troubled if he thought any member of his family was responsible for killing her. I think it was more personal to do with him – some sadness or despair. I'm not entirely sure what.'

'Let's hope he makes it through and then we can ask him', said Wilcox. 'If he dies, Bellweather will probably hold us responsible.'

'One thing his removal to hospital makes easier, is that we can now question Mrs Fincham without him getting in the way. Interesting that she's the one who repeatedly threatens suicide and he's the one who gets on and does it. Let's hope he hasn't been successful.'

Chapter Forty-Four

VERITY FINCHAM WAS WATCHING television in the sitting room when they called round later that day. An elderly couple were being shown around apartments in Spain – homes in the sun or whatever – and looking in delight at the kitchen fittings and handkerchief-sized pools. Murphy could see that, if you had to retire, somewhere warm was preferable, but the prospect was still alarming. She wondered if Verity was making plans.

They had delayed this visit until confirmation had come from the hospital that Edward Fincham was out of danger. Murphy didn't want Verity to claim that she couldn't talk to them because she was too worried about her husband. As it was, she was stretched out on the sofa in some sort of loungewear and didn't move when Dorothy showed them in.

'Thank you for seeing us, Mrs Fincham' said Murphy. 'Do you think we could have the TV off for a few minutes?'

Verity swung her feet down, pressed a button on the remote and folded her arms.

'I'm sure you're relieved to hear that your husband is OK' said Murphy. 'Have you managed to see him yet?'

'Not yet' she replied. 'He needs to rest.'

'Yes, of course.' Murphy absorbed the implied rebuke. 'Do you have any idea what can have caused him to take an overdose?'

She frowned. 'None whatsoever. But surely it's not a police matter.'

'No, it's not', said Murphy. 'If the attempt had been successful, we would have had reason to investigate but, as it is, it's not a matter for us.'

'In that case, why are you here?' For the first time Murphy saw a flicker of fear.

'We're here about another matter. The death of Billy Jukes in 2004.'

Verity sighed. 'But we've been over all that. I explained it to the police at the time and again to you just a few days ago. There's nothing more to say about it.'

'I think there's quite a lot more to say about it.' Murphy made eye contact with Verity and held it. 'This issue is never going to go away. The police backed away in 2004, but we're not going to do that. And I can't think you want it hanging around your neck forever. It's time to tell the truth.'

'I told the truth in the first place.'

'No, you didn't. Somebody drowned Billy in the pond and the only person with the opportunity to do it was you. I could also hazard a guess at why you did it. Do you want me to tell you?'

Verity dropped her head into her hands, and for several seconds the only sound was the ticking of the carriage clock on the mantelpiece. Murphy wondered whether she would now demand a lawyer.

She raised her head and when she spoke it was in a whisper.

'I was going out early to feed the geese. Dorothy and I take it in turns and it was my turn that day. I didn't expect to see anybody, certainly not any of the kids. But there was this kid, Billy, standing in the doorway to the barn with a shocked look on his face. I went up to him and then I saw... I saw... what he was looking at. I had wondered sometimes, seeing the looks passing between them, but I always dismissed it. I just knew that I couldn't let him tell anybody. All their lives would be ruined.'

Tears were running down her face now. Tears for her children or for the child she had killed? Murphy suspected the former.

'What did you do?'

'I took him by the arm and told him I needed his help. I said one of the dogs was drowning and he had to help me. I told him to be very quiet and not wake anybody else. I knew he couldn't swim. I led him into the pond and said the dog had gone under further in. I pulled him a long way out of his depth and waited for him to stop resurfacing. Then I pulled him out and called for Dorothy.'

Wilcox switched off the record function on his phone, stood up and read Verity Fincham her rights.

***

Edward Fincham had been given a private room. 'Probably has BUPA' said Wilcox. A nurse was in attendance. 'Five minutes' she said warningly, and left the room.

He was looking grey and frail and shrunken. His hospital pyjamas had been buttoned up incorrectly so there was a spare buttonhole under the lapel. It was the sort of stupid detail Murphy always noticed and itched to fix, but on this occasion, maybe not.

'Thank you for coming in' he said. 'I'm trying to get out of here, but they won't give me my clothes.'

'I think you almost died, sir' said Murphy. 'In fact, if it hadn't been for Dorothy, you would have done. So they probably figure you need a bit more rest. You will know that your wife has confessed to the murder of Billy Jukes.'

'Yes' he said. 'So I assume I will be charged with perverting the course of justice.'

'Did you know she had done it?'

'No, not at all. I couldn't believe she would have done such a thing. But equally, no other explanation made sense. So I always wondered. I had my suspicions about Sebastian and Phoebe. That's why I made sure she went to Edinburgh. I didn't want her following him to Durham. It was such a relief when she got married. I knew that would be the end of it.'

'Did Effie know all this?

'I don't think she can have known anything. I didn't actually *know*. But she could certainly have suspected.'

'Did she come to see you about it?

'No. And if she had, I wouldn't have been open to any blackmail attempt. There was no need. If she and Hugo split up, we would have made her a decent settlement.'

'Yes, I rather thought that', said Murphy.

'My wife. Can I see her when I get out of here? I'll need to arrange representation for her.'

'Of course. We'll let you know when she's been charged.'

The nurse was back in the room waving a finger. Time was up.

***

Wilcox was silent on the way back to the station. Murphy could tell he was still processing it, so she kept quiet.

'What I don't understand' he said finally, 'is how you thought of it. I mean Sebastian and Phoebe. Such a thing would never have occurred to me.'

'You just need a bit longer in the job, Kevin. Keep practising and eventually you'll have an imagination as depraved as mine. There were a lot of pointers along the way. They were very close as children, she carried on visiting him at university, presumably sleeping in his room. And Sebastian, despite all that easy charm and being so attractive to women – yes he is, believe me – didn't seem to have any other relationships.'

'It just seems so ... backward.'

'Exactly. It's something we associate with primitive societies, or very remote societies, where there aren't too many options. And here's a highly sophisticated family, with all the options in the world. There's a lesson in there somewhere. Poor Phoebe. No wonder she didn't want to get too close to Effie. Effie was smart. She could have worked out what was going on if she had put her mind to it – in fact maybe she had. She probably wouldn't have backed off from talking about it either. So Phoebe was to some extent to blame for Billy's death – but not for the reason she thought.'

'From talking to Sebastian' said Wilcox, 'it sounds like Andrew knows about it.'

'I think he does and that's why he's protective of her. She's very lucky to have met somebody like him, and his family sound very normal. That's what she needs.'

Wilcox immediately thought of Andrew's nan and wondered whether 'normal' really covered it, but decided to keep his thoughts to himself.

***

Back at the station, Bellweather also seemed to be in a state of shock. The arrest of a retired judge's wife on a murder charge was not something he had anticipated. For some minutes he just sat and said nothing. Then he roused himself to speak.

'Good result of course. Cleared up a cold case. Although actually it wasn't...'

Murphy could see the cogs going round. It wasn't a cold case because it had been written off at the time as an accident. So solving it wouldn't do anything for his clearup rate. Time to get out of the way before he finished that thought.

'Few things still to sort out' she declared, and dragged Wilcox off with her.

He was still looking thoughtful. 'So, as far as we know, the only member of that family who was not involved in anything bad' he ventured, 'was his honour.'

'Yes' said Murphy. 'Wife beating, marital rape, incest, murder. Proper Greek tragedy, all in one family. But he may have been responsible for beating Hugo when he was a kid. That may have led to a lot of the other stuff. If Hugo had not been beaten, he may not have bullied Sebastian and Sebastian and Phoebe may not have formed their over-close relationship. Also, he may not have abused Effie, and that could have led to a different outcome. So I don't absolve his honour from any of this.'

'I guess this will at least be closure for Billy's parents' said Wilcox. 'But we still don't know who killed Effie or Kate.'

'No, we don't. More work to do' said Murphy.

Chapter Forty-Five

Effie Fincham's funeral had been arranged to take place in the church where she had been married. Murphy called her father who explained why he had agreed to this.

'We have no family left in Manchester' he said. 'We have no roots in Maidenhead, so this was the only place left. I'm letting them organise it, but I'm giving a eulogy. It's all I can do for her now.'

It was a damp, grey morning but the church was half full. Pretty good turnout for a funeral. Looking around, Murphy spotted Edward Fincham with Hugo and Dorothy. Sitting behind them were Olivia and Pete. On the other side of the aisle were a scattering of young people and a few rows further back Jackson sat alone. No sign of Sebastian or Phoebe. Edward was still looking frail and Dorothy kept a grip on his arm when the congregation stood up to sing 'Abide with me'. Hugo, who had no doubt been dreading this occasion, then walked to the front and described his beautiful, sociable wife and how much he missed her. Should have treated her better when he had her, thought Murphy, but she still couldn't decide whether or not he was a killer.

Bernie Watson then walked up and leaned on the lectern.

'I'm here to bury my child' he said. 'It's the worst thing that can happen to a parent. Effie was my only child and I brought her up as a single parent – not so common then as it is now. She was a beautiful child and she became a beautiful woman – and clever too. I was proud of her when she got her degree and I was so happy when she gave birth to my grandchild. She really loved Mabel and I loved both of them. But you can't protect your children from everything' his voice was starting to break here, 'and you can't control which other people they may associate with. I hope whoever took Effie's life will obtain forgiveness from God. They won't get it from me.'

The vicar paled at this. Bernie walked back to his place and the vicar signalled urgently to the organist to strike up the next hymn.

Murphy thought Bernie had done rather well and looked around to gauge the effect of his speech. Edward and Hugo were standing ramrod straight and expressionless, Dorothy was looking distressed. Olivia was definitely crying.

Twenty minutes later the coffin was on its way to the crematorium and people began filing out of the church.

Murphy stationed herself at a short distance, sheltering under a tree, from where she could observe everybody as they came out. The rain was now falling in earnest and umbrellas were going up. Bernie came over and stood with her. He put his umbrella up to cover them both.

'I hope this case hasn't been dropped' he said.

'This case definitely won't be dropped' said Murphy. 'It's taking a while to unravel, but we'll get there.'

They stood and watched people file out. Edward, Hugo, Dorothy, Olivia. All of them looked in her direction and then turned away. Murphy thought it was probably Bernie that they didn't want to confront. All their social skills were as nothing when up against his righteous anger. Maybe none of them had killed her, but he had managed to make them feel guilty just the same.

'I think they're doing refreshments back at the house' she told him.

He tossed his head. 'They can stuff their refreshments. I'm collecting her ashes and then I'm going home.'

She was cheered by his resilience. His loss was so much worse than anything Edward Fincham could believe himself to have suffered, but he hadn't resorted to any overdoses.

'Take care' she said. 'We'll be in touch.'

She made her way out of the churchyard, dodging the puddles which were filling up fast, and got into her car. The person she most wanted to speak to now was Edward Fincham, but not today, with other people around. She wanted him on his own.

***

Murphy found she rather agreed with Bernie about stuffing the refreshments, but on the other hand it was an opportunity to observe the players at close quarters. Was there anything left to find out about them? Possibly.

She pulled up outside the house and rang the bell. The door was opened by the usual woman in apron and trainers and today she seemed to be wearing a black dress under the apron. Murphy had no need to explain her presence. In fact, just as the door opened, the vicar appeared behind her, so they went in together. They were directed into a sitting room which Murphy had not seen before. The walls were a muted olive green, covered in bookshelves and pictures, some of which she could see had been hung to hide cracks in the walls. The rugs were threadbare, the sofas looked like they had lost most of their stuffing and the fire, which was burning up with quite a roar, was monopolised by an elderly-looking sheepdog lying on a moth-eaten blanket. Murphy loved it, in spite of herself. Here was a room you could relax in. Unfortunately, apart from the dog, the only person disposed to relax appeared to be the vicar, and she thought she detected on his part some disappointment that alcoholic beverages were not on offer.

Everybody else was showing the strain. They were mourning the passing of somebody whose passing most of them did not much mourn. The only exceptions were probably Olivia and Bernie, who had in any case absented himself. The absence of Verity was not being referred to, but it hung there, and they were all touched by the shame of it. Murphy's appearance served only to underline this, and she expected them to be unwilling to engage with her. She accepted a coffee from Dorothy and remarked upon the absence of Sebastian.

'He's in Bristol' said Dorothy. 'Visiting suppliers.'

'Shame he had to go today' said Murphy insincerely. 'I thought he quite liked Effie.'

'Yes' said Dorothy. 'To be honest none of us know what to do with ourselves right now. I think he wanted to get away.'

Murphy nodded in what she hoped was an understanding fashion. 'And how is Mr Fincham doing?'

Dorothy looked across at him, pinned into a corner by the vicar. Murphy wondered if he was being pressured for donations.

'He seems to be doing OK' said Dorothy. 'No long-term physical effects, anyway. The domestic situation will take a bit of getting used to.'

Murphy thought the domestic situation would probably be greatly eased by the removal of Verity, currently on remand and awaiting sentencing, but perhaps it would be tactless to say so. At that moment Hugo looked across, noticed her and quickly looked away.

'I imagine this has been very shocking for Hugo' she mused.

'Indeed' said Dorothy. 'He will need a lot of support in looking after Mabel.'

Olivia had been talking to Hugo and now appeared to be leaving. Murphy decided to catch her up.

'I must get on. Thanks for the coffee.' Dorothy nodded and Murphy made her way out, following Olivia to the drive.

'This is a sad day for you' she observed.

'Yes' said Olivia. 'Even sadder for Effie's dad. I thought he probably wouldn't come back to the house.'

'I think it would have been a bit strained if he had' said Murphy. 'Hugo seems to be bearing up OK.'

Olivia stopped by her car. 'I think the marriage was on the way out anyway' she said. 'So now he doesn't really know how to react.'

'Well the sooner we clear up what happened to her the better' said Murphy brightly. 'Pete didn't come today?'

Olivia fumbled with her keys. 'No, he had to work. I was lucky to find a babysitter or I'd have had to bring Ben.' She had the door open now.

'Take care' said Murphy and unlocked her own car.

***

Back at the station Wesley had been busy. Permission had been obtained from the social media companies and they could now access the accounts for both Effie Fincham and Kate Black.

'You take Effie' said Murphy. 'I'll start on Kate.'

Kate Black's Facebook page was much as Murphy would have expected. Lots of photos of her beautiful daughters, photos of her with Martina and Geraldine, holding up cocktails, sitting on beaches, her with other people they had yet to identify, older photos of what looked like her and her husband. A record of a life – or at least a record of the good bits. No sign of anybody called Richard.

Whatsapp was a bit different, and here he was. A photo of him, just his face, with windswept cliffs in the background. Could be Cornwall. And was that him or some unsuspecting Italian? Murphy thought it was probably Italians who had their photos nicked most often because, let's face it, they were the best-looking people. This was certainly a good-looking mature man. Time to put a trace on his phone number.

Richard Brewster had exchanged a number of Whatsapp messages with Kate Black. He described himself as a retired musician living in Polperro and sent pictures of a large house by the sea. They had exchanged a few thoughts about Mahler and Stravinsky. On the face of it, all pretty innocent. However, he expressed the desire to come up to London to visit her and she responded by saying she didn't think that would work too well, so it was fair to conclude that he was keener than she was. Did he maybe turn up unannounced,

Murphy wondered, and turn nasty when he found he wasn't welcome?

More information came through a few minutes later. The mobile number was registered to a Richard Brewster who lived, not in Polperro, but in St Mazan, near Bodmin – one of those small towns that tourists drive through on their way to places like Polperro.

'If we phone him, that will give him warning' said Wilcox, 'but it's a long way to travel to interview him.'

Murphy nodded. 'Yes, we have to act with due regard to the departmental budget, and he may turn out to have nothing to do with it. But we have to follow it up.'

'Zoom' said Wilcox. 'Let's interview him on Zoom. We can always follow up with a visit if we need to.'

'Good idea' said Murphy. 'Call him up. See if you can fix it for this afternoon.

Chapter Forty-Six

THEY SPENT THE REST of the morning going through Effie Fincham's social media accounts and there was a lot of it. Murphy decided to concentrate on the last six months, but even that time period was extensively recorded – every outfit, every place, every purchase, every meal, every random thought. The more interesting shots were those of Mabel, who at least was not pouting or sucking in her cheeks. Hugo featured very little. He had obviously made it his business to stay out of the way of Effie's iPhone, and who could blame him?

'There's two thoughts I have about this' said Murphy. 'The first is that when you look at this lot, you'd think the person posting didn't have a brain in their head, whereas we know that she was at least a graduate. The other is that the best way to hide a relevant fact is to submerge it in a sea of dross, so I think we, or maybe you, will have to go through all this lot again, and read between the lines a bit, see what we've missed.'

Wilcox nodded resignedly, stretched his legs and yawned.

***

Richard Brewster appeared on the screen promptly at 3pm with none of the fiddling around that usually accompanied Zoom meetings. He was obviously familiar with the medium. Wilcox held their badges up to the camera and he checked them over and nodded. He was a cheerful-looking man of late middle age, with something about his posture that looked strange and a barking noise that emerged when he opened his mouth.

'Mr Brewster, could you move away from the camera a bit' said Murphy.

He did so and they could see that he was actually sitting in a wheelchair. Next to him sat a medium-sized dog of indeterminate breed with ill-matched ears, who barked at them again.

'That'll do, Riley' said his owner.

The room behind him was covered in bookshelves and Murphy thought she could see two pianos.

'Thank you for agreeing to be in touch with us Mr Brewster' Murphy began. We want to talk to you about Kate Black.'

'Do you mean the Kate Black I've been in touch with?'

'That's right. Do you know what's happened to her?'

'You mean she's the Kate Black...? Oh, no. I read about it but I thought it's not an unusual name. I hoped it wasn't her – although of course it had to be some poor person. That's awful. She was a lovely person.'

'So we're hoping you might be able to help us' said Murphy. 'We know you exchanged Whatsapp messages with her, but maybe you spoke to her on the phone as well?'

He pulled out a large white handkerchief and wiped his eyes.

'Yes' he said. 'As you can see, I can't get around too easily. Fell down the stairs at the Festival Hall and damaged my spine. So I had to leave my lovely house in Polperro and move somewhere I could get round in a wheelchair. My wife had died by then and my son had moved to New Zealand. So it was important to me to stay independent somehow. I have a good pension, so I'm luckier than most, but life does get lonely. So I enrolled on a few dating sites, not really to find a wife or girlfriend, I don't have much to offer in that sort of relationship, but just to find somebody I could be in touch with. And I came across Kate. She wasn't a musician but she knew a lot about music. She used to go to concerts a lot with her husband. So we recommended different pieces to each other, she actually got me interested in Rameau. Not a composer I'd encountered very much. And we both liked books and current affairs. If we'd met thirty years ago, we might have been a great match.'

'Did you suggest going to visit her?' asked Wilcox.

'Yes, just a joke really. I said Riley and I would fight our way onto the train and the tube and appear at her door with a lovely bottle of Merlot. She said please not Merlot, red wine gives her migraines, make it a nice Sauvignon instead, and I said of course. We were laughing about it. She knew I wouldn't really be able to do it. But now I wish I had. Maybe we could have saved her.'

Chapter Forty-Seven

EDWARD FINCHAM WAS SITTING in an armchair, not at his desk. He was wearing what Murphy thought were probably chinos and a grey sweater. The sweater matched his face, which was pale with faint stubble shadowing his jaw. The suicide attempt had obviously affected him physically, but the bigger change seemed to be mental or spiritual. The fight had gone out of him. Dorothy sat next to him, picking bobbles and bits of fluff off the sleeve of a sweater which looked like it had come to serious harm in the washing machine. Neither of them were looking their best. Murphy was glad that Dorothy was in the room – she wouldn't have wanted to be accused of harassing somebody vulnerable.

'As you will know, Mr Fincham' she began, 'your wife has pleaded guilty to the 2004 murder, so there will be no trial. This will save Billy Jukes' family any further trauma. There is at least now closure for them.'

He nodded. 'Yes, I'm glad about that. They should never have had to suffer the uncertainty for so long.'

'And now' said Murphy, 'there's somebody else I want to ask you about. Kate Boswell.'

The effect was immediate. His gaze shot up and his eyes filled with tears. It was some minutes before he spoke.

'It was so many years ago. A different lifetime. But I've never forgotten her.'

'I think' said Murphy, 'that she never forgot you. She had a long happy marriage and two daughters that she obviously loved very much, but when her husband died she found herself alone. Did you announce Hugo's marriage in the *Times*?'

He nodded wordlessly.

'She was a regular *Times* reader. She'd obviously put in the time to learn the ins and outs of the cryptic crossword. I think she scanned the births, marriages etc, as people do, and saw the name Fincham – well it's not that common is it? – and thought about you again. Olivia Atwell met her and thought she looked familiar but couldn't place her. I think she may have seen her at Effie's wedding. After all, Church of England weddings are public events, anybody can attend. So I think Kate saw Effie marry Hugo, she knew the house they would be living in – she'd probably even been there at some time in the distant past, had she?' He nodded again.

'I think Kate saw Effie as her means to re-establish contact with you. I don't know how she contrived to rush for a cab at the same moment as Effie – it may have involved a bit of surveillance and a few failed attempts. But once she managed that, it was easy. Effie was a friendly, trusting sort of girl. If she hadn't suggested sharing the cab, Kate could have made the suggestion herself. Then from Effie she got the up-to-date news about you and Verity and learned about the vineyard. And she must have wondered if, now that you were retired and the children were grown up, maybe you could see each other again. So she expressed interest in the vineyard and of course Effie brought her on a wine tour. She only caught sight of you from a distance, but she signed the visitors book as 'Kate Boswell Black' and she put her full address and phone number. That put the ball in your court.'

'I saw her name there' he whispered. 'I thought very hard about getting in touch.'

'It's a pity you didn't' said Murphy. 'You might have saved her life. Because somebody else recognised her name didn't they?'

His shoulders shook and Murphy realised he was crying.

'It was quite brazen' she said, surprising herself with the word she used to hear when she was young, usually referring to girls whose skirts were considered too short. 'Many people might think of doing such a thing, but 99.9% of them wouldn't actually do it. It's the action of somebody for whom the normal boundaries don't apply, maybe because they've been indulged and protected for too long, but also because they've violated those boundaries once already.'

He was sobbing openly now and Murphy wondered momentarily whether to carry on or give him time to recover. But, sod it, he was responsible for most of this, and he was still alive, so not that deserving of sympathy.

'So there's Kate' she said, 'at home alone, minding her own business. And there's a knock on the door. I think her assailant would have contrived to get into the building by tailgating somebody who had input the code or waiting for somebody else to come out. When you're a respectable-looking person you can get away with these things. I don't think they would have chosen to ring ahead and ask for entry. So Kate opens the door and there's Verity with a bottle of wine – love interest's wife bearing peace offering, or whatever. We know her assailant brought the wine because Kate Black didn't drink red wine. So her visitor wasn't anybody who knew her well or had ever been drinking with her. I'm sure it wasn't a welcome visit, but she's hardly going to refuse to let Verity in, they're two polite, sophisticated women, after all. I think we can all guess how the rest of it unfolded. Kate welcomes her in, lots of strained small talk, Verity admires the view, Kate collects glasses and they go out onto the balcony. All very civilised. Kate opens the bottle. Maybe, as it's a red, Verity suggests they let it breathe for a few moments. She won't want to accept a glass, that would mean removing her gloves. They admire the sunset and then Kate decides to take a photo. That's a really bad idea. It would only have taken Verity a matter of seconds to whack her hard on the head and tip her over the balcony. Verity's quite strong for an invalid isn't she? Does she have a home gym?'

It was Dorothy who replied. 'Yes' she said. 'In the basement.'

Chapter Forty-Eight

Detective Inspector Wellesley was there when they got back to the incident room and Bellweather was looking as pleased with himself as if he had personally been responsible for setting the bones in question. The plaster cast was now off and Wellesley was walking with a stick, but remarkably cheerful.

'I'm just so glad to get out of the house' he said to Murphy. 'Have you ever watched daytime TV? I swear to God, it actually destroys brain cells. After two days I couldn't look at it any more. But I hear you've had lots of excitement here.'

'We absolutely have' she said. 'We've got ex-Justice Fincham's wife in custody for one murder and I'm about to charge her with another one.'

'Whaat?' That was Bellweather. 'Surely not.'

'Yes, surely' said Murphy. 'And I'm pretty sure she'll plead guilty to this one too. Her husband is instructing the family lawyer and that's what they'll recommend. She wouldn't do too well in court.'

'That's phenomenal' said Wellesley. 'Two murders solved in a week. You should be a shoo-in for promotion.'

There was a grinding noise from behind Wellesley. It was Bellweather's jaws. He turned, marched into his office and slammed the door.

'I must call Martina and Geraldine' said Murphy. 'Let them know that Kate's death was not due to anything they did.'

'Well we've still got one case left' said Wilcox. 'We still don't know who killed Effie Fincham.'

'I've got an idea about that' said Murphy. 'I don't like it, but I think it's the truth'

One of the uniformed PCs called over at that moment. 'That other car you asked me about? It did turn up on the ANPR. Come and have a look.'

They went over squinted at the murky picture on the screen. 'And there's the evidence' said Murphy.

PART THREE

Chapter Forty-Nine

THERE ARE SOME BITS I missed out in my earlier narrative, although everything I wrote there was true.

Effie and I had a strong bond and I loved her in very many ways. It's only people you love who really have the power to hurt you.

When Effie arrived that evening and showed me her bruises, she actually told me everything she suspected. I wasn't sure it was true, but it was certainly what she believed.

What I believed was that she and Pete were seeing each other again. I had suspected it for a while, just looks passing between them, but I had tried to ignore it. I couldn't believe she would do that, after so many years, and us having Ben. But that was Effie. All blokes were fair game.

So when Pete offered her a lift home, I put Ben in his car seat and followed in my car. I parked some way away and walked up to the door and I could see their silhouette on the blind. When I saw him cuddling Mabel, it was like the ultimate betrayal. He was Mabel's dad. I could see it immediately. That's why Mabel had looked familiar to me.

He'd taken up with me in order to stay close to Effie. It had always been about her.

I went back to my car and sat and waited. Lots of other bits were connecting in my brain. I remembered the district nurse at the wedding talking about Hugo having had mumps. So maybe Hugo was infertile. She had been happy when Pete and I got together. That meant she still had access to him. She had married Hugo for the money, but she never intended to stay with him, and once he started roughing her up it was time to go. And being Effie, there had to be somebody else on standby.

After about twenty minutes I saw Pete drive off. Then I took Ben in his car seat and went and knocked on Effie's door. She was wearing a beautiful silk kimono and she was pretty surprised to see me, but she let me in. I told her what I suspected and she didn't deny it. She didn't even think it was a big deal.

'The thing is, Livy' she said, 'you were right. You were right when you said I shouldn't chuck Pete. I should have listened to you. He was the one for me all along. I realise it's a bit awkward now, but I'm sure we can sort it all out.'

'Sort it all out? What are you talking about? Pete's my partner. We have a child.'

'Yes, I'm sorry about that. I don't think we expected you to have a child. But Livy, it will be OK. I'm going to get some decent money out of Hugo and we'll make sure you're OK. To be honest, I think Hugo quite likes you...'

It was at this point that I lost control and grabbed her by the shoulders. Maybe I thought I could shake her awake, get her to drop this crazy scenario she had constructed.

'This is bullshit Effie. It's not going to happen.'

'Darling it's already happened. I'm sorry you had to find out this way.'

I was so angry that, before I knew it, my hands had slid inwards to her throat. It was a cold night and I was still wearing my leather driving gloves. You have to be quite strong to strangle someone, but Effie had a pretty skinny neck and I have a strong grip. I wasn't in the rowing team for nothing. The middle-aged detective with the purple hair made that point. Clever of her, I thought.

When I let go, Effie fell on the floor and it was if I suddenly woke up at that point. I wasn't sure whether she was dead, in one way I hoped not. I knew I needed to get out fast and I was thinking clearly enough to have the idea of making it look like a robbery. I grabbed a bunch of silverware and stuffed it into Ben's car seat. A few days later I dumped it in the office at the vineyard. If the police didn't buy the robbery scenario, it would serve to incriminate one of the Finchams, probably Hugo.

When I got back to the house, Pete's car was there and he was probably already asleep upstairs. I knew he wouldn't have looked in on us when he came in, for fear of waking Ben. Not waking Ben was a big part of our lives. It wasn't until the police came round the next day that I knew for certain that Effie was dead. And the sense of loss that I felt was totally genuine. Not that my behaviour is thereby excused. I'm not making any bid for sympathy here.

When they took me into custody (when it was clear that my denials were not going to hold water) I asked the detective with the purple hair when she had first suspected me. She said that when she looked at the christening photos she saw Pete and Effie with their heads together in what looked like more than polite conversation. I think she was right about that. I thought the same, although I tried to ignore it at the time. And, of course, I had told her that Effie wanted to leave Hugo and that Effie had always had lots of boyfriends, so she said that she started wondering if Effie had somebody else in mind. At first she thought it might be Sebastian, but he was still only interested in Phoebe, even if their affair was pretty much history. So then she wondered about Pete, which was what he had been questioned about in the first place. If Pete had come with me to the funeral, in his car, I may have gotten away with it. It was when she saw my car that day, and realised that I had a car of my own, that she decided to check the CCTV for it, and then it was over.

Pete and I are totally finished of course, but we still have Ben and he is the priority. I am hoping Pete will bring him to see me occasionally, while he is young enough not to realise that this is a prison. Pete is going to take a paternity test and try for custody of Mabel. He is actually her only remaining parent. This means that, instead of having two women on the go, he will become a lone parent of two children. He may be very successful at it. He's going to make sure that Mabel gets to see her other grandad – Effie's dad – which is probably more than the Finchams would do.

I'm on remand now, awaiting sentencing. I decided to plead guilty. I couldn't face a trial and I didn't want to put Effie's dad through it either.

The detective with the purple hair (actually a lot of it's grown out now, and I must stop calling her that. It's Detective Inspector Murphy) came to see me yesterday. She told me that Ben is fine, which is really all I care about. Apparently, Sebastian has gone off to California to work at a vineyard and the one at Fawcett Hall is now being run by Hugo and his dad, which means his dad will have to muck in and do some work. Probably be good for him. But they'll miss Sebastian. Can't see either of those two being much good at all the chitchat involved in the wine tours. That would need someone like Effie.

Afterword

Indie authors don't have the promotional clout of the big publishers, but we do have the goodwill of our readers to help us.

If you enjoyed this book I would be very grateful if you could spend a few minutes leaving a review on the book's Amazon page. It can be as short as you like.

Many thanks,

Eva Maclean

And perhaps you would like to stay in touch by joining my Book Club.

A vicious poisoning. A group of old army comrades. A serial killer on the loose?

Killing Time is a prequel novella dealing with events prior to Miranda Murphy joining the police force. The novella is offered free to members of my Book Club. To sign up and get your free novella go to https://evamaclean.com

THE SECOND NOVEL IN the DI Miranda Murphy series, *Dead Cool,* is now available on Amazon.

Rush hour. A packed tube station. A body on the tracks. Looks like accident or suicide. Because who would want to kill a man who was already dying?

Printed in Great Britain
by Amazon

43544273R00189